COVER-UP

COVER-UP

LaErtes Muldrow

ISBN: 978-1-962313-02-5 (Paperback Edition)
ISBN: 978-1-962313-03-2 (Hardcover Edition)
ISBN: 978-1-962313-01-8 (E-book Edition)

Book Ordering Information

Vintage Ink Solutions, US
Address: 1968 S. Coast Hwy Laguna Beach, CA 92651
Phone Number: (949) 538-2236 ext 1001
Email: info@vintageinksolutions.com
www.vintageinksolutions.com

Printed in the United States of America

Contents

INTRODUCTION

You are about to experience "COVER-UP" - a futuristic fantasy mystery. If you're looking for "The Great American Novel," this is not it! I am no scholar, no intellectual, nor am I a high maintenance poet or word slinger, so I won't be dazzling you with exceptional award winning prose. I'm a normal person, just like most of you. In fact, I'm a movie buff, and one of my goals is to see my stories become moving pictures. When adapting a book into moving images so much is lost from the creative words to image representation. I keep my wording simple, leaving plenty of room for creative screenwriting without loss of theme. My stories read very much like an e-book: the chapters and paragraphs are the epitome of brevity. My writing style is akin to the simplistic oral traditions of storytelling where villagers gathered around a favorite location for stories about their heritage, history, lineage, myths, legends, fantasies, or current affairs. This style I call "Minimal-Listic," meaning lack of rhetoric, non-redundant, with less prose, for a genre called "Horra/Thrilla/Fantasy." Like the Elder Storytellers before me, I spin stories giving you just enough information to see images, which hopefully will engage your own imagination into supplying the additional movie elements from your hearts, minds, and souls.

This Minimal-Listic approach takes you from point 'a' to 'z' as directly and quickly as possible, via a strong entertainingly rich and creative story, so you can return to your usual life.

Be warned though, some of my stories are not for the timid or meek.

Enough said, enjoy your brief escape into…

"COVER-UP!"

—LāErtes Muldrow

Chapter 1

Eight overlapping heartbeats filled his ears, all beating out of sync with each other. Together they sounded like tribal African drums each beating to their own chaotic rhythm, all but one. Donovan's heart beat to a calm consistent thump-pa— thump-pa—thump-pa, no variations—no missed beats…a rhythm that would soon shock the world into a frenzy. He was the invisible man when compared to the hype everyone else got. No one remembered or associated his name to any major wins during the track season. He'd only performed well enough be placed in event after event, and that's just the way he wanted it; "*Actions speak louder than words, baby!*" He remembered his father had taught him that. Donovan had come to get his and then, like a ghost, he'd be gone!

His confidence level was off the charts. He was poetry in motion to watch. He went into a palpable Zen trance as he approached the starting mark. Squatting down to assume the position, he kicked his legs behind him to loosen his muscles, while a few drops of sweat fell to the track, splashing in all directions in front of him as he settled into the starter's blocks. With a smirk, a sense of calm came over him as he slightly glanced to the left, then slowly to the right of his lane realizing his competitors had no clue what he was about to do.

Each of his events followed one right after the other so there was never enough time between events for the paparazzi to get an interview. All they had to report from was the instant replay images, and the new Planetary Records Donovan had set in every event he competed in. Setting new Planetary Records was his main goals, because along with them came the unquestionable distinction of being known as "The Fastest Man on the Planet!"

Donovan was going for Platinum!!

Since athletes were bigger, stronger, faster, and competed in multiple events, the crowing glory was lifted from Gold to Platinum. When a single athlete won gold medals in seven separate events and set new Planetary Records in those events, the next event that athlete won elevated them to Platinum status, and that supreme athlete was crowned with a 100% Platinum Tiara, adorned with platinum leaves, then ceremonially introduced to the planet as "The Olympian."

A loud shot rang out and a deafening roar came from the sold-out crowd of spectators. It was standing room only and they were about to witness a performance that would be talked about for decades to come. The rest of the pack appeared to be moving in slow motion as one runner was attracting all the attention. The planet's record was 9.5 seconds, and had been set before Donovan came on the scene. He was about to destroy that record. Donovan was the type of person who loved to be shrouded in mystery, an enigma...the invisible man. And this time, history was about to be made in the blink of an eye.

Donovan didn't hear the crowd; all he heard was the initial gunshot. All he felt was the sensation of inertia, as he sliced through the atmosphere that tried to slow him down.

Not this day!

This was D-day—Donovan's Day, his time to show the planet what they had never seen before. His feet barely touched the track; he was one with the wind as he blazed through the ribbon, grabbing it with an outstretched hand—ending the famed 100-meter sprint.

The stadium fell into a hush. The only sound heard were the stadium flags flapping in the wind. All eyes stared at the mega-panels, anxiously waiting for the time to be displayed. There was no doubt that everyone had witnessed something remarkable and a first in the history of track and field.

They had already witnessed Donovan setting new planetary records in the 100m, 400m, 800m, 110m hurdles, 400m hurdles, the long jump, the high jump, and the triple jump over the course of the last few days of the Hawaiian Summer Olympic Games of 2020.

No single athlete had set more records at the Olympics since Michael Phelps, who had the help of great teammates early in the 21st century, or when Marion Jones stole her gold by pumping herself full of steroids, or before her when Michael Johnson blazed the field —both competing back in the late 20th century.

But it was a new day!

Donovan Mocion was on the scene now and when he competed all existing records disappeared.

His parents were scientists and reverse mirror images of each other— creation's yin and yang.

His mother specialized in Biotechnology, Genetic Engineering, and Advanced Artificial Intelligence Systems Programming.

His father's specialties were Biochemistry, Tissue Regeneration, Nanotechnology, and Advanced Artificial Intelligent Systems Development.

Both were brilliant and globally renowned in their fields.

Donovan got his brilliance honestly; brilliance was in his blood. Not only was he a planetary-class athlete, he maintained a 5.0 GPA, and was always on the Dean's list for excellence at the University of Washington, and was well on his way towards achieving his doctorate in psychology, specializing in the cognitive, developmental, educational, evolutionary, and experimental. Many major behavioral science institutions were already clamoring to recruit him for highly specialized research projects, as well as top-secret government funded projects, upon his graduation. Donovan always spent more time in the books than on the field or socializing.

Donovan stood 6'7, and weighted 300lbs, with a sculpturesque physique that would shame Adonis. His unique almond-shaped green eyes, golden brown complexion, and curly off-black hair made him the fantasy of many admirers, both male and female. He was a private, driven man who loved to keep his secrets, and to surprise people when he was good and ready. And that was exactly what he was doing.

Everyone knew he was fast and an excellent athlete. Just being at the Olympics proved that, but this was his time to pull out all the stops and race the clock—to out distance the measuring tape.

Donovan was in the zone—his zone! And the only person who knew what was going to happen was Donovan himself.

The first eye contact Donovan made after this, his final race, was with his loving parents. He saw the tears of joy running down his mother's cheeks, and the satisfying smirk that his father always gave him when he was especially proud of Donovan's achievements. Donovan, full of pride and accomplishment, trotted over to where they were standing, and the three of them focused their attention on the mega-panel where images of the runners at the starting line were being shown.

The runner in the middle of the pack had sprung off to an unbelievable lead.

What appeared to be smoke, but was really dust, came from his running shoes as he blazed through the finish line, splitting the winner's tape. There had been no jockeying back and forth for position; Donovan just dusted the entire field as though they were standing still, and when his time was posted the entire stadium went "WOO!" as they read…

7.5 seconds in the 100 meters…A new planetary record!

"No person on earth has ever run from zero to 100 meters this fast before.

7.5 seconds!!!" shouted announcers in every language over the stadium's public address system.

"Donovan Mocion—THE FASTEST MAN ALIVE!!!"

The stadium was in an uproar. Flashbulbs were popping and people were jumping up and down yelling and screaming, "Donovan! Donovan! Donovan!"

The mega-panels all around the stadium were replaying the race as Donovan jogged his victory lap proudly waving the Stars and Stripes and bowing his head to the spectators.

Donovan was the only one who knew he was holding back while he raced his way to planetary records and the history books. He knew the value of pacing himself. He had only given the crowd what he wanted to give them, but not all he had to give. Donovan had plans to be around and set even more planetary records in the near future.

As far as he was concerned, before his career was through, no one would remember any of the other fabulously gifted speedsters and hurdlers like Jessie Owens in '36, Wilma Rudolf in '60, Willie Davenport, Tommie Smith, and John Carlos in '68, or the likes of Carl Lewis in '84, Florence Griffith Joyner in '88, Gail Devers, and Jackie Joyner-Kersee in '92, all fabulous athletes who had come before him.

He had his sights set on becoming the greatest sprinter/hurdler/jumper of all time.

And that night, his 20th birthday, he had accomplished all of this! Donovan Mocion…"THE OLYMPIAN!"

At this moment, during this space and time, Donovan Mocion, was on top of the world.

Donovan's parents came down from the stands after the award ceremonies. His mother, Vanessa, ran to greet him with kisses and hugs saying, "Ah, baby— you did it! I'm so proud of you."

Donovan returned his mother's loving hugs while asking his approaching father, "Well, what did you think, Dad?"

"I think you left their dicks in the dirt, son," answered his dad, Donald. "Don, do you have to be so crude all the time. What if someone heard you?"

remarked Vanessa, acting embarrassed. She wasn't though; Don's frankness was part of her attraction to him.

"Just keeping it real, baby!" answered Donald, "No shame in my game." "Let's get out of here," said Donovan, not one for all the hoopla that surrounded festivities like this.

Donovan always shied away from victory parties and interviews; there weren't many paparazzi photos of him, either. He kept a very low profile, even while training. The coaches didn't really know the extent of his abilities. Donovan only showed his coaches just enough to please them, but not enough to make news headlines.

"Don't you want to stay and soak in all these accolades?" asked a proud, smiling Vanessa.

"Nah, I'd prefer a private celebration with just you and dad. I'm just glad everything is over," answered a drained Donovan.

"Ok by me. Let's hit the jet," said Donald.

The Mocions quietly slipped away from the Olympic gaiety, jumped into a waiting limo, and soon arrived at their jet. Neither Donald nor Vanessa recognized the pilot, co-pilot, or flight attendant who greeted them there.

"Where's our flight crew?" asked a concerned Donald in a stern voice. "And who are you?" questioned Vanessa, equally concerned about who these strangers were.

"Mr. and Mrs. Mocion, I'm your replacement pilot, Jim Kovac. This is my co-pilot Enrique Salones, and your flight attendant, Leidra Lawson. It seems your regular crew came down with botulism and was rushed to the hospital. But, don't worry, they're doing well. As soon as Global Pharmaceuticals got the news they immediately dispatched us as your replacement flight crew."

"Is that right?" said a skeptical Donald, who reluctantly introduced them to his family. As Donovan was about to be introduced to Leidra, she interrupted by saying, "And you of course must be Donovan! The man of the hour...The Olympian!"

Leidra placed her arm around his shoulder, draping herself over him as she escorted him to a seat onboard the jet.

"It's a pleasure meeting such a physical perfection as you. If there is anything I can do to make your flight more pleasurable, anything, at all," looking Donovan straight in his eyes and licking her lips, "don't hesitate to take full advantage of all my services."

Donovan looked at his dad and his dad winked at him.

Vanessa, catching the wink, looked at Donald and scowled at him, while mouthing the words, "You dog!"

A weary Donovan looked at them both, shook his head, then calmly took a seat and strapped himself in for take-off. Within minutes the Gulfstream Jet was taxiing down the runway, picking up speed as the G-force pushed its passengers back into their plush leather seats.

The take-off was Donovan's favorite part of air travel. He loved hearing the power of the engines, feeling himself being forced into his seat by the pure power of speed. Take-off, to him, felt like leaving the starting block and separating from the earth. The in-between part of flying, traveling from point A to point B, Donovan could do without.

After the plane climbed to 41,000 feet and leveled out, Leidra popped open a bottle of Veuve Clicquot Brut Champagne from France to toast Donovan's victories. This was the happiest moments of his young life. All he had sacrificed and trained for had come to pass; he was living his dreams.

Donovan, only 20 years old and legally still under age, said, "Now this is what I'm talkin' 'bout," and whole-heartedly accepted his toast, and several more made by his proud, loving parents before a deep sleep overcame the three of them.

Chapter 2

1 hour later into the flight, came the raspy voice of Big Jim, the pilot, over the PA system, momentarily drowning out the hissing sound made by the jet's forced air system that recycled the breathable air inside the plane. "Is everything secured back there? We're almost at our rendezvous location."

Enrique, the co-pilot, stopped what he was doing and casually walked over to the cabin's intercom and replied, "The last knots are being tied as we speak. The doctors are ready to go. What about the kid?"

"Leave him!" came Big Jim's harsh reply.

"What a waste...," said Leidra, the flight attendant, who was straddling Donovan's lap, drooling like a spider with a fly caught in her web. Thinking to herself, "*There's so much pleasure I could have with him.*"

"You freak, get your mind out of the gutter," snapped Enrique. "Just make sure he's strapped in…don't want him missing the fireworks."

"Yum-yum…that's exactly what I had in mind. I could explode all over this fine specimen," teased Leidra, looking at Enrique grinning, as she placed two fingers between her moist full lips, sucked on them—pausing to feel her body tremble from the erotic x-rated thoughts racing through her imagination. She slowly pulled her fingers from her lips, giving them a long lick, while seductively staring at Enrique. Then she did a grind into the kid's lap like she was riding a bucking bronco.

Enrique, mesmerized, looked on, licking his own lips and rubbing his crotch; he was getting aroused at the sight of Leidra teasing him. He always had the hots for Leidra, any time and any place

Leidra just oozed of sex, all 6 feet of her lean sexy slinky physic, wearing short cropped raven black hair which she loved changing colors the way most women changed their shoes. Her striking bluer than blue eyes could turn cold as ice, or beckon, come *take* me now, with the blink of one of her naturally long eyelashes. She was the type of woman that one look from her made most men and women want her to become their Sugar Baby. Hell, she could have written books or conducted seminars on the subject—Sugar Baby 101. She only had three things on her mind, sex, money, and death.

She was as deadly as they came. All three of them were - they were all mercenaries. They were brought in when big companies wanted people found, or in this case, lost.

Big Jim Kovac, immune to Leidra's magic because his sexual appetite mirrored certain members of the clergy, was the leader of the trio; ex-Navy Seal, ex-Special Forces, smuggler, assassin, and the pilot. He first became treacherous, then infamous, for running Black Ops in third world countries. He was merciless, cunning, and deadly. People weren't people to him; they were just entries on his to-do list.

Enrique Salones was Big Jim's right-hand man, a walking hard on, connected throughout every smelly, dirt-tasting, third world rat hole there was. If any type of high-tech gadgetry needed to be delivered anywhere on the planet, Enrique was "your Huckleberry" - a jack-of-all-trades and go-to guy.

Leidra Dawson was the femme fatale of the trio.

An independent flight team for hire was their cover. Corporations employed them to fly V.I.P. clients. They worked mostly for Global Pharmaceuticals, or one of its many subsidiaries. This current assignment was a Global Pharmaceuticals' sanction—a snatch, vaporize, and be-gone operation.

A loud beeping blared from the navigation equipment announcing the plane had reached its rendezvous co-ordinance far out at sea, in a radar-blind spot assuring no electronic eyes or ears witnessed what was about to happen. Big Jim reached overhead, turned off the alarm, and began to jettison the plane's fuel. Then he flipped a switch on the plane's backlit control panel, engaging the autopilot pre- programmed to fly the plane further out to sea after they had bailed out, and then crash the jet into the ocean. He pulled a small briefcase from a side locker, placed it in the pilot's seat, opened it, punched in 15 minutes on a digital display, and then hurriedly made his way through the cockpit door into the plane's cabin, announcing, "We're here…chop-chop. Let's get this party jumping."

"All is good-to-go on this end," replied Enrique.

"What a team, what a team!" said Big Jim with a smile as Leidra began helping him put his parachute on.

The two doctors already had their chutes on, and so did Leidra and Enrique.

The kid, like his doctor parents, was still unconscious from the drugs Leidra had given them right after take-off.

"Damn! Why is deadweight so heavy?" asked Leidra as she struggled with the female doctor's limp body.

"Hell if I know! But if you think she's heavy, come over here and try opening this damn outer door," answered Enrique, huffing and puffing, fighting to get it open.

Then, like a popped balloon darting around a room, the rushing wind blasted into the little jet's cabin, hitting Enrique in the face, forcing him to shut his eyes and take a few clumsy steps back from the door to regroup. "Damn!" Enrique said. "Atmosphere—what a rush!"

The smell from the plane's jettisoned fuel filled the cabin while Leidra, with a hand from Big Jim, got the female doctor positioned at the opened outer door.

Leidra stared blindly into the pitch-blackness. It was like looking into a forbidden world of the unknown—and the unknown excited her. She liked it…a lot!

Leidra and Enrique were each connected piggyback to a doctor. Just before she jumped out, Leidra turned, faced the inside of the plane, and blew a kiss to her comrades in crime, and in what seemed like slow motion at first, then, within the blink of an eye, vanished into the black abyss of night.

Next, Big Jim helped Enrique position the male doctor at the door, then said, "I'll see you on the deck, Esse," and Enrique, just as suddenly, disappeared from sight.

After giving the aircraft the once-over, Big Jim did a superman dive through the aircraft door into the black howling night.

The five of them quietly floated down towards distant shimmering lights below. There was no moon glow this night and few stars were shining, but that was no problem as the night vision gear they wore allowed them to see everything.

They had made this type of drop many times before; it was second nature to them. They created very little splashing as they slid into the warm tropical waters which felt like stepping into a heated swimming pool, but instead of tasting the pool's chlorine, they tasted the salty water of the ocean.

Their pickup boat had been patiently awaiting their arrival. Once they were all onboard, several crewmen took the unconscious bodies of the doctors and immediately transferred them to a waiting submarine that silently submerged back into the deep black waters of the night.

Dripping wet, Big Jim, Enrique, and Leidra were handed towels as they looked up through low-hanging clouds into the black sky at the flickering lights from the perfectly good airplane they had jumped from.

The boat gently rocked back and forth to the rhythm of the ocean as Big Jim raised his watch, tapped on the face, and then announced, "Won't be much longer now!"

CHAPTER 3

Donovan slowly regained consciousness with no idea where he was. He rubbed both hands over his face and eyes hoping the touch would clear his groggy head. The fumes from the jet's fuel were suffocating, and he gagged several times, having dry heaves, and each time he tried to open his eyes, they burned from the toxic vapors of the fuel. He finally got his eyes to work by squinting to get a little focus, and he looked around the cabin of the empty plane. Questions popped into his mind with no available answers.

"*Where the hell am I*?" was the first clear thought to enter his head, quickly followed by, "What's going on…where is everybody?" as his mind became sharper.

In the cockpit, peacefully sitting in the captain's seat, was an instrument of total destruction, calmly counting down to a point that would bring an abrupt end to the abandoned little jet's existence. The display on the device read 1 minute 10 seconds - 9 seconds - 8 seconds…

Suddenly, Donovan noticed the sound of rushing air and felt the brisk force of wind rushing around the cabin from somewhere. He let his ears lead him to the source of rushing air and, to his horror; he saw the opened cabin door. The sight of this shot his blood pressure through the roof, sending his heart into a pounding panic.

Donovan called out, "Mom…Dad," but no reply came. "Is anybody here?"

Donovan leapt from his seat in the back of the cabin and sprinted to the cockpit door yelling, "Can anybody hear me?" When he looked into the cockpit, he fell to his knees in shock…

…No one was there!

In the captain's seat was the detonation device with its readout displaying 1:00 minute, then 59 seconds – 58 seconds – 57 seconds….

"Oh, shit!!!" yelled Donovan. He instinctively glanced at the altimeter winding down as he sprang to his feet. He realized he was at a safe altitude to bail out and he started running back towards the cabin, tripping over his own feet and smashing into the galley wall, almost knocking himself out.

30 seconds, 29, 28, 27….

Donovan shook his head from side to side to clear his mind, and reached up to an open storage compartment, grabbed a safety parachute, and strapped it on while still on his knees. Then, he was up and off again, streaking towards the open outer door…

20 seconds, 19, 18, 17….

The thought of the device counting down in the cockpit caused him to leap towards the outer door, but before he reached it the plane took a drastic nose dive, following the programming of the automatic pilot. The dive left Donovan in a weightless state floating about the empty cabin.

10 seconds, 9, 8…

Donovan used anything firm he could pus off to propel himself closer to the open outer door and the unknown safety it represented. No matter what was outside, he thought, "*It's got to be better than blowing up inside this plane*!" The incoming rush of air was now Donovan's enemy as it kept pushing him back while he struggled with all his might to reach the open aircraft door.

5 seconds, 4, 3, 2….

Floating peacefully on gentle waves safely aboard the rendezvous boat, the flight crew's eyes were all skyward. "How long do you think it's got before lighting up the night?" asked a smiling, wide-eyed Leidra, getting sexually excited about the impending doom of the helpless Gulfstream. She draped her arms around Enrique's neck, rubbing her body firmly against his.

"I'd say a few seconds," answered Big Jim nonchalantly, as he turned his back to the sky, and headed below deck.

"Well, shit! I can't wait. I've always been a sucker for a good fireworks show," said Leidra as she spun around Enrique's neck, swinging her hips from side to side, and grinding her round, shapely butt into his crotch, giving him an instant erection.

Enrique grabbed a handful of Leidra's booty, squeezing until she moaned out loud in pleasure, then he said, "Yeah, baby, I got just the tool to tighten up those loose hips of yours, and as soon as this fireworks show ends, I'll give you some real explosions."

"Hey, check it out - I can see it!" Leidra shouted, looking up into the black sky, spotting the flashing safety lights of the little Gulfstream.

"Showtime!" announced Enrique.

The plane spiraling down toward the ocean, burst into a brilliant fireball and then shattered into millions of pieces as it crashed into the rock hard water. The only sounds heard were a tremendous boom from the explosion and the splashing of debris onto the ocean's surface.

"Fantastic!" shouted a jubilant, jumping up and down, arms stretched to the sky, swishing her hips from side to side, cheering Leidra, who turned toward Enrique and said, "Nothing like fireworks over the ocean at night to set the mood." Then, in a wide-eyed surprised expression of someone who just accidentally passed gas in an elevator, she said in a high-pitched school girl's voice, "Oh my…I'm dripping wet!" Instantly, those surprised, wide eyes turned seductive as Leidra, now speaking in a lower, sexier tone said, "First act's over—now for the main event," and she grabbed Enrique by the huge bulge in his pants and lead the way below deck.

Chapter 4

"Man! Did anybody else see that?" shouted Cedrick, an overzealous young rookie air traffic controller, peering into his scope and blinking his eyes over and over, and then rubbing them, not wanting to believe what he just witnessed.

"What, what, what…see what, what, what…see what?" asked Karl, a jittery, caffeine-addicted co-worker, as he nervously peeked and jumped from scope to scope, leaping around the tower like he was trying to escape a flying saucer attempting to beam him up.

"Dude, I was tracking this little Gulfstream Jet out of Hawaii when she did a nose dive and disappeared," explained Cedrick with a bewildered expression onhis face. Cedrick had only been on the job a few months and he was overly determined not to make any mistakes.

"She didn't hit anything, did she?" asked the supervisor, Doreen, whose wide hips bounced off the equipment and caused chairs to screech as they were pushed across the concrete floor, while she clumsily made her way to Cedrick's station for a closer look.

"No way! She was flying solo - clear for miles around," replied Cedrick. "Well, call out the Coast Guard and give 'em the last known position of the little fella; let them check for survivors. Then backtrack the bird and get me all the info on it you can," instructed Doreen. "And Karl…," she said in a louder voice pointing her finger with an extended, multi-colored fake nail on it towards him, "Switch to decaf!"

"Yeah, yeah, yeah, yeah, yeah, I'll do just that," replied a twitching Karl. "I'm all over it!" said Cedrick as he quickly began backtracking the Gulfstream Jet's flight plan.

A couple of minutes later what he discovered lifted him straight out of his chair and he shouted, "Dude… gnarly!" He blasted into the Doreen's office, announcing, "Houston, we have a problem!"

Looking up from her desk, frowning because of his dramatics, Doreen said, "Cedrick, can you not be so damned dramatic for once? Just tell me, in English, what you've got."

"Sorry, Boss!" acknowledged Cedrick, attempting to calm himself down. "Well, what we have here is a private jet owned by Global Pharmaceuticals. It says here that the passengers' list is classified Top Secret, and in the event of an emergency, a media blackout is demanded. It says to contact Global Pharmaceuticals STAT!!!"

Under her breath, Doreen said, "Oh, shit. What the hell is that damned company up to this time?" Then, in a take-charge tone, she instructed, "Contact the Coast Guard; fill them in on whose bird it was, then bring them up to speed on the instructions of Global Pharmaceuticals. Once that's done, you'll need to save all data from the incident into a Global Pharmaceuticals Eyes Only file. Next, inform the Coast Guard to do likewise. None of us want those bastards from Global Pharmaceuticals crawling up our butts claiming we didn't follow their protocol."

Cedrick giggled to himself as he thought, *"Somebody is gonna have a lot of crawling to get up all that ass you got."* Then he said aloud, "I'm all over it!" and off he went, eagerly following Doreen's instructions to the letter.

By the time the Coast Guard arrived, it was daybreak and the water was choppy. The debris from the Gulfstream Jet could be seen floating on top of the water for miles around. The rendezvousing vessels from the night before had long since disappeared without a trace.

"Rescue 1, this is Rescue 3, come back." "Go ahead, R-3."

"It's a real mess out here, but we got lucky…got ourselves a live one. He's pretty busted up, but at least he's still breathing. We're gonna air-vac him to the nearest trauma center."

"Copy, R-3."

"R-1 out!"

CHAPTER 5

Global Pharmaceuticals was the planet's leader in pharmaceutical development, biochemical and immunochemical development, organic tissue development, generic and organic DNA development, and scientific research and development.

Since the early 21st century, after they enigmatically developed the only cure for the deadly RAGE outbreak, Global Pharmaceuticals maintained the cutting edge over the planet's technology, agriculture, and health care. And they made no secrets about being the planet's number one supplier of military weapon systems, either. Through its major subsidiary companies all over the globe, Global Pharmaceuticals had controlling stock in crystalline-based artificial intelligence, advanced computer systems development, cryogenics rejuvenation advancement, and molecular nanotechnology applications and development.

Taking a lesson from the great Microsoft scandal of the late 20th Century, Global Pharmaceuticals had no need to have its name on every new innovation released to the world. As long as Global Pharmaceuticals held major stock in that innovation, they were content. This strategy eliminated nagging governmental critics against corporate monopolization.

Global Pharmaceuticals also owned several major sporting franchises, including the National Football League's World Champion Pittsburgh Steelmen.

Headquartered in Exton, Pennsylvania, Global Pharmaceuticals purchased the entire city of Exton, which ultimately became their central hub of operations. This massive facility put Langley, Virginia, home of the CIA, to shame. The entire city of Exton was practically a militarized zone, patrolled by Global Pharmaceuticals' private armed forces who were notorious for having itchy trigger fingers and backed with enough legal power to cover up anything deemed "minor indiscretions," which covered beatings, shootings, and highly questionable fatalities.

Global Pharmaceuticals had developed, and forcefully perpetuated, the mystique of being untouchable and above the law!

Negative rumors spread worldwide about their illegal conduct and inhumane experimentation on animals and, even worse, people. In reply, the company spared no expense on damage control propaganda against those rumors. Rebellious insurgents looked at a colossus like Global Pharmaceuticals as the devil in disguise, and were always seeking avenues to undermine its commanding control over the lives of the masses. Global Pharmaceuticals kept a close eye on these groups. The main reason for such close attention was that Global Pharmaceuticals had many skeletons and catastrophic secrets in their closet, secrets that the company was willing to, and had, killed to keep.

Secrets aside, Global Pharmaceuticals was built on integrity; not its own, but the integrity of its subsidiary companies, which constituted the foundational footprint of the Global Pharmaceuticals' empire.

Global Pharmaceuticals' Chief Executive Officer was Francine Katrina Bovier. She executed the company's public and private operations with military precision and authority. She drilled the message into her subordinates that, *"It's better to be feared than respected!"* And she always achieved her goals; everyone who worked under her feared her.

Francine began life as a "sweet-pea," the apple of her parent's eye, a daddy's girl from birth. And from birth her parents molded her to become a leader in the business world. Francine was truly an alpha creation. She had no brothers or sisters to experience sharing or caring, which caused her to miss out on many important social lessons. Francine never learned how to play well with others, but she did learn how to dominate them. Francine studied people's strengths and weaknesses, then quickly adapted her actions to use those weaknesses, and even strengths, to her advantage. She was extremely brilliant, a prodigy. At the age of 17, Francine was on the verge of obtaining her Doctorate in Business and Corporate Administration.

With wide-eyes, she would lovingly follow her daddy everywhere, especially to work where he was a high-level executive on the board of directors for a world class corporation. Days before her 18th birthday, a tragic accident claimed both her parents' lives. The circumstances surrounding their deaths reeked of cover-up and being alone in the world, with no relatives to fill her with adulation or to depend on, Francine's life dove into a downward spiral of self- shutdown and self-destruction.

In college Francine was extremely arrogant and openly showed her distain towards her older collegiate peers. Spitefully, her shunned classmates chose *now*, the most vulnerable period in her life, to strike back at her for treating them like they were sub-classed, regarded as insignificant peons to be abused at her leisure. They knew if she was warned, *"You shouldn't try that!"* she would do just the opposite. Usually, no matter what, Francine came out on top. But this time they caught her off her game. She was weak and needing something to make the pain from her parents' death disappear; something that would stop her from feeling, so her vengeful classmates systematically introduced her to drugs, specifically the type that would destroy her life even further than the deaths of her parents had.

Francine became a willing subject in her own destruction by allowing herself to be victimized. Her classmates, under the guise of helping her relieve the pain from grief, introduced her to marijuana and alcohol. While high on these drugs she was now susceptible to other drugs, and these rich kids, the college's so-called upper echelon group and future leaders of industry, introduced Francine to cocaine and ice, making sure to issue her a stern warning not to try any harder drugs, knowing for certain that Francine's self-righteous, nothing-is-greater-than-me ego would kick in to seal her doom.

Unlike her classmates, Francine didn't use these drugs as party favors, she used them for one reason only…to escape reality. In short order, Francine surrendered all self-control to a daily cocktail of cocaine, heroine, and any psychotropic substance available. She dropped out of college and began a life dedicated to the achievement of her next high. For years Francine lived a fearless, drugged-out existence, more than willing to perform whatever degrading act it took to maintain her high. Issues of health, food, housing, and appearance were on her back burner.

Shockingly, Francine remained extremely attractive. Her outward beauty was the main reason she stayed hooked on drugs for so many years. All drug dealers wanted a beautiful showpiece hanging off their arms, at their beck and call. A pretty piece of meat willing to perform any and all freakish sexual acts in exchange for supplying that always-needed, *next* body rush—*next* mind buzz—that total numbness which drugs temporarily supplied while stealing her precious life and soul.

Francine never stayed with any one dealer very long. After she learned as much as she could from one, she moved up the drug dealers' invisible ladder of success to the next higher-level dealer. Some of these moves were forced upon her because of a dealer's death or incarceration. During one of these upgrades, she met a dealer who became very special to her. He reminded Francine of her late father, not in age or appearance, but in wisdom. Another special thing about him was he wasn't an addict or a pimp.

He taught Francine the value of prosperity over addiction, to acknowledge her fears, and to use her mind to control those fears.

This man fascinated Francine; he wasn't about keeping her on her back, legs to the sky. When she looked into his eyes she could tell he was seeing *her*, and that he really cared about *her.* She had finally found someone who believed in what dwelled beneath her surface, someone who saw the hidden abilities she had suppressed during years of drug, alcohol, and sexual addictions, someone who wanted to help her face her parents' death the right way, as well as overcome any other fears she had.

As far as Francine was concerned, this man saved her life by exposing her to the next level of existence. Along with what she had learned from her father, she had him to thank for her current position of authority and power as CEO of Global Pharmaceuticals.

CHAPTER 6

The news media was eating its young after the Hawaiian Olympics because not a single wire service had seen or heard from 'The Fastest Human Alive' since he was crowned 'The Olympian' months ago. Donovan Mocion had simply fallen off the face of the planet.

Not even the tabloids had a lead on him.

This lack of information was just what Global Pharmaceuticals wanted. Now they could release whatever propaganda suited their needs. They finally broke the story.

"After shocking the planet with his performance at the Summer Olympics, the newly-crowned Olympian, Donovan Mocion, and his entire family fell victims to an unfortunate plane crash following the closing ceremonies.

Donovan Mocion's parents, globally renowned scientists—both holders of the coveted DuPont Chair in Genetics - Drs. Vanessa and Donald Mocion's bodies were not recovered and are presumed dead.

Search and Rescue located Donovan floating a mile from the crash site, still alive, badly injured, and unconscious.

For the past 90 days, he has been treated at an undisclosed medical center and is reported to be in critical condition.

A total of five people are believed to have perished in the crash. Along with the Mocions was a three-member flight crew whose names have not been released.

More details about this tragic airplane crash to follow. Stay tuned to the Global Pharmaceuticals News Network for the latest breaking news on this and other planetary matters."

At the Global Pharmaceuticals Headquarters there were many questions needing answers regarding the tragic loss and the CEO, Francine Katrina Bovier, was summoned by the Board of Directors to update its members. The Board of Directors consisted of the highest-ranking executives from all the subsidiary companies under the Global Pharmaceuticals umbrella.

Francine had prepared an award-winning song and dance routine well in advance, so she was more than ready to present it to the Board of Directors.

"Ladies and gentlemen of the board, we have suffered a tremendous loss. Two of our most gifted and accomplished scientists, Drs. Vanessa and Donald Mocion, were taken from us in the tragic crash of one of our Gulfstream aircrafts." Francine held her head down and took in a deep breath as though grieving, then continued, "The FAA has investigated the incident and discovered a problem with the plane's fuel system. The complete report is contained in the documents on the table in front of each one of you. As a result of the FAA's findings, our remaining fleet has been re-inspected for similar issues and all have been cleared for flight."

With a dazzling, disarming smile she proudly announced, "Members of the board…our fleet is safe!"

Quickly becoming somber again, she continued, "Unfortunately, that same tragedy left the Mocion's only son, Donovan, comatose, and a paraplegic for the remainder of his life."

"The facts are the Mocion family was returning from the recently held Olympics in Hawaii were their only son, Donovan, achieved Platinum Awards and earned the title of Olympian. Unfortunately, the world will be deprived of his future contributions in competitive sports as our doctors sadly report that he will never compete, or walk, again." Francine let the room become silent, allowing the members to soak in the moment of grief, and then continued in her most magnanimous manner. "Members of the Board, I propose that Global Pharmaceuticals absorb all medical expenses for Donovan. I also have no doubt that the company will handle all funeral arrangements, and costs, of our irreplaceable, devoted scientists, even though their bodies have not been recovered. I feel this service will bring a sense of closure to a dreadful event, while relieving a tremendous financial burden from the shoulders of young Donovan. I also suggest the services be postponed until Donovan is healthy enough to personally attend."

Francine glanced around the board table and saw that every board member agreed with her proposal. "*Good!*" she said to herself. *"They went for the easy part. Now let's see if they'll swallow the rest."*

"As most of you are well aware, the Mocions were developing new applications for micro-nanotechnology combined with tissue regeneration. I've already reassigned the project and will personally oversee development, assuring we remain on target for approval by both the Food and Drug Administration (FDA) and Planetary Health Federation (PHF).

"I can reassure all subsidiaries and departments that this devastating loss will not diminish Global Pharmaceuticals' pursuit of excellence.

"Global Pharmaceuticals will maintain our leading edge in all phases of operations and credibility led by you, our trusted Board of Directors, and of course continue to increase our profit margin for our devoted stockholders. Thank you all for attending."

A round of applause was given, and the chairman adjourned the meeting.

A pleased Francine left the meeting, as usual, with the Board of Directors eating out of her hand. Now she had to put the next phase of her master plan into effect.

"Time to call in some favors..."

Chapter 7

Global Pharmaceuticals in Exton, P.A., was a mammoth facility. Only a few key personnel were privy to every entrance. Several of these entrances were military in appearance, and in pure military fashion IDs were required to gain entry, while other entrances looked like normal upscale businesses. There was one entryway, however, that went unnoticed by most eyes. It was in a desolate location out in the boonies where dust devils randomly sprouted up and tossed tumbleweeds into the air and along the ground. The only sign of any past life was a dilapidated water tower standing sentry over the termite-ridden remains of a rickety wooden barn. Surrounding the site was a rusty weather beaten chain link fence, with nothing else visible for miles. Anyone gaining access would not have noticed the multiple cameras recording every possible angle of the seemingly deserted compound after arriving at the retractable gate. This gate required a 16 digit alphanumeric code to access a dirt road leading to the water tower, which stood directly across from the old barn's wooden doors. These doors were barricaded by 5 retractable remote controlled bollards that appeared from beneath the ground when the barn doors were approached.

A remote controlled pole, looking like those at ancient drive-in theaters which once held speakers to be placed inside car windows to hear movie soundtracks, rose from the ground on the driver's side. A panel opened and a scanning device quickly scanned the driver's pupils. Once approved, the barn door silently opened, allowing entrance into the empty barn. Inside was one lone security booth surrounded by cameras, with one guard barking instructions to step out of the vehicle and move forward to another scanning device, this time a handprint scanner. After approval, an inner door opened revealing an elevator. The elevator's control panel had color-coded numbers to choose from, starting with the color white, and the number 0.

This futuristic elevator, with its soft lighting and glowing shades of deep blues and rich burgundies, made no sound and seemed to glide on air while heading in one extremely fast direction — down. This down was not a normal 'straight-down' though, it was angled and the descent felt like sliding along one side of a "V," speeding toward its tip and the many sublevels below.

These sublevels were color-coded, and backlit, displaying a glowing Biohazard symbol, then the floor number. Once past Bio-Level 1, the floor numbers, and health risks, increased.

BL 1- Minimal Biohazard - Study of Low-Risk infectious agents w/cures: Pneumococcus, Salmonella.

BL 2 - Moderate Biohazard - Study of Moderate-Risk infectious agents w/cures: Hepatitis, Lyme disease, Influenza.

BL 3 - High Biohazard - Study of High-Risk infectious agents w/cures: Anthrax, Typhus, HIV, RAGE.

BL 4 - Extreme Biohazard - Study of Maximum Security infectious agents w/ NO CURES: Ebola, Lassa, Hanta, and Motula.

BL 5 - Bioweapons Development.

The Cloning Projects was below that- color-coded blue, occupying levels CL 6 – CL 9.

This was followed by cryogenic experimentation and preservation, color- coded green, occupying levels KL 10 – KL 15.

Next, color-coded black, were levels XL 16 – XL 19 which were housing, restaurants, nightclubs, chapels, gymnasiums, sports parks, holographic entertainment suites, employee medical facilities, household stores, and storage.

The last color and accessible level was color-coded red - DL 20 - Molecular Deatomizer, also known throughout the facility as the "Disposal!"

This color-coded subterranean facility, known only to Global Pharmaceuticals' top executives, scientists, and other crucial employees, was named...

The ***CONE.***

The Cone is where all that does not exist—EXISTS.

Where all those illegal experiments that didn't happen—HAPPEN.

The Cone was the place that, if its existence was known by those not authorized, that knowledge resulted in DEATH!

No one spoke of the Cone by name...EVER!

The Cone was a separate world inside itself, created deep underground, utilizing untapped energy from the earth's core. Those who worked there seldom saw the light of day, and they preferred it that way. Those workers were a specialized group of individuals; men and women who preferred the subterranean lifestyle to surface living. To help maintain sanity, there were 3-dimensioned cityscape views throughout the facility and living quarters, and depending on the mood of that individual, they could be changed to any scenic representation, on or off the planet, complete with atmospheric details and real time soundscapes.

The most brilliant of the brilliant the planet has produced, alive or dead, at one time or another had been involved with what went on inside the Cone, either with or without their direct knowledge. Their lives were, and had been, dedicated to achieving that which was collectively thought to be unachievable.

A handful of Global Pharmaceuticals' most powerful where privy to the Cone's unavowed location. Francine Katrina Bovier was one of those powerful few. Francine made one of her unannounced special trips from the elite 50-story Mahogany Towers of Global Pharmaceuticals, down to the non-existent subterranean Cone to 'put the fear of Francine' into the scientists, and for an update on her pet project.

Global Pharmaceuticals' top scientists had spent months trying to complete the Mocion's Human Enhancement Formula, each time with the same disastrous results, the loss of lives, but each time they got a little closer to the results they were after.

Francine stormed through the office door in her usual storm trooper manner, skeptical about any results, and using her patented, "I'm tried of failure!" tone of voice, announced, "I better hear some exceptional news from you two brainiacs today!" while glowering into the eyes of her subordinates, Drs. Wiley and Hothan, giving them her best imitation of a rabid animal out for the kill.

Drs. Diane Wiley and Louise Hothan had been friends for as long as they could remember. Not "special friends" like lovers, but like big sister/little sister friends. Diane was a few years older than Louise, which lent itself to her having a protective, bossy, big sister mentality. This was just fine as far as Louise was concerned because she had a tendency to doubt her abilities under pressure and babble when called upon for direct answers. Both grew up in the small town of Sandwich, Illinois, where they discovered they had similar interests in life. Those life interests developed into a great working team, so they encouraged each other to shoot for the stars in all endeavors. Both were graduates from Massachusetts Institute of Technology (MIT) with Ph.D.s in Biological Engineering, Biology, Mental and Cognitive Sciences, Health Sciences and Technology, Physics, and Chemistry. They were both brilliant and very respected in their fields, as were all scientists working in the Cone facility.

Dr. Diane Wiley, the older of the two, was in her early 40s, and stood 5' 2" tall. She had a medium build, was shapely but cushiony, and had curly off-blond hair with darker streaks to bring out her light baby blue eyes. Her rather large nose distanced those baby blues perfectly, making her overall pale, white-skinned face very attractive. Professionally she was very by-the-book, an anal retentive type whose career was her life, and she lived for her work in the Cone.

Dr. Louise Hothan, the younger of the two, was in her late 30s and stood 6' tall with long auburn, almost black hair, which she consistently worn in a ponytail because she was too insecure to try anything different. She too had pale white skin. Everyone who worked in the subterranean facility had a ghost-like appearance no matter what their individual ethnicity; all Cone staff was sunlight deficient.

Dr. Hothan, contrary to Dr. Wiley, let her heart motivate some of her reasoning and decision making processes. She had model-like features with almond-shaped, steaming, dark brown penetrating eyes. Her beauty got in her way sometimes because some colleagues didn't take her seriously. Her beauty blinded them, but her brilliance spoke for itself. After all, she *did* work in the Cone!

Drs. Wiley and Hothan were originally assistants to the Mocions, then, after the tragic plane crash, they were both promoted to complete the Mocion's project. As brilliant as they were, they could not come up with the 'xyz' of the final formula. No one seemed able to, but the last thing they wanted to do was let Francine know this, so while looking Francine directly in the eyes, Dr. Wiley, trying to give her best look of confidence and hoping Francine couldn't hear her pounding heart beating like a percussionist playing congas inside her chest, replied, "We've achieved partial success."

She knew full well she'd better start her update report to Francine in a positive direction, before her personal frustrations over not being able to reproduce the Mocion's work revealed themselves.

Then she added, "But, I just don't understand it! The Mocion's notes are precisely detailed, and we've followed them right down to the last molecular structure...unless they intentionally left a key equation out. It can't be that impossible to extrapolate the concluding sequences producing the final equation." She ran her fingers through her curly brown streaked hair in frustration while adding, "Perhaps it's the subjects we've been using. They are, after all, the dredges, homeless, death row criminals, and outcasts of society."

Eager to place the blame on someone, or something, other than themselves, Dr. Hothan added, "Yes, I think it's time we acquired more suitable subjects.

These current subjects have contaminated their bodies for so long that rejection to the process is only logical."

"I do not like what I'm hearing," said Francine, tapping her foot on the floor in what could only be described as a controlled mini-temper tantrum. Francine threw both hands up in the air, causing her expensive silver bracelets to create a ringing sound as she stormed out of the lab in a huff saying over her shoulder, "Do the best you can. Run the damned advertisements!"

The only reason Francine was being so nice to Drs. Wiley and Hothan was because she knew full well that the Mocions had intentionally withheld that final equation, preventing their formula from working, and if she couldn't get that equation soon, the entire project would have to be scrapped and taken back to formula.

Drs. Wiley and Hothan were more confused by Francine's actions and comments than by the Mocion's formula.

Dr. Hothan, in disbelief of Francine's actions, said, "She must be medicated!"

"Totally! She's never been that accepting about a failure before," added Dr.

Wiley.

"I read somewhere that true genius is getting from the letter A to the letter Z, and not needing the rest of the alphabet," began Dr. Hothan as they left their office and returned to the main lab. Dr. Hothan had a habit of spouting out trivial information when she felt inadequate about her abilities.

"If those are the ground rules for true genius—where does that leave us?" replied Dr. Wiley.

They both stopped and looked at each other.

"Clearly, not in the same league as the Mocions," admitted Dr. Hothan. "Well, who is?" replied Dr. Wiley as they entered the lab through automatic opening doors.

Dr. Hothan, in an attempt to put a positive spin on their work over the last few months, offered up, "We have had relative successes, which puts us closer than we were months ago when we were dropped into this mess. I think posting advertisements for volunteers is our best option."

"We've got nothing to lose now," added Dr. Wiley. "Besides, we just got the approval to do so by the HNIC."

Dr. Hothan stopped in her tracks, looked Dr. Wiley square in the eyes, and then they both burst into uncontrollable laughter. After a minute or so, Dr. Hothan managed to say through her laughter, "You...better not...EVER... let her hear... you...call her that!" And then she finished, "Not if you want to stay alive."

They both immediately stopped laughing as they recalled some of the horror stories floating around about those who had angered Francine Katrina Bovier.

Chapter 8

Global Pharmaceuticals launched an advertising campaign in every major newspaper announcing…

"MEDICAL RESEARCH VOLUNTEERS NEEDED!

IF YOU ARE A VETERAN SUFFERING FROM THE FOLLOWING AILMENTS:

Shakes, Tremors, Gulf Vapors Syndrome, Iraqi Neuromuscular Disorder, Iranian Bowel Disorder, Societal Reintegration Disorder, Osteogenesis Imperfecta (OI), Osteoporosis, Arthritis Pain (Any Form), Muscle Weakness, Joint Laxity, or Limited Range of Motion Conditions.

> *We are conducting Clinical Trials for a revolutionary new treatment that will, once perfected, permanently eliminate all the above disorders, syndromes, and pains.*
>
> *Living and food accommodations will be provided for accepted applicants.*
>
> *The minimum duration of these clinical trials is 90-days. At the conclusion of the studies, candidates will receive $30,000.00 Tax Free compensation. After payout, those eligible will receive Unemployment Insurance compensation. They will also receive a lifetime supply of medication developed through these trials.*
>
> *Those interested in qualifying please report to…"*

This ad reached the hands of disabled veteran, Malik Jamerson, who had been part of an insurgent team sent to extinguish the reignited gulf oil field fires.

Terrorists of the global economy knew that greed would eventually approve the return to the gulf to extinguish these fires. At the time, unknown to the global economic decision makers, those fields were booby trapped by a chemical weapon concealed within the vapors of the burning oil, causing irreparable damage to anyone exposed.

Several months after initial contact, the afflicted would start suffering from what they thought was the onset of osteoarthritis or rheumatoid arthritis. Then, when medications by western doctors were prescribed, those meds unknowingly increased the speed of deterioration, causing the patient to live a life of unbearable pain and suffering. This malady became known as the Gulf Vapors Syndrome. The GVS caused the joints' fluids to evaporate. Next, the cartilage would wear out. Then, the joints deteriorated to a bone-grinding-against-bone condition, and finally frozen joints followed by immobility.

When Malik saw the newspaper ad his spirits soared with hopefulness, which was an emotion he had not experienced in many years, and he quickly made his way to the interview site across town.

Hundreds of people had flocked into the vacant, damp, and musty warehouse along the docks to apply. The place looked like an orthopedic mash unit/insane asylum, complete with people using wheelchairs, crutches, walkers and canes. The only thing missing was padded rooms. The pain of those suffering could be felt in an instant. The ambient noise was all moans and groans, and the place reeked from over-the-counter ointments, salves, and the horrible odor of homemade cures people had created in hopes of eliminating their chronic pains. Those not in pain were moving around, twitching and fussing out loud at invisible people, or cursing at any stranger who looked at them the wrong way. The place was like a circus or a zoo, holding the souls of once proud people now reduced to tormented dying bodies that were falling apart.

Slowly Malik made his way, one step at a time, to the counter.

"My name is Malik Jamerson and I'm here about the ad," Malik eagerly announced to a big, round faced, round bodied, balding, fat, white guy. He was the type who was mad at the world for allowing his life to turn out the way it had, making it his life's mission to ruin as many people's days as possible. He sat slouching like an over-fed bulldog at a counter that was safely secured behind 6" of protective glass; without looking up from his girly magazine, he pointed a chewed-up #2 pencil at a red and black plastic number dispenser on a stand next to the window, and then smugly said, "Take a number!"

Then he shoved some papers through the open slot at the bottom of the protective glass, wrinkling most of them, and instructed, "Answer airry single question on dhese forms. When you get 'err done, bring 'em back and put 'em in dhat dhere in-slot." He pointed the same chewed-up pencil at a little slot on the far wall with a black printed label reading 'Completed Forms.' "Dhen take a seat - yo number ell be called soon as yo answers get checked."

Then, to Malik's surprise, the guy looked up in disgust from his magazine, revealing big, red, bubble eyes, and gave Malik the once-over from top to bottom and said, "It's free coffee 'n' snacks on dhat table back dere... NEXT!"

> Malik thought, *"I hate coming to these damn 'cattle-calls,' and sitting in shitty uncomfortable-ass little chairs. At lease they picked the perfect weather for it. It's been pouring down rain all over the planet for the last 3 weeks now. And nobody can convince me that it's not due to all those upper atmosphere experiments going on. Fixing the ozone my ass! This planet's in trouble and soon we'll either have to live underground, underwater, or on a different planet."*

Malik sat squirming from side to side, trying to keep his butt from falling asleep for over an hour, and just when he had taken all he could take, he heard his number called.

"Number 28, number 28."

Malik looked in the direction of the voice and discovered that a cute, petite little redhead with a tight hourglass figure, long athletic legs, muscular calves, toned thighs, and a nice round booty, was behind the sweet voice calling his number.

"*Things are looking up!*" he thought, then said, "Here…I'm number 28," waving his number in the air, walking towards the hot little package calling him.

"I'm Kara. Please follow me," and she turned and began walking away.

Malik paused a second, then stayed a couple of feet behind her; this gave him the perfect vantage point for checking out the outstanding package seductively strutting in front of him.

"*She's outrageous!*" he thought. He also figured that since he was tailgating this hot little number, he had been accepted for the trials.

Kara, who Malik was now drooling over, led him to a small office where 3 other people were sitting: a rather attractive woman in a wheelchair, and two other scruffy homeless looking people. Malik decided to take a seat next to the woman in the wheelchair, since her beauty, along with Kara's, improved the view in the shabby little office.

"Good afternoon. You can refer to me as Kara, and I'd like to welcome you, our qualified applicants, to this fantastic research opportunity. We're going to start by keeping this project as clinical as possible. So, from here to trial's end you will only be addressed by the random numbers you selected at your arrival. Now, so that the rest of you will know who is who, you will begin by sharing with the group your personal number, starting with you." Kara pointed to one of the scruffy two who had gravitated to the back on the room, each to a corner with several empty chairs between them.

"Who, me? Oh, oh, oh…my name is Ar…"

Kara blurted out, "Stop!" She immediately cut him off. "All we need know is your number."

"OH, oh, oh, oh, OK, my number is 5."

His given name was Arturo Zanzibar. While fighting in the Bio-Conflict of Iran, Arturo had been leading a squad on a covert assault behind the enemy's stronghold when a "Disassociation Nerve Gas" was released on his squad. After he returned from duty, the DNG's side effects left him unable to cope with the social demands of society. He suffered from Societal Reintegration Disorder. Arturo became one of the many causalities of war, wandering the world, living a nomadic life of survival by any means possible.

"Thank you!" said Kara, who then announced with an uppity attitude, "People, this is how it works. You will only be referred to by your number, and you are only to respond to your number. Now, is that clear?"

None of the four applicants replied.

"Fine! I'll take your silence as compliance. Now, you, in the far left corner…"

"ME?" asked the other scruffy looking candidate. "Yes, you! Please, tell the group your number." "Fif-tee-3!" came a loud abrupt reply.

The name was really Camille Giuseppe. After the United States' "Who's The Boss" military campaign against North Korea ended in turmoil earlier in the decade, Camille was released from active duty due to Shakes and Tremors, a condition many soldiers fell victim to during that conflict. They were prone to sudden uncontrollable panic outbursts, some to the point of violence, and others had even been known to commit murder, or even suicide. It was a roll of the dice that determined the individual's reaction to pressure under any given circumstance.

Next, Kara looked to the woman in the wheelchair, and in a less intimidating tone she asked, "And your number?"

"37…," she softly, nervously, replied, then she cleared her throat and answered more loudly, "My number is 37."

Claudia Rawlins was her given name. She had enlisted in the Planetary Forces several months ago, wanting to do her part in protecting the planet against terrorists'

attacks. Unfortunately for Claudia, a few weeks into basic training, while she was going through a simple obstacle course, she broke both arms as she swung from one bar to another.

While in the hospital, it was discovered that she suffered from a form of Osteogenesis Imperfecta. As a result of this genetic disorder, she was immediately discharged from the service without compensation. She soon wound up needing a wheelchair just to get around. As far as she was concerned, she had nothing to loose.

Finally, Kara walked in front of Malik, sat on top of a desk at the front center of the room, and crossed her legs, teasing him, while simultaneously sending the message, "You will never get any of this!"

"And you?" she asked seductively, raising her left eyebrow, with a quasi- smile on her lips.

Malik, slouched down in his chair, almost to where his knees were touching Kara's crossed legs, and slowly began swinging his legs open and then closed as he said, "You've already got my number!"

"I most certainly do!" she said as she abruptly stood up, took a step, turned, pulling her hair from her face with her left hand, then waved her right hand over the group as if displaying a prize on a game show, saying, "Why don't you give it to the other members of the group so they'll know what to call you?"

"Why don't you two just get a room!?" came a vocal outburst from the back of the room where numbers 53 and 5 were located.

Malik stood up directly in front of Kara, giving her an exclusive view of the bulge in his pants, turned around, giving Kara a back view, said, "28," and then calmly sat back down.

"There you have it," began Kara, "Our ALPHA CLINICAL TRIALS group. Here and after your group will be referred to as A.C.T. Now, before you launch all your questions at me, let me say this…ALL YOUR QUESTIONS WILL BE ANSWERED INDIVIDUALLY ONCE YOU ARRIVE AT THE MEDICAL

RESEARCH FACILITY! So, let's be on our way. If you will follow me," and she looked at 28 holding her finger out, curling it at him in a suggestive come-and-get- this manner, with 28 following behind her like a puppy dog in heat.

He thought to himself, "*Hell, I may be in pain, but I'm not dead! I'd gladly hit that!*"

A.C.T. was loaded into a van with no windows then transported to a private hanger where they drove straight onto a waiting military-type aircraft. They were unloaded from the van and given individual seats aboard the aircraft which, like the van, also had no windows. Once the plane reached cruising altitude, Kara calmly walked over to 28's seat, squatted down beside him, and allowed him and him alone to view under her skirt and between her thighs to see she wasn't wearing any underwear. She leaned in and whispered in his ear, "Follow me!"

She led him to an isolated area in the plane where she initiated 28 into the ranks of "The Mile High Club." An hour later 28 returned to his seat wearing a huge smile on his face and reeking from the smell of sex. The smell did not go unnoticed by the other members of A.C.T., but whatever comments or thoughts the other members had, they kept them to themselves.

A few minutes later the plane landed at Global Pharmaceuticals' private airport in Exton. Kara reappeared looking a bit frazzled, making sure each group member was back on board the windowless van. 28 was the last to climb into the van, so Kara gave his hand an affectionate squeeze, and when he turned his head to look at her, she gave him a sexy wink, then blew him a kiss before closing the van's door behind him. She watched and let out a sigh of remembered pleasure as the van slowly rolled off the plane and continued its trip to the Cone facility.

Chapter 9

Inside the Cone facility, Global Pharmaceuticals' scientists had conducted experiments on primates with a variety of successes and failures. Time constraints pressured the shot-callers, mainly Francine Katrina Bovier, to approve human trials of the Human Enhancement Formula in its current, as-is stage.

Francine insisted on maintaining the Mocions' schedule of development as if they were still running the project. The known dangerous and deadly side effects were insignificant in her final decision to proceed.

Each member of A.C.T. had been blindfolded until they were securely inside the elevator leading down into the Cone facility. The speed of their descent, along with the flashing color-coded lights, made them all light-headed until the elevator stopped, which almost made them throw up on XL 10, the first floor of the research division. As their heads cleared, they were met by the formidable Rovena Budnski.

Lab Supervisor Rovena Budnski — the 'n' in her last name was silent, but since she was always in everybody's business, behind her back she was called, "Butt-In-Skee." She was also given the nickname Roe. She was a short, round, thin-lipped, nosy and overbearing, multiple-wig-wearing German woman in her 40s, with a loud nagging voice – almost like fingernails on a chalkboard.

She smelled of garlic and always demanded things be done her way, getting angry at the slightest deviation. She had been passed over too many times to count for promotions because of her Gestapo-like attitude. It seemed she had reached her highest position as the Head Laboratory Supervisor.

Nobody could tell her that she wasn't good at what she did and she knew it.

If she wasn't, she wouldn't be working in this facility or standing outside the elevator awaiting the new arrivals — "New Meat," as she referred to them. Roe greeted the members of A.C.T. in her take-charge manner as soon as the doors of the elevator opened.

"I am Lab Supervisor Rovena Budnski," she said sternly. Then she loudly announced, "Now, before any of you "New Meat" abuse my last name – the 'n' is silent and I pronounce it Budski. I am... The Head Lab Supervisor," and waving her arm over her head in a single motion she turned and ordered, "Follow me!" like she was leading an assault on an invisible enemy.

She marched A.C.T. into a meeting room, and once they were seated, she proceeded to blast their ears off by indoctrinating them into the facility dos and don'ts. Once this torture was completed, she announced, "Now, Meat, this way to your individual domiciles, and remember...look sharp while being treated in my facility. I will not tolerate any back-sliding!" and away she marched, with A.C.T. closely following her through a maze of unsettling dimly lit corridors lined with concrete and steel. The facility smelled sterile, like it had been rubbed down with disinfectant. It had a very cold, very hard, ominous and frightening aura about it. There was also the faint stench of decaying flesh present, not enough to be a real bother, yet enough to be aware of it.

A.C.T. was completely blown away when they entered their individual quarters. There were plush wall-to-wall carpets, luxurious king-sized beds, a variety of living, oxygen-producing plants, tranquil, peaceful colors throughout off-set by texture-covered walls with hanging digitized changeable art displays, and elegantly appointed furnishings with electronically changeable wall panel artificial views of any viewscape, including their accompanying sounds, plus an unlimited library of any type of music they wanted to hear. Their accommodations were no less than those of the highest-rated hotels.

Once settled, they each received a phone call informing them that a guide would be sent to collect them for "questions and answers" in the meeting room. The pleasant voice over the phone added, "And don't worry, the guide won't be Budnski."

A.C.T. soon realized that if Budnski had her way, the research facility would be run like a Nazi concentration camp. Thank goodness she was only in charge in her imagination. Everyone else at the facility treated A.C.T. like they were special guests on vacation at a 10-Star Resort, complete with 24-hour room service and No Tipping Required.

When A.C.T. entered the sterile concrete-surfaced meeting room, sitting at a round stone-topped table were Drs. Diane Wiley and Louise Hothan, along with four empty chairs and writing tablets on the table in front of them.

"Come on in, come on in. Please, sit down and make yourselves comfortable. I am Dr. Hothan."

"And I'm Dr. Wiley. Contrary to the impression one of our colleges has given you… we won't mention any names…"

"Butt-In-Skee!" coughed Dr. Hothan.

"…we run this clinical control group," continued Dr. Wiley, "and we want your experience here to be as beneficial and as pleasant for you as possible. We can imagine that you are full of questions and we would be happy to answer them."

"As best we can," added Dr. Hothan.

"Before you ask your questions, let us explain just what it is we are trying to achieve with these treatments," said Dr. Wiley.

"First and foremost, we believe we have discovered a release from your daily extreme chronic pain. We also believe we have a serum that will strengthen your weak muscles, and return flexibility to your joints. The serum will enhance your mobility and agility beyond your imagination, as well. And finally, the serum will promote a mental sense of well-being and improve your overall emotional health. Now, Dr. Hothan, will you please go into a little more detail?"

"Absolutely. We have conducted treatments on primates with inspiring results. Based on those results, we have concluded that the serum is ready for human trial—our target species. Now, let me speak a little about the side effects."

53 interrupted by asking, "Yo… is it true, like a… I'm gonna get paid 30 large for being a guinea pig?"

"Why, yes, you are. All of you will receive $30,000.00, tax free, for your participation in these trials," answered Dr. Hothan with a smile.

"Dat's what I'm talkin' 'bout," said 5, giving 53 a high-five.

"That's all I need to know," said 53. "Can I go now? I ordered pizza from the menu in my room just before I got phoned to come here."

"Yeah…me, too! I ordered prime-rib," added 5.

"Well, certainly, if that's all you needed to know. We'll send for you when we're ready to begin," answered Dr. Wiley.

53 and 5 bolted from the table with large smiles on their faces, giggling between the two of them until they turned around and saw a sour-faced Rovena Budnski waiting to escort them back to their quarters. She had already made up her mind to despise these two for being scruffy and grungy looking. To her, all grungy looking people were a plague on society, non-contributors to the higher development of the species, and they all should be experimented on—to their deaths if necessary.

28 and 37 looked at each other, smiled, and shook their heads at the actions of 53 and 5.

37 asked in her soft spoken voice, "Please, tell me about those side effects." "Yeah, what about them?" asked 28 in a more matter-of-fact tone.

The doctors were secretly hoping the entire A.C.T. group only wanted to get paid and had no questions to ask. That would have made their day. They were prepared to answer certain questions, if need be. But in no way were they going to tell A.C.T. the true details involving the horrible deaths all prior human subjects had experienced.

"To answer your question," began Dr. Hothan, "in the primates, we discovered that the serum lasted for 10 hours, followed by a withdrawal period lasting various lengths of time, but no longer than 2 hours. During that period, the subject became agitated, showed some aggressive tendencies, and was in a constant sexually aroused condition."

37 thought, *"With what I've seen about 28, sexually aroused is his normal condition."*

28 caught 37 looking at him and winked at her.

37 shyly smiled and blushed as she lowered her head, looking into her empty lap.

"What! Is that it?" asked 28. "Are those the only side effects?"

"Well, there was another side effect, but we believe it was due to the serum being formulated for primates and not humans," added Dr. Wiley. "And just what was that?" asked 37.

"After the primate passed through the withdrawal period, all positive signs of benefits from the serum were gone, and there were conclusive signs of aging in primate subject,." admitted Dr. Wiley, who was hoping she wouldn't be asked, *"What was the aging rate?"*

"We've made adjustments to the serum and we're confident that we will achieve the positive results intended," Dr. Hothan quickly injected. "Are you two ok with that?" she asked, sounding truly concerned.

The room became quiet for a couple of moments as 37 and 28 did some individual soul-searching.

Finally 37 broke the silence by saying, "Well, I'm here to help get the bugs out of something that will be of great benefit to mankind, so I'm still in!"

"Me, too!" announced 28, noticing what a nice shape 37 had sitting in that wheelchair of hers.

Over the next seven days, A.C.T. was prodded, poked, rammed, jammed, scraped, and scanned. Fluids were withdrawn, chemicals were injected, and their systems were completely flushed out from every orifice. When these preliminary cleansing/screening tests were completed, the scientist knew more about their test subjects' bodies and minds than each test subject ever would, and much more than a couple of them wanted revealed.

With the test results, Drs. Wiley and Hothan calculated how much Human Enhancement Formula was appropriate for each test subject. And so, the moment of truth was at hand. The injections were scheduled for 10 am the following morning.

"Back to your cages, Guinea Pigs, and get some rest. The experiment begins tomorrow and remember…I expect all Meat to be on its best behavior at all times in my facility!" ordered Budnski.

Chapter 10

'The Fastest Man Alive,' crowned The Olympian at the Hawaiian Olympics Games of 2020, Donovan Mocion's single greatest accomplishment was being the sole survivor of a devastating plane crash. He lay in a coma at Cedars-Sinai Medical Center in Beverly Hills, California, for 9 months and counting. Although he was oblivious to what was going on around him, inside his mind was actively replaying flashbacks of his life. He recalled nothing from high school or his formative years except two board games: chess and Chinese checkers. Both games had taught him strategy. Chinese checkers showed him how to be ruthless and single-minded of purpose and chess taught him the art of deception in achieving his personal goals. Randomly laced between these flashbacks was additional information that didn't fit the lessons of either game; perhaps he wasn't ready to wrap his mind around those particular flashbacks, yet.

Donovan's college years supplied clearer images. He was never a 'people person' and didn't care what others thought of him. When he knew he could do something, even if he'd never tried it before, there was no hesitation in proving it or boastfully announcing, "I own that!"

Especially when it came to academia; Donovan existed ahead of the curve in all his studies. His logic and facts were incontestable.

His self-awareness about his own brilliance angered his competitors while they struggled to come up with answers during scholastic decathlon competitions. Donovan always upstaged everyone with his uncanny ability to instantly recall obscure facts about every topic.

On the flip side, Donovan could always be counted on to demonstrate that his people skills were at the bottom of the curve. Still, there was something special about him, and everyone around him saw it, too.

Donovan's comatose mind-flashes recalled his first slap from a pretty girl...

At a pep rally before a major track meet, a beautiful girl had been seductively flirting with him from across the room. Not knowing her name, he put his best "Mac-daddy" persona on, strutted across the floor to her and simply said, "I know you're feeling me. You've made that straight up clear. Now, I like getting right to the point, so let's go somewhere so I can 'hit it!'"

A frown came across her face as she stared at him, her mouth open in shock and disbelief over what she had just heard! Never before had she been hit on so crudely. In response, she laid a vicious slap across Donovan's face.

"Damn, girl... what you getting all insulted 'bout?" he asked while rubbing his stinging face. "History has already proved that if it dresses like a - - -."

Donovan intentionally didn't finish for effect; instead, he looked her up and down, smiling his approval of her exquisite front view.

"And if it acts like a - - -."

He gently took her hand and smoothly twirled her around as he relished her dramatic curves.

"Then it must be a…"

But before he got the final word out she placed her forefinger to his lips, took Donovan by the hand, and led him to her dorm room for the night.

Donovan tried hanging on to this flashback for as long as he could, but it quickly faded. Next, he was in a conversation with his father, who was telling him, "Son, when it comes to physically showing off, make sure you carefully pick the time and place to display your real abilities, and understand this, son... *"The press is never your friend! Therefore, when you choose to make headlines, make sure you're at the top of your game so the media has no choice but to kiss your entire ass!"* Donovan could feel the laughter he and his father enjoyed after that little lesson on how to treat the paparazzi.

Then he flashed on his mother telling him, *"Well, baby boy, if you know* you're weak in a subject, then do all you can to strengthen that weakness. Go out of your way to absorb everything about the subject you can—that will make you stronger!"

Something else flashed through Donovan's brain— so intense it caused him to physically jerk in his hospital bed. It was his first movement since he had been fished out of the ocean months ago. In his coma he sensed something tragic had happened. In his mind Donovan kept seeing bright flashing lights, hearing a loud roar, and feeling the force of wind blowing his body in all directions. Then he realized he was falling and he opened his eyes, sat straight up in his hospital bed, and yelled at the top of his lungs,

"WHAT'S HAPPENING TO ME?"

Chapter 11

Consciousness unfolded slowly for Donovan. A swirling blurred image kept appearing, disappearing, and reappearing in front of him. His eyes fought to focus on a bright flashing light that he couldn't quite make out, but there was one thing he was certain of. There was an atrocious, eye-watering smell.

His unconscious mind recalled a trip to southern California. He was riding through a little city named Lake Elsinore where, during the summer months, the heat evaporated the lake down to a third its normal size, and when that happened it gave off a horrendously foul stench. But worse still was on the way back to LA, traveling north on the I-15, passing endless corrals of cattle, along with an active slaughter house. The suffocating smell of cow dung, mixed with putrid, pungent decaying flesh, made choices like not breathing, rolling up the windows in over 100 degree heat without air-conditioning, or even tolerating someone smoking tobacco, all more enjoyable experiences.

The odor Donovan was experiencing now was far, far worse than any of those memories! He turned his head from side to side trying to avoid the smell, but something kept putting his nose directly in this aroma's foul path. He tried to speak but his mouth wasn't cooperating. He only managed to puff out indistinguishable sounds. "Ba… Ba…Ba…," he kept repeating. "Ba…Ba…Ba!"

Marla Givens, the nurse who was leaning over him, shining a light into his eyes, said to the orderly standing next to her, "Jimbo, he keeps trying to say something but I can't make it out. Can you?"

Jimbo listened closely, shrugged his shoulders and shook his head from side to side, then replied, "Nope!"

Donovan kept trying to speak, and this time he managed a different sound. "Add…add…add."

Donovan's eyes were slowly coming into focus, but his sense of smell was continuously being bombarded by something dreadful. He tried holding his breath to avoid it, but that only worked for a short while. Gradually, other faculties started returning and he began putting together the words being spoken, and as the blurred swirling images slowed down, he finally made out the words "Can you hear me?"

Donovan tried his best to respond, but the only thing fully functional was still his sense of smell. Then, as if someone had turned on the lights, his vision locked into focus and he recognized from where the dreadful aroma was emanating, and this time his mouth cooperated with his mind and he managed to shout out, "Baaaaad," then there was a slight pause, after which followed the word "BREATH!!"

Marla bolted straight up and turned towards Jimbo, who was doing all he could to hold back his laughter, until he managed to say, "I think he's complaining about your breath."

By now Donovan's vocal skills had returned sufficiently enough for him to clearly say, "Bad breath…YOU!" while looking directly at Marla.

Jimbo burst into laughter and said to Marla, "Wait till the word gets out that your breath was so bad it woke up a comatose patient!" and he left the room, laughing uncontrollably down the hallway.

Poor Marla, embarrassed, blushing, and feelings hurt, covered her mouth with her hand while innocently saying under her breath, "I've got an appointment to get my gingivitis taken care of today!" Marla had developed a crush on Donovan over the past several months; secretly, she enjoyed the way Donovan's body reacted to her touch so whenever she could, she'd come by his room to check on him. This visit was right before her dentist appointment.

Marla left Donovan's room not knowing which emotions to feel, excitement over him being awake or hurt feelings over Donovan's comments. She decided to be excited over him being awake and hurried to the nurses' station to inform them of Donovan's status.

"Can you see me? Can you hear me?" asked a face moving in and out of focus.

"Barely," was Donovan's reply. "Where am I?" he asked Nurse Johnson, who was now leaning over him.

"You're at Cedars-Sinai Medical Center, in Beverly Hills, California."

"California!" repeated Donovan in bewilderment. "How'd I get here? Where are my parents?" this question came abruptly, not giving the nurse time to answer his first. Donovan anxiously looked around the room for his parents, then shouted as loudly as he could in his weakened state, "MOM!! DAD!!!"

Sadly, they were nowhere near to hear their baby's cries.

Head Nurse Johnson intentionally avoided eye contact with Donovan by looking at his chart while saying, "I'll go get your doctor for you," and she quickly turned and left his room, not wanting to feel his pain.

Donovan tried speaking to her again but his mouth couldn't respond fast enough to catch the nurse before she was out the door.

He looked around and discovered he was alone in a private room. There were no flowers, no cards, no balloons, and no clue that anyone knew he was alive. He tried to sit up again but he couldn't move. He noticed an attendant's call button by his side so he began pushing it when a small Oriental man with keen features, salt and pepper hair, wire rim glasses, a bright smile and kind face, dressed in a white lab coat walked through the door.

"Hello, I'm Dr. Andrew Kim and I've been treating you for the last 9 months."

"9… months?" a shocked Donovan repeated slowly. "Where are my parents?

Dr. Kim momentarily hung his head down, then looked Donovan directly in the eyes and said, "I'm sorry to inform you that their bodies were never recovered from the plane crash. You are the sole survivor."

"What! What plane crash?" Donovan tried to yell but he was too weak, and a look of disbelief, dread, and desperation covered his face. The power of these emotions was too much for him to bear and Donovan passed out.

The next time Donovan opened his eyes it was the next day. This time the first person he saw was Dr. Kim.

"I wanted to be here as soon as you came around. There are some vital health issues I need to discuss with you. First of all, how are you feeling today?"

"Like SHIT!" answered Donovan, unable to come up with a more accurate description for how he felt. "My head is clearer than the last time I saw you, but I can't feel anything below my waist."

Dr. Kim replied, "That's the first thing on my list of issues to talk over with you. I realize that you have suffered a tragic loss, and I'm afraid my news will only make it worse."

"WORSE!?" Donovan repeated in an exasperated tone. "You tell me my parents, the only souls who love me, and who I love, are dead. How much worse could it be?"

Dr. Kim continued calmly, "I'm afraid a lot worse." He took a deep breath to ready himself. He could feel Donovan's suspense overflowing, see the horror building in his eyes. *"This is the part of my job that I hate the most,"* thought Dr.

Kim to himself.

"Donovan, you've suffered a paralyzing spinal cord injury and have lost the use of your legs—***permanently!"***

Donovan's mind hung on the words "***paralyzing***" and "***permanently.***" Then he launched a massive assault of invisible flying eye daggers toward the doctor as he squeezed his bedrails in disbelief.

"That can't be!" he shouted. "I'm a world class athlete—the best! I want a second opinion," demanded Donovan.

"Mine is the fourth opinion. You have already been seen by all the top medical leaders in spinal cord injuries. They brought you to me as your last hope. I hate to tell you this, but I concur with the findings of my expert colleagues. Your spine has been crushed at the base," said Dr. Kim, calmly and sadly.

Donovan looked blindly into space and tears from his soul poured down his face. He closed his eyes and drifted off to some unknown place within, blotting out everything else Dr. Kim was saying. Finally, Donovan said to Dr. Kim, "Please, Dr. Kim, I need to be alone right now. Can we pick this up later?"

"Sure," said Dr. Kim. "We'll pick this up after I've finished my rounds. We need to discuss your injuries in detail, and your options."

"Options! What fucking options!?" Donovan shouted angrily while he violently shook his bed railings.

Dr. Kim had been through this same scenario with other Spinal Cord Injury patients, and each time it weighed heavy on his heart. He completely understood Donovan's emotional and physical outburst and he quietly left the room without replying.

Donovan's whole world, all his life's plans, and worst of all, his beloved mother and father, had been ripped apart and he couldn't even remember how it had happened. He felt more helpless than he had ever felt before. Donovan was devastated, terrified, and destroyed. Being active one day and paralyzed the next sent him into a depression with nothing but a bottomless pit waiting.

Donovan went to sleep and slept the sleep of the dead where he dreamed dreams of competing, dreams of doing things with his life that now he'd never be able to do. He had devoted all of his life to studying, to track and field, and to his beloved parents. He had no close friends. In fact, the only friends he had, had been killed in that plane crash. Now his whole world was empty, useless and shattered just like his spine. Donovan felt his whole life had been yanked away from him and he wallowed in self-pity, bitterness, and depression. He quietly asked the Creator the most commonly asked questions from someone in his position…

"Why me?"

"What is there to live for?"

"Why didn't I just die?"

CHAPTER 12

As promised, after Dr. Kim completed his hospital rounds for the day, he went back to see Donovan, determined to explain in complete detail the reality of his spinal cord injury. He entered Donovan's room and found him staring off into space with a blank expression on his face.

"Hello, Donovan. How are you doing this afternoon?"

Donovan continued staring into space and didn't acknowledge the doctor's presence.

"Well, Donovan, you need to listen carefully to what I'm about to explain to you. These are the details of SCI."

"SCI?" interrupted Donovan.

"Spinal Cord Injury and exactly how you are affected. I will explain it to you as though you are a child. Please, I realize you are highly intelligent, so don't allow yourself to be insulted by this approach. Are you ready?"

Donovan, not sure he really wanted to hear this, replied, "I'm listening— let's go!" Dr. Kim gave Donovan a smile of encouragement, and began. "Donovan, let me explain the nervous system and its groups of nerves. Your nervous system is composed of the central nervous system, the cranial nerves, and the peripheral nerves. The brain and spinal cord together form the central nervous system. The cranial nerves connect the brain to the head. The four groups of nerves that branch from the cervical, thoracic, lumbar, and sacral regions of the spinal cord are called the peripheral nerves."

"This is how you talk to a child? Damn, Doc, what kind of children do you know?" Donovan asked sarcastically, already convinced he didn't want to hear this lecture.

"Well, none really," answered Dr. Kim. "Stay with me here, I'm doing my best."

"Sorry, Doc. Please, continue."

Dr. Kim regrouped and continued.

"The brain's primary role is to function as the body's control center. This organ receives and interprets nerve signals from every part of the body and initiates the appropriate responses. These responses include adjustments in internal bodily functions such as heart rate, temperature, movement, speech, emotions and consciousness. You still with me?" asked Dr. Kim with a smile.

"So far, so good," answered Donovan.

"Great, let's move on," said Dr. Kim. "Now, the spinal cord is a cylinder of nerve tissue that runs down the center canal in the spine. The nerve fibers in the spinal cord transmit sensory information toward the brain and motor signals to the appropriate parts of the body. The spinal cord also handles some automatic motor responses to sensory information by itself.

"There are 5 pairs of nerves called the sacral spinal nerves. They are medically identified by their alpha numerical designations of S1 through S5. These nerves, S1 through S5, control the thighs and lower parts of the legs, the feet, most of the external genital organs, and the area around the anus. This is where your damage is. Your S5 is crushed, and all information stops at this damage point and does not travel any further. You're lucky because you still have control over your erectile organ, your bladder and your bowels; most SCIs loose that control. I'd say you're lucky to be alive," added Dr. Kim.

> "*Lucky...*" thought Donovan, *"how lucky is a person who's lost his entire family, lost his mobility, and lost all independence after just tasting his dreams? How lucky is it to come out of a coma to a stranger telling you that your parents are dead and you will never walk again? Yeah, I'm lucky all right!"*

Donovan had no more words for the doctor. He just closed his eyes, pulled the covers over his head, and withdrew into that place within where only he had access. When he opened his eyes again, he was all alone in his room, just as he was all alone in his life.

Every time he attempted to move his lower extremities, the cruel reality of his destroyed life haunted him. Every time he needed to use the bathroom, it became a major production requiring assistance from others.

To Donovan, this wasn't a life— he wished he *was dead!*

Chapter 13

Cedars-Sinai Medical Center in Beverly Hills, California, was a world- renowned medical facility. Its medical director, Dr. Rozelyn Harris, received a memo directly from the desk of the Francine Katrina Bovier, CEO of Global Pharmaceuticals, authorizing any and all treatments for Donavan Mocion.

Rozelyn and Francine had quite the history between them, all the way back to the days when Francine was cleaning up her addictions. Francine's mentor had contacted Rozelyn to set up recovery treatment for her. He, Francine, and Rozelyn also had a tumultuous history between the three of them.

Once Francine became sober, she and Rozelyn developed a *special* relationship with each other and, whenever possible, one would help out the other, until Francine went back to school completing her doctored in business and started climbing the corporate ladder of ruthlessness. Rozelyn wasn't willing to conduct business with the same ferociousness as Francine, and their relationship deteriorated the higher Francine rose in the corporate world.

While Francine was in the recovery center she saw an old 20th century American movie classic titled The Godfather. That movie alone made a tremendous impact on how Francine would later conduct herself in her business, as well as her personal, life. She took the blueprint from Don Vito Corleone and incorporated it into her way of life. Whenever Francine did someone a favor she let it be clearly understood that she had done this favor and a favor was owed her in return. That return favor might not come the same day, the next day, or even the next year, but she fully expected to redeem that favor at some future point and at any cost. Francine, just like Don Vito Corleone, made offers that had better *not* be refused. The word was out on the streets, and in the corporate world, that refusing to return a Francine Katrina Bovier favor could mean the loss of life.

Rozelyn, along with many other high-ranking business officials who thought they were close friends of Francine, now took unquestioned orders from her in fear of the consequences to themselves or someone they cared about. Francine learned early the value of conducting business with people in extremely high, and sometimes even lower, places.

The memo also requested weekly reports on Donovan's condition be couriered, "Eyes Only," to the CEO of Global Pharmaceuticals. Rozelyn knew this wasn't a request, but a direct order from Cedars-Sinai's parent company, and more powerful still, Francine Katrina Bovier. So, with the obedience of a lab monkey trained to push the right button in order to get a treat, Rozelyn blindly set the necessary wheels into motion.

Within the hour Dr. Kim reported to Rozelyn's office. "Morning, Andrew."

"Morning to you, Roz. What I can do for you today?"

"I understand you're treating a patient named Donovan Mocion. How is he doing?"

"Physically, he's recovering as well as can be expected. He suffered massive spinal cord injuries; I'll get you a copy of his charts."

"Thanks, Andrew, I'd appreciate that."

"Emotionally though, he's deeply depressed from the traumatic events, and he refuses to allow himself to grieve the death of his parents. We've got him on a battery of anti-inflammatory, anti-depression, and pain medications. In my opinion, Mr. Mocion will never walk again; as yet, he doesn't accept that fact. His life was devoted to becoming a supreme athlete, and now the reality of being a paraplegic is something he refuses to acknowledge, thus, his depression. His reaction is a common occurrence for athletes who have sustained this type of tremendous physical and emotional loss. I've suggested a grief counselor to him, which he adamantly refused. My only recommendation at this juncture is for him to begin physical therapy, whether he wants to or not."

"I see. Well, Andrew, this one is a 'need-to-know' case. I need to be directly in the loop, and you'll need to prepare yourself for receiving outside instructions on this patient. It seems the people up the food chain have taken a special interest in our Mr. Donovan Mocion."

Dr. Kim knew Dr. Harris could only be referring Global Pharmaceuticals. Rozelyn opened a card caddy sitting on the left side of her desk near her sat-phone and flipped through it until she came across the card she wanted. Then she stared at it a few seconds thinking, *"We haven't spoke in quite a while. This should be interesting,"* and she quickly handed the card to Dr. Kim, as if the card might somehow read her thoughts, and said, "I want this therapist used on the Mocion case, but make it look like an extensive search had been done before a final decision was made."

Dr. Kim took the card, looked at the company and the name on the card, and nodded his head in agreement saying, "This was my first choice."

"Great minds think alike," replied Dr. Harris with a smile.

"I'll have my office make the arrangements. Good day, Roz," said Dr. Kim. "I hope so, Andrew," replied Dr. Harris, "I truly hope so."

Chapter 14

Up and down the west coast whenever the question, "Which physical therapy company has done the most good for their patients?" was asked, there was one company at the top of everyone's short list, and that was New U Physical Therapy Centers, with thriving locations in Seattle, Portland, San Francisco, Oakland, Monterey, and several southern California locations in the Los Angeles, Beverly Hills, San Diego, LaJolla and Del Mar areas.

Most of their business came from professional sport franchises. Over the past 10 years, New U had successfully rehabilitated athletes of mixed martial arts, baseball, basketball, hockey, and football. Players who thought their careers were over due to serious injuries during their regular seasons were given second chances after receiving therapy from New U. This kind of success rate kept New U Physical Therapy Centers fully booked. New U's quality of service and success rates were so outstanding that professional sport franchises hired therapists from New U as staff trainers during their regular seasons. New U's success results also reached into the upper echelon hospitals and medical centers throughout the west coast.

The next morning a smiling Dr. Kim went into Donovan's room saying, "How is our patient doing?"

"ADSS," came the lifeless response from Donovan, lying there with a blank expression on his face, staring into nothingness.

"ADSS?" asked Dr. Kim.

"Another Day—Same Shit," informed Donovan lifelessly.

Dr. Kim had gotten used to this negative attitude and sarcasm, so he completely ignored Donovan and announced, "Over the past few months you've been stuck in this room except for mandatory trips for treatment. Well, today things are going to change. I want you to meet Myron."

Dr. Kim moved to the side and then motioned with his hand, like a matador waving his cape at a bull, for someone to enter.

That someone was Myron Hammond, a self-made entrepreneur who became wealthy at a very young age by maximizing his natural born hustling abilities. As a young man, Myron learned the value of supply and demand on the streets of the San Francisco Bay Area. In other words, he supplied those who supplied thestreets anything the streets needed. His tenacity as a hustler paid off greatly after a car accident left him with broken arms, a broken leg, a broken wrist, and a sprained back, disabling him for nearly a year. During his physical therapy treatments he had an epiphany that changed his life goals and he decided to become a physical therapist. Not just any physical therapist, but one who treated elite athletes, those with money to burn and the willingness to become better than they were before their injuries. Myron was an excellent athlete himself, standing 6' 2" tall, weighting 225 lbs, and his lean, sculptured, muscular physique looked suited to be a model working the runway. His skin was as smooth and dark as a moonless night, his bright hazel eyes like stars in the night, and his glowing smile with his trademark baldhead lit up every room he entered. Myron excelled in track and field, baseball, gymnastics, and mixed martial arts. He could have turned professional in any of those disciplines but at that time, the money he made from the streets was too good to give up. Myron was a brilliant businessman who knew how to save his money. He took some of that saved money and invested in a higher education for himself. Majoring in Sports Medicine and minoring in Psychology, he earned Master's Degrees in both. After graduation he opened his first New U Physical Therapy Center. Over the next several years his investment really paid off and he owned facilities throughout the west coast.

Dr. Kim said to Donovan, "Donovan, this is Myron; he's going to become your new best friend. Myron is one of, if not the best physical therapist in the country."

Myron maneuvered his way into Donovan's room pushing a wheelchair, and rolled it over to the bed, then extended his fist to Donovan, expecting a pound in return. Donovan just glared at him and that wheelchair, completely ignoring Myron's peace gesture, and sarcastically asked, "Why don't you both take a seat, spin around, and the two of you can get the hell out of here?"

Dr. Kim smiled and said, "Glad to see you're getting stronger. I'll just leave you three alone to get acquainted. Donovan, I'll check in on you later."

Before he left he turned to Myron and placed a sympathetic arm around his shoulder, leading him towards Donovan's door, while quietly saying, "You've got your work cut out with this one."

When they reached the doorway, Donovan shouted out, "Hey! You guys forgot your ride!" pointing his extended middle finger at the wheelchair sitting by the side of his bed. Over their shoulders Dr. Kim and Myron glanced back at Donovan, not bothering to respond. Myron smiled at Dr. Kim and then said, "See you later, Doc."

Myron was confidant; he had worked miracles before with some of the most stubborn patients, so he turned around and gave Donovan a smile, and then said, "Donovan, in little to no time you'll be burning up the halls in this chair and I'll have to nickname you *'Smoke.'*"

"Is that right? Don't hold your breath!" came Donovan's dubious reply.

Myron walked back to the wheelchair bedside Donovan's bed, placed his hands on the push grips, paused a minute, then slowly moved around, and sat down in the wheelchair, all while staring Donovan straight in the eye.

"The two of you look good together. Now, why don't you spin around in that chair and leave me the hell alone?"

Myron just sat there in the wheelchair staring into Donovan's eyes. "What? You just gonna sit there and stare at me?"

Then in the soft, kind, reassuring voice of wisdom and experience, just above a whisper, Myron said, "Listen up. I know who you are and what you accomplished in Hawaii. I had front row seats for all your events. I would tell you I'm a fan, and that I'm extremely proud of you, but your attitude is so fucked up right now you wouldn't be able to hear my true appreciation. So, allow yourself to hear this. Donovan, I've been at this for a long time, and I've shared the pain and suffering right along with my patients. I won't bullshit you by saying I know how you feel, because I don't know the type of hell you're going through right now. I'll just tell you this—I know from experience how it feels to be laid up, and to lose the ones you love. Believe me; I can help you deal with this, but you'll have to work with me, not against me, to put your life back together. Donovan, I guarantee you, somewhere along our journey together doors will open for you, and through those doors you will discover another Donovan. Hey, who knows, if you're not a complete asshole, we could even become friends. But for now, you need to get your ass out of that bed and into this wheelchair. There's a new world for you to discover and it's time you got started!"

Donovan had his head hanging down, letting his fingers pick mindlessly at invisible pieces of lint on his sheet, feeling like a child being scolded. But inside Donovan was tired - tired of being helpless, tired of feeling sorry for himself. He thought about what Myron had just told him, and he knew if he was going to survive, going to live, it was now or never. Donovan slowly lifted his head and stared deep into Myron's eyes without saying a word, and for the next few moments they just stared at each other, allowing an invisible bond to be created. He felt as though Myron was feeding him energy, energy to lift his spirits, and help him rebuild his life.

"Maybe this guy can help me," he thought. *"Anything is an improvement over wasting away in this bed!"* Finally, Donovan asked, "Are you always that damn long-winded? Because if you are, we'll never get anything done."

And for the first time in months, Donovan smiled.

Myron smiled back and replied, "Only when necessary. But for now, I'll explain exactly how we're going to work this magic—first of all, before you get into any pain zones I'll tell you what to expect, pain-wise, on a scale from 4 – 10."

"From 4 – 10. What happened to 0 - 3?" asked Donovan.

"Well, you might not believe it, but this very moment you're actually feeling pain level 4, but the drugs you're on are covering that up. Donovan, I promise you, before we're finished you're going to be thankful for those drugs."

Then Myron gave Donovan a wink of trust.

"Shit!" said Donovan, "I'm already thankful for them," and out came a tiny laugh.

Donovan's eyes lit up; he was truly startled by his ability to laugh, and for the first time since he regained consciousness, the sensation of hope slowly seeped into his heart.

"Didn't know you had that in you, did you? Well, there's a lot more of *that* to experience. I guarantee!" reassured Myron, flashing a huge smile for Donovan.

For their first session together, Myron had Donovan practicing getting in and out his wheelchair, and then taught him how to maneuver it without hurting himself. After Myron saw that Donovan had mastered those skills, with a tilt from his head in the direction he wanted Donovan to go, he said, "Alright, let's take it for a spin," and out the door of Donovan's room they went. Donovan looked up and gave Myron a surprised puppy dog look, as he wheeled himself through the door.

"You just made it through one of those doors I was talking about," announced Myron as he walked next to Donovan in his wheelchair.

"Where to now?" asked a pumped-up, willing-to-go-anywhere Donovan who found himself excited about being mobile again.

"Thought I'd give you the hundred dollar tour of the place," replied Myron with a smile.

The first thing Donovan noticed once he rolled into the hallway was the opaque, under lit, acrylic, marble-looking floors with the multiple colored inlaid lines.

"This place must be enormous. I take it these color-coded lines in the floor are to guide people to their different destinations."

"Correct!" Then Myron pointed to a view panel display and said, "For those who are colorblind these displays will help them navigate throughout the facility."

"What happens if you're colorblind and can't read English?"

Myron looked down at Donovan with a smirk and said, "I'd love to say that person was SOL, but, check this out." Myron approached the view panel and tapped on it. A virtual keyboard appeared within the screen, along with a dropdown menu for selecting the preferred language.

"Any other questions?"

"Yeah. Does SOL mean what I think it does?" "And what is that?" asked Myron.

"Shit Out-of Luck," replied Donovan followed by a mischievous smirk of his own.

"Exactly!" said Myron with a wink.

"I felt you spoke my language," said Donovan with a wink of approval. "Yeah, I caught your ADSS acronym back there with Dr. Kim."

They both laughed and continued the tour.

Myron led Donovan into the rehabilitation and therapy wing of the facility, which was nothing less than a state-of-the-art Olympic-style training facility. It was massive! There were several swimming pools of various depths, sizes, and shapes, along with every type of exercise equipment known to man. Donovan's eyes became as round as silver dollars. He was completely impressed with the grandeur of this department.

Then without warning, sadness came over his face, and a single tear ran down his cheek, because in his heart he had no choice but to accept his paralyzed condition.

Myron had seen that look before and could sense the emotions Donovan was experiencing. "Don't sweat it, bro. We're gonna take it one moment at a time until you've developed everything you'll need to enjoy life again. But now, I've got a surprise for you."

Donovan barely heard what Myron was saying. He had drifted back into that isolated place within. He was so oblivious to what was happening around him that he didn't notice that Myron, who had been walking beside him throughout the tour, was now pushing him to the next destination. Donovan forced himself back into the moment by asking Myron, "Did I hear you say something about a surprise?"

Myron, pleased with Donovan's ability to control his negative emotions, replied, "As a matter of fact I did. You must be hungry after rolling yourself around all morning, and believe me, there is far too much to see in one tour. So, I thought I'd take you to one of the best places here to eat."

"Good idea," replied Donovan as he dried his face on his shirt sleeve.

They took an elevator up a few floors and then got off on a secluded-looking floor with a circular nurse's station surrounded by four sets of double doors. Each door had a name plate on it, and one of the name plates read "MOCION." Myron hit an activation button and double doors slid open revealing a private suite full of living plants and all the electronic devices the late 21st century had to offer. The suite was specially equipped for paraplegics, which included a special lift device in the main living area for getting in and out of bed, and a similar device in the bathroom to make personal hygiene as easy and convenient as possible.

"These are your new digs," began Myron. "You now have your own personal nurse and orderly who will show you how to care for yourself and use every piece of equipment in this suite."

Donovan's jaw had fallen open and almost dropped into his lap as soon as the doors had opened. He was in awe - speechless. He couldn't believe this was a hospital room, and though he was beat from his tour, he slowly rolled over to a wall of windows and looked outside. Donovan's view overlooked a forest which was full of color and life.

Donovan looked back at Myron and said, "I've got a view…of a forest!"

And tears flowed down his cheeks again, only this time they were tears of joy and gratitude. He saw a note hanging from one of the plants and when he opened it the message read, "This is the least we could do. Don't worry about a thing. We've got you covered!" Global Pharmaceuticals.

After Donovan was securely back in his bed, a grinning Myron said, "You did good for your first day, my man, but now it is time for me to get on with my day."

"Will you be here tomorrow?" asked Donovan, sounding like a young wide- eyed kid asking his big brother to take him to the park again tomorrow.

"Oh, yeah!" said Myron, as he extended his fist to Donovan once again. This time Donovan gladly gave Myron's fist a pound.

"I've got news for you, Donovan. The healthier you get, the more time we'll spend together. Soon you'll be dreading our sessions."

"Only if you get long-winded again," said an appreciative Donovan, feeling like he had a new outlook on life.

"See you tomorrow," said Myron as he turned and left the room.

After lunch Dr. Kim dropped by to visit Donovan.

"Hello, Dr. Kim." said a perky Donovan. "How's it hangin'?"

"Down and to the left," replied Dr. Kim, showing his smart-ass, humorous side. "What happened to you? Did Myron light a fire under you?"

"Well, yes, he did," replied Donovan with a changed attitude. "Dr. Kim, I need to apologize for being such an asshole over the last few months."

"Think nothing of it. You were expected to be an asshole for a few months, but now it's time for you to get on with living."

"My feelings exactly," agreed a smiling Donovan. "My, my, it smiles. Good for you, Donovan."

Donovan settled back into his bed, but before the doctor left the room, he quickly called out "Dr. Kim?"

The doctor turned back and faced Donovan. "THANKS!"

Dr. Kim gave Donovan a nod, and then walked away.

Over the next few months, Myron became the big brother Donovan never had, and in many ways, Donovan became his little brother. Donovan, now able to manipulate the wheelchair with ease, began tooling around the medical center after his therapy sessions without Myron. While cruising the hallways, mobile and somewhat independent, one of the first things Myron ever said to him ran through Donovan's mind, "*In little to no time you'll be burning up the halls in this chair and I'll have to nickname you 'Smoke'.*" Donovan couldn't shake that name from his mind; he liked it — *Smoke.*

Chapter 15

Drs. Wiley and Hothan were looking down from the observation booth, overseeing the four monitoring bays in the procedures lab below. Over the past few weeks of testing and evaluating the Alpha Clinical Trials subjects, the doctors had modified their version of the Mocions' Human Enhancement Formula. They had both spent sleepless nights anticipating what effects those changes would produce. Neither of them wanted the unthinkable task of reporting failure to their boss.

Their operations support team consisted of 2 telemetry-monitoring technicians for each subject and Kevin Mathews, the lead technician, reported any changes or anomalies directly to Drs. Wiley and Hothan. All technicians on the procedure floor, as well as in the booth, wore communication earpieces. There were also several very large, heavily muscled orderlies on the floor wearing earpieces too, their jobs were to subdue and restrain any test subject who experienced a violent reaction to the serum. In the past, a test subject became so violent that he began destroying the lab and attacking the personnel. Unfortunately, euthanasia was needed to protect the research personnel from that subject.

The observation booth technicians gave the telemetry equipment the final once-over, then Kevin informed Drs. Wiley and Hothan that everything was ready.

The procedure lab looked more like a physical training facility, with exercise and medical evaluation equipment strategically placed throughout. Each test subject had an exclusive procedure team of their own consisting of a medical doctor, a nurse, and two orderlies, with Der Fuhrer, Rovena "Roe" Budnski scrutinizing them all in her usual domineering Gestapo manner.

Dressed in gowns, the A.C.T. subjects arrived at 0900 hrs, and were quickly prepped and strapped onto their individual monitoring tables awaiting their 10 o'clock injections. With nothing to lose but their individual disorders, they were taking this, the big day, peacefully and in good spirits on the outside.

"How are the subjects' readings?" asked a calm, cool, and collected Dr.

Wiley.

"Slight elevations across the board for all the test subjects," reported Kevin.

"Just a little anxiety," reassured Dr. Hothan. "Nothing to be concerned about." Dr. Hothan presented her best professional demure for all to see, but inside she was a mess and wished she had taken a zonnotal to quiet her nerves.

1000 hrs was announced by Kevin.

Dr. Wiley gave the green light for the injections to proceed. A special device, much like those for lethal injections, was used to administer the serum. Each subject, with their own individually formulated units, received injections at precisely the same time.

After the injections had been administered Dr. Wiley, with wide eyes, turned to Dr. Hothan and said, "No turning back now!"

"Here we go again!" replied Dr. Hothan under her breath, with a nervous look on her face.

The red phone buzzed and Dr. Wiley answered it. A female voice on the other end asked, "Are we on schedule?" It was Francine.

"Yes, we are," replied a confidant Dr. Wiley.

"Keep me posted!" ordered Francine, then the line went dead. Dr. Wiley slowly returned the handset to its base.

"Was that her?" asked Dr. Hothan in a sheepish tone, watching every move Dr. Wiley had made.

"Who else?" answered Dr. Wiley. "Mark each subject's reaction times for later reference," reminded Dr. Wiley to all test subject monitoring technicians.

"The subjects' heart rates and body temperatures are rising," abruptly announced Budnski, before Kevin had the chance to report to the doctors.

Kevin glared down at Roe for butting in to his responsibilities, while under his breath he was calling her every type of *bitch* he could think of.

The two doctors observed the change in telemetry readings, then looked at each other and said, "SHOWTIME!"

"Time?" asked Dr. Wiley.

"1002 hrs," answered Budnski, again before Kevin had the chance to reply, then she turned to him and said over her communications set, "Pick up the pace, Kevin! You've got to be fast, fast, fast when you work for me!"

Roe was higher up the food chain than Kevin, so all he could do in retaliation was imagine Roe being body-slammed, or worse.

Subject 53 was the first to speak saying, "YO, Docs! Like, I'm feeling sum- n here—I'm get-n a little heated inside."

"Me, too!" added 5, "I'm feeling this shit kick in…what a body rush." "I can feel my bones tingling," said 37.

"Ahhhh," went 28. "This is the first time in years that I've had no pain in my joints."

The two doctors looked at each other again, both hopeful that, "*Maybe this is going to work after all.*"

"Time?" asked Dr. Hothan.

"1005 hrs," reported Kevin, catching Roe off guard, into someone else's business, and not paying attention to the doctor's question.

Roe gave Kevin a look to kill, and to demonstrate her domination, said, "I think we should get them on their feet so we can run them through some tests."

"No! Not yet, Roe. We will tell *you* when!" ordered Dr. Wiley over the P.A. in a stern voice of authority— putting Roe back in check. "The subjects are in a state of flux. We must wait until they stabilize."

Subject 5 turned to 53 and jokingly repeated, "We're in flux— any idea what that means?"

"The Flux if I know," answered 53 with a giggle.

Roe glared up at the control booth frowning and began mouthing something.

Any one who read lips understood that Roe mouthed, *"You fucking cunts…you both can kiss my big ass. You two don't know what the fuck you're doing. You retarded slits!"*

Kevin, having read Roe's lips switched to the doctor's private line and asked them if they wanted to know what Roe mouthed.

Both doctors had observed Roe mouthing something, while giving them the evil eye, and answered a resounding "NO!"

Dr. Hothan leaned over and whispered in Dr. Wiley's ear about Roe, "That damn bitch is going to give me a headache before this day is over."

"You and me both," replied Dr. Wiley, "you and me both." "I've got a spike in my readings," announced 53's monitor. "So do I!" shouted 5's monitor.

"The adrenalin levels for these two are going off the charts. Something major is happening," reported Kevin.

Over the last several days, Budnski figured she had gotten each subject's personality type categorized, so she didn't think anything strange about the sounds 53 and 5 were beginning to make. In her opinion, they were the dredges of society and goof-offs of the group, here to get paid and have a good time, so their grunts and groans where them being funny and nothing to be concerned about.

Budnski, in her usual loud obnoxious voice, began barking insults at 53 and 5, "Settle down, Meat! This is not a game. Knock off those ridiculous antics!" Then, like a storm trooper, she charged across the lab towards them dead set on literally ripping them some new ones.

"Doctors! Subject 53's alpha waves have just gone off the chart. I've never seen anything like this before," reported a nervous, excited Kevin.

The doctors focused their attention on 53 down below, and what they saw sent chills up their spines. 53 was in more than flux. Some type of physical transformation was taking place. 53 was shaking from side to side so rapidly a blur effect was created. Once that stopped 53 began making throaty, guttural noises, like those of a large primate. In fact, 53 was taking on the appearance of a primitive humanoid. 53's normally scruffy physique was quickly transforming into rippling muscles, and as it grew in size the treatment gown was ripped to shreds.

53's feet were now hanging off the monitor table. Its hands, feet, and head became oversized, and a dense dark fur began growing over the entire body, with a finer, lighter facial hair. Each fingernail and toenail became a thick dark claw. 53's nostrils expanded and began flaring in and out, needing more air intake to supply its huge chest cavity. Its jaw line protruded down, and squared off, like the demons or villains in the Marvel comic strips. Its teeth, both top and bottom, grew into rows of jagged fangs, like those of sharks, and its mouth became several times the normal size. 53's eyes were glazed and dead looking, and they bulged from their sockets, perfectly round in diameter, jet-black with no eyelids. 53 could no longer be considered human but something that predated man's current evolution— something that looked as though it would consider man as prey and nothing more than its food.

Up in the observation booth everyone was maintaining their composure.

"TIME?" yelled out Dr. Hothan

"1015 hrs," replied Kevin, shocked at what he was witnessing.

Down on the procedure floor, Rovena Budnski was so wrapped up in shouting obscenities at 53 and 5 that she didn't notice the transformation happening to them until she was right in their faces, and by then it was too late! Like snapping sewing thread, 53 broke his straps, and with unbelievable speed pounced on Budnski, snatching the 200 lb round mound into the air like a feather, and then body-slammed her on top of its monitoring table.

Looking down from his safe viewpoint, Kevin smiled his approval and calmly said, "Awesome!"

Budnski, who was in a kind of out-of-control denial shock, was yelling orders for 53 to get back on its table, and cursing at the top of her voice until 53 yanked her left arm out its socket, tearing it away from her body, and took a huge bite from it. Then, in what looked like disgust, 53 spit the piece from its mouth as though Budnski's flesh was tainted, spoiled food.

Budnski stopped giving orders and wailed in intense agony.

53 seemed to enjoy the wailing Budnski was making and placed its left claw on Budnski's chest, digging it deep into her breast, holding her in place, and began slowly slicing at her belly with its right claw sending Budnski into louder screams of excruciating pain.

By this time 5 had transformed into a similar looking creature, although slightly smaller in scale and with breasts. Subject 5 broke free, sniffing at the air, and once it smelled Budnski's blood and flesh, it immediately looked in her direction, drooling slime and licking its jagged fangs. Ferociously, the beast snapped its jaws at the air, sounding like the clanging of a steel bear trap every time its mouth closed, until finally, it released an ear-shattering roar that shook the lab's windows, then in the blink of an eye, it pounced on Roe and began devouring her fresh, bleeding flesh.

Dr. Wiley looked at Dr. Hothan and they briefly smiled as if justice was being served, and the main course was Lab Supervisor Rovena "Roe" Budnski. But their smiles were short-lived as Kevin shouted, "Doctors! We have to do something about this!"

"Time?" asked Dr. Wiley.

"1017 hrs," replied Kevin.

"Knock the subjects out! All of them!" ordered Dr. Hothan.

Each test subject had been outfitted with a tranquilizing injection device that could be remotely triggered, if needed.

53 and 5's remote injections did nothing but add more intensity to the horrific feeding frenzy they were unleashing on Budnski.

When Dr. Hothan saw that the injections had no effect on subjects 53 and 5, she announced over the facilities main P.A., "Condition Red—Condition Red!" and a loud alarm sounded which startled the two beasts, causing them to leap into the air away from Budnski. When they landed they caught sight of their reflections in a wall of mirrors and they froze like stone statues, shocked. They turned and looked at one another, then looked back into the mirrors just in time to notice several orderlies sneaking up on them with nets in their hands. Both beasts turned to face their attackers and, with blinding speed, they both grabbed an arm and leg of the same orderly and yanked him into 5 pieces. His head was left screaming as his torso bounced around the floor of the procedure lab until he finally bled out.

While the action was unfolding at other end of the lab, the remaining unharmed floor personnel quickly and quietly removed themselves and subjects 28 and 37 to safety outside the lab. 28 and 37 were oblivious to what was happening; they had peacefully gone to sleep once the precautionary tranquilizers were remotely triggered.

At first the security orderlies froze from their initial shock, but once they gathered themselves, they sprung into action and tried containing 53 and 5 with brute force. This action enraged the beasts who easily escaped by leaping away from their assailants. 53 and 5 went on the assault. They focused their deadly attention on these new victims. 53 quickly separated two orderlies from the rest, like a predator separates its prey from a pack, and simultaneously drove his claws deep into the chests of both men, lifting them skyward, and then brutally smashed them, head first, into the concrete floor, splattering skulls, brains, flesh, bones, and blood all over the lab. 5 caught another orderly and tossed him across the room like a rag doll, smashing him against the concrete wall of the lab.

Immediately facility security stormed into the procedures lab and repeatedly shot 5 and 53 with tasers, and additional tranquilizers until they fell to the floor, unconscious. They were quickly restrained, removed from the lab, and placed in quarantine.

"Man," said a security member, "What the hell is that smell coming from these things?"

"Hell if I know!" replied another, "Smelled to me like decaying flesh and feces."

Rovena "Roe" Budnski, Lab Supervisor, lay on 53's monitoring table in a beyond shock state, babbling something incomprehensible. Still managing to have the last words, until she slowly, and painfully, expired.

Immediately the red speaker phone buzzed.

"What the hell is going on down there?" asked the voice over the speakerphone.

"Two of our subjects had negative reactions to the serum. They reverted to some form of cannibalistic humanoids. We had to tranquilize and taser them," Dr. Wiley calmly answered.

"Where are they now?" asked Francine.

"In quarantine," came Dr. Wiley's reply.

"And the other two? What condition are they in?" asked Francine.

"They're doing well. We knocked them out before they knew what was going on. We're still monitoring the effects of the serum on them while they sleep," informed Dr. Wiley.

"Good! I hear we lost Rovena Budnski…is that true?"

"Yes, I'm afraid it is," answered Dr. Wiley.

"Great! I never liked that bitch! Can you carry on the experiment without her?" "Absolutely!" answered Dr. Wiley.

"We could promote Kevin Mathews to lab supervisor," Dr. Hothan, who had a secret little crush on him, promptly suggested. She and Kevin exchanged glances and she gave him a hot-for-you wink.

"Good idea. Get me copies of your current reports and analyses, STAT!

Send all remains to Disposal then resume the experiment without delay!"

The phone line went dead.

CHAPTER 16

Getting nowhere fast trying to replicate the Mocions' work, Francine decided to try a different approach, and she called Dr. Harris at Cedars-Sinai in California to turn up the heat on their prized patient, Donovan Mocion.

"Roz? Fran. How goes things out there?"

"I'm getting an update out to you now," replied Rozelyn in a quasi-friendly manner. Rozelyn knew it was better to stay friendly with the devil rather than having the devil as her enemy.

"Wonderful, dear. Then it's appropriate to say I'll be hearing from you before lunch with that report?" Francine's summarization was more of an order than question.

"Absolutely! You can instruct me on how to proceed from there," replied Rozelyn, not wanting to keep the conservation going any longer than she needed to. Talking to Francine had a way of ruining Rozelyn's day. It wasn't that Rozelyn couldn't stand up for herself. Everyone who worked with Dr. Harris knew she was tough, and a fierce fighter for what she believed in, but up against Francine she was totally out-gunned, just like everyone else under Francine's thumb.

As soon as Dr. Harris got off the phone, she summoned Dr. Kim to her office.

Rozelyn knew that shit always flows down hill, but she was not about to mess on her people the way Francine did.

Dr. Kim, anticipating a 90-day update, already had it prepared. Myron had given Dr. Kim his 90-day evaluation on Donovan the day before. When Dr. Kim walked into Dr. Harris's office, he had a file in hand and presented it to her saying, "Here's the 90-day report on patient Donovan Mocion, for your review."

"Thank you, Andrew." She took the file and placed it on top of the lateral mahogany filing cabinet behind her. "What are your personal medical insights on the patient? Off the record, so to speak."

Dr. Kim was not sure whom he was really talking to, Dr. Harris or her superiors, knowing perfectly well that meant Francine Katrina Bovier, so he decided to keep his response safe and professional.

"The patient has made remarkable progress as far as his physical recovery goes. Myron has him on a 5 day a week floor exercise program so strenuous a perfectly healthy athlete would have difficulty performing. It's amazing!" said a smiling, truly excited Dr. Kim. "It looks like an elaborate gymnastic floor exercise performed as a slow, smooth, fluid, power routine. Donovan begins seated on the floor with his hands at his sides then moves into a handstand, holds it perfectly motionless for a few seconds, switches to one hand, holds it, and then does the same with other hand, then back into a handstand. He does a complete 360-degree spin in that handstand, holds it perfectly still again, and finally, slowly lowers himself back into the seated position where he began. I'd give the routine a 10 point score if I were judging it. Donovan is phenomenal; I can see why he was a supreme Olympic athlete. Myron's physical therapy techniques are revolutionary; he even has Donovan running on his hands back and forth on the parallel bars from two different positions; arms extended below the bars, and arms extended above the bars. For a cool down Donovan swims 100 laps in the pool each day.

Physically, Donovan is a miraculous specimen. If I didn't personally know for sure, I'd say he was a machine—his lower extremities show no atrophy and he's displaying a full range of motion, when moved by someone else, of course. And what's more, he still has great muscle tone throughout his entire lower extremities.

"The bad news is Donovan suffers from emotional trauma, and has repressed all conscious memory of the plane crash, the deaths of his parents, even the events of the Olympics. He hasn't allowed himself to go through any grieving process, either. Subconsciously however, his situation is worse. He suffers from a condition known as Night Terror. I believe he's reliving the accident in his dreams and that's causing these episodes. The nurses report that every night he wakes up screaming and dripping with sweat. This is a very serious emotional condition and, if not addressed, could cause a psychotic breakdown."

"Any ideas how we can get through to him?" asked Dr. Harris.

"Myron Hammond, Donovan's physical therapist is also a trained, licensed, active psychiatrist, and since he and Donovan have bonded, I believed Myron is the best person to help Donovan with this condition before a psychosis develops."

"Will you discuss the issue with Mr. Hammond? Then, get back to me with his response. I'll bring myself up to speed by studying your detailed report on the patient."

"Consider it done," said Dr. Kim. As he was leaving Dr. Harris' office, he called his secretary and began instructing her on retaining Myron Hammond as psychiatrist for Donovan Mocion.

As soon as Dr. Kim was out her door, Roz began to briefly daydream about her past, which included Myron. She quickly shook her head, getting rid of the thoughts and dove into Donovan's medical report.

Her intuition was sending up red flags about this Donovan Mocion project.

She had no idea just how deep the rabbit hole went. She knew for a fact it was deeper than she wanted to go, especially since it had Francine Katrina Bovier's personal attention. That in itself was already deeper than she wanted to be. After she finished reviewing Dr. Kim's report on Donovan, she called Francine.

"Very interesting indeed," said Francine after hearing Roz's synopsis of Donovan's update. "Send me the data by courier," ordered Francine. "By the way, I think it was a great idea to use Myron Hammond for this patient. It sounds to me like the patient is healthy enough to travel. Is that a correct assumption?"

"I would have to concur," commented Dr. Harris.

"Excellent! Now this is what I want you to do," began Francine.

Chapter 17

Myron had no problem accepting the offer to be Donovan's psychiatrist. He agreed he was the best person for the job. He always included psychiatric therapy when he dealt with his more severely injured patients. Myron thought, *"Hell, if they wanted to pay me for something I normally include for free—hey…I'll take the money."* Besides, he had a special interest in Donovan's recovery. Myron was well aware of Donovan's emotional state, and had already planned an approach for helping him.

By now Donovan was able to pop wheelies and do donuts in his wheelchair. He was especially proud to show off these skills each time he saw Myron for their PT sessions.

"Man, I've gotten so good at controlling these two wheels, I think it's time to take you up on that nickname," said a smiling Donovan, demonstrating his skills by continuously spinning in 360 degrees while he spoke to Myron.

"Nickname?" so preoccupied with the intensive level of emotions the upcoming session would take Donovan to, Myron momentarily forgot all about any nickname.

"Yeah, nickname! You're slipping Myron. Don't tell me that steel trap you call a brain has forgotten something. Well, let me refresh your memory. You told me the first time we met, and I quote, "*In little to no time you'll be burning up the halls in this chair and I'll have to nickname you 'Smoke.'"*

"Well?" Donovan extended both hands out to his side as if waiting for applause, said, "Give it up, give it up," then displayed a wheel stand, and did a couple of reverse back-to-back 360s and said, "What do you think? Am I smokin' or what?"

Myron laughed and then said, "You definitely have earned the nickname, all right."

"That's what I'm talkin' 'bout!" replied Donovan, "From this moment on, when you feel like it, you can call me *Smoke.*"

Myron knew what he was about to say would completely change Donovan's mood, but it was the perfect segue into a difficult emotional area, so he begin by saying, "I guess I'm gonna have to sign you up for the Special Olympics."

Donovan, caught in the middle of a 360 spin, shifted his weight just a tad too far backwards and toppled over, landing flat on his back. Donovan just laid there, motionless, with the wheelchair's little front wheels up in the air, rolling slowly to a stop.

A shocked Myron, immediately feeling responsible for this tumble, rushed over to Donovan and helped right him and his chair, exclaiming, "Donovan, Donovan, you alright?"

"Damn, bro! You really know how to bring a guy down," said Donovan as he gathered himself back in his chair, a slight look of betrayal on his face.

Myron, on his knees in front of Donovan, checking his eyes for any signs of trauma, was relieved to see his friend was ok and said, "Look, Donovan. Being able to do these little tricks is all well and good, but there is deeper work we have to start on today, and it's not going to be easy. Now, I believe you're strong enough to handle the issues you've been avoiding, and today we'll begin that journey, together."

Donovan knew what Myron was getting at, and said with his head down, "I guess they finally told you about my nightmares."

"Yeah, they told me. But what hurts me is that you didn't tell me yourself. I was under the impression that you and I were the home team, brother-to-brother!"

"Am I your brother?" asked Donovan as he lifted his head, looking Myron in the eyes.

"Donovan, you're the closest thing to a real brother I've ever had. We can get through this together, but only if you let me in. Will you do that? Will you let me help you?" asked Myron, now squatting in front of Donovan's chair so they were eye to eye.

Donovan, not once loosing eye contact with Myron, lifted his right hand and placed it on top of Myron's bald head, rubbed it a couple of times, smiled and answered, "Yes!" Then, jokingly, Donovan asked Myron, "Are you my genie?"

Myron chuckled a few times, smiled at Donovan, then said, "At your service!"

Chapter 18

The next day Donovan was sitting in his window appreciating the wonderful forest view from his hospital room when Myron entered, looked around for Donovan, saw him at the window, walked over and stood beside him. "Great view you got here!"

"Yeah, it is," answered Donovan in a quasi-dreamlike state.

"How'd you sleep last night?" asked a concerned Myron.

"Well, you know, ANSS," replied Donovan still entranced by the view out his window.

"Let me see, ANSS…Another Night Same Shit?" guessed Myron with a smile.

"You got it! These night terrors are kicking my butt!"

"Come on, let's go. I've got something for you to see and someone for you to meet who can change your life." Myron turned around and headed toward the door with Donovan following and asking, "Where we goin'? Myron, where we goin'?"

"You'll find out," replied Myron mysteriously, "Just keep up!"

"But, Myron, where we goin'? You're not going to tell me, are you? Where we goin'?" Donovan asked repeatedly, sounding like a little brother trying to get a secret from his bigger brother.

They went through the main building, out into a courtyard, and then to the other side of the facility to a group of 1-story buildings Donovan had never seen before. The smell, however, gave him clues as to what awaited inside. "Are we going to see puppies? I like puppies," kidded Donovan in a slow, hollow, 'dee-de- dee' sounding voice.

"I bet you do, you smart ass!" replied Myron as he held the door open so Donovan could wheel himself inside the building.

When they reached the reception desk, JaDonna RaDea Bush, Director of the Helping Hands Program for Assisted Living, met them.

"Well, well, this must be the incomparable Donovan Mocion," she said, extending her hand and greeting Donovan with a great big smile, along with a pair of the biggest, brightest, roundest eyes he had ever seen.

JaDonna stood 4' 10" tall and was a tiny, wiry, energetic soul. She had cocoa brown skin and her dark brown, closely cut hair was almost bald on a perfectly round head. She had dark, bushy, slightly arched eyebrows, a small, round, button nose, luscious full lips with the top lip forming a kissable "M" shape, pierced ears adorned with African-styled earrings, a small, cute, rounded chin with fully developed perky medium-sized breasts that looked large on a woman of her stature.

"Follow me," said JaDonna, and she turned to lead the way.

Donovan thought, *"Damn, this little beauty is the same height as me in my wheel chair*!" Then he couldn't help but notice after JaDonna turned around she had one of the most perfectly round, plump behinds he had ever seen.

Feeling some heat tingling in his groin area, he thought to himself, "*Well, alright! I must be getting better.*"

JaDonna led them through several hallways then finally to an electric glass double door that automatically opened when they stopped in front of it.

"Donovan, this is my training facility," she said as she moved to the side and waved him in like a game show hostess displaying a prize.

Donovan was taken aback by what he saw…a lab filled with.........

monkeys!

JaDonna saw Donovan tensing up and figured talking to him would help calm him down, so she said, "These monkeys are known as Capuchin Monkeys. Originally they're from southern Central America, around Costa Rica, Paraguay, and Trinidad."

Once Donovan began relaxing she continued, "They are very smart monkeys. You've probably heard about them used as pets or trained performers, but here at Helping Hand, we use them as therapy animals, and helpers for paraplegics."

By now Donovan had pieced together what Myron was up to. Since he had overcome his initial shock, he decided to go along since Myron had never misled him before, which earned Donovan's irrefutable trust and unconditional belief.

"These little fellas weight between 3 and 8 pounds. They vary between 12 to 22 inches in head and body length and the length of their tails is approximately the same length. Their usual life span is between 15 to 20 years."

Myron glanced down at Donovan to see his reaction and was pleased to see that Donovan was going with it.

"Monkeys are devoted helpmates, giving their disabled companions independence, dignity, and love. Believe it or not, sometimes they pick the people they want to help," informed JaDonna, and without warning two monkeys jumped right into Donovan's lap and got right up in his face, looking him straight in the eyes. Donovan tensed up, afraid to move, and his eyes became as big as silver dollars. He had an, "Am I about to be eaten?" expression on his face. He was so terrified that all he could do was sit there, motionless, listening to his heart beating uncontrollably. He tried to speak, but no words came out of his wide-open mouth, which he did managed to shut before the monkeys put something unexpected in it.

"It looks like you have been chosen, Donovan. I guess I should make the formal introductions," said JaDonna, fighting back her laughter. "The larger little guy, trying to shake your hand is Topaz, a male, and the smaller one, hugging you, is Jade, a female."

JaDonna stretched out her arms calling Topaz and Jade to her. Topaz, who never refused the open arms of a lady, quickly jumped towards JaDonna's arms, while Jade decided to snuggle even closer to Donovan. Topaz, seeing this, decided he was not going to be outdone by Jade, so he jumped back into Donovan's lap, and this time he grabbed Donovan's hand and placed it on his head. Donovan did what came natural and began petting them as they snuggled in his lap like babies with their parent.

"Oh, yeah, you've been chosen...big time!" announced JaDonna. What happened next shocked both Myron and JaDonna.

"Tell me more about these little guys," requested Donovan while he enjoyed cuddling with Topaz and Jade.

"As I was about to say, continued JaDonna, our little monkey helpers are trained to perform simple everyday tasks like getting something to eat or drink, retrieving items dropped or out of reach, turning lights on or off, tasks that we take for granted. As you can see, these little fellas are affectionate, responsive companions who can brighten a disabled individual's outlook on life, and help him become more independent."

"So, Donovan," said Myron, "here's the plan. Three times a week, more if you and JaDonna can work it out, you'll have sessions learning how to work with Topaz and Jade. It will be Topaz and Jade, right JaDonna?"

"Absolutely, that choice has already been made!" answered JaDonna with an approving grin.

"Donovan, why don't you, Topaz, and Jade get to know each other while I go handle some other business? JaDonna will keep you company and be available to answer any questions," said Myron, who turned and left the four of them alone.

"Take your time," said Donovan, "I've got my hands full with these two," and he spent the rest of the morning getting to know Topaz and Jade.

Chapter 19

For the next therapy session, Myron convinced Donovan to take part in a futuristic sleep disorder treatment. Their specialty was dream capturing by administering miniscule charges of electricity to precise locations of the brain while the subject slept, then sensory transmitting electrodes sent digitized information to monitoring and decrypting devices for audio and video reconstruction, allowing others to see and hear the subject's dreams.

Myron explained to Donovan what the procedure entailed and that it was designed to help subjects recall suppressed memories via their dreams or, in Donovan's case, night terrors.

Still a bit skeptical, Donovan said, "I thought you had forgotten about my night terrors. It's been a few sessions since we talked about them."

"No, I didn't forget, I just needed to give all those pain meds a chance to leave your system before you could undergo this type of specialized treatment," explained Myron. "And you thought I forgot. Well, don't sweat it. I'll be with you every step of the way. We're a team, remember?"

"Hmm," said Donovan, "Yeah, we're a team alright, but it sounds like I'm the one who'll be getting juiced in the head."

"Look, Donovan, if I didn't think this would work, you wouldn't be here.

Besides, I come here from time to time and get it done just to get a look at my dreams. People can't remember 90% of what they dream. This technique will change all of that for those who can afford it," said Myron.

"Who said I could afford it?" asked Donovan.

"Hell man, I thought you knew. Some big-time company is paying your tab.

The sky's not the limit as far as you're concerned," informed Myron. "But, hey, don't let that concern you right now. You need to focus on what's in front of you."

"Yeah, you're right," agreed Donovan, still nervous about this dream reading technique.

The technicians at the Sleep Center showed Donovan to his room, and then attached what, to Donovan, seemed like hundreds of miniaturized exterior wireless neurotrophic electrodes to his head, and dozens more wireless electrode transmitters over the rest of his body and feet. Not only could they transmit data, some of them delivered tiny electrical charges at key memory locations of the brain.

Donovan thought they would be uncomfortable, but they weren't.

"You doing ok, Mr. Mocion?" asked a technician. "Not too uncomfortable are they?"

"No, surprising enough, they're not. They're kind of warm," answered a still slightly nervous Donovan.

"Well, the heat you're feeling comes from the adhesive holding those leads to your skin," explained the tech. "We don't want any of them to fall off while you're sleeping. We'd hate to wake you up just to reconnect a lead."

"Can you hear me, Mr. Mocion?" came a voice through speakers mounted in the ceiling of the room.

"Yeah, I can hear you. Who and where are you?" asked Donovan, looking up at the ceiling.

"I'm Dr. Tzmatsu, your controller for this session. I'm across the hall in the Telemetry Control Room with Myron."

"Can you hear me, bro?" asked Myron. "Didn't want you to think I'd abandoned you, leaving you in the hands of strangers."

"Can you guys hear me? Stupid question! Of course you can hear me, we're talking. Sorry, guys, must be my nerves," babbled Donovan.

"That's usually the case for everybody their first time doing this. We've got a little something that's going to take those nervous jitters away," replied Dr.

Tzmatsu as a technician entered the room and approached Donovan with a tiny syringe in his hand.

"Just a tiny prick and we can get this show on the road," said the grinning technician.

Donovan looked at the technician apprehensively, until he heard Myron's voice say, "It's ok, bro, you've been filled with far worse meds over the last several months. This will only make you a little drowsy. Your lack of sleep will do the rest."

Dr. Tzmatsu looked at Donovan's telemetry readings and said, "Our boy's a little excited," pointing out a specific line of display to Myron.

"Yeah, I see. Once he gets that shot in him, those readings will drop," added Myron with a grin on his face. "Mine did," he recalled.

"Sweet dreams," said the technician as he turned out the lights and closed Donovan's door behind him.

A little panic came over Donovan at first, causing his telemetry readings to spike. When Myron saw this he said, "I gotcha, bro. You're not alone!" and Donovan's readings calmed down.

Donovan's room wasn't completely dark. Some nightlights were strategically placed around the room throwing off just enough light so the camera could monitor Donovan's facial expressions. They brightened up the image in the control booth so they had a great picture of their sleeping subject.

REM sleep was what they were waiting for. In that state, physical, rapid eye movement under the subject's closed eyelids occurred, which was one of the indicators that the subject was dreaming.

The other indicator was all the telemetry equipment Donovan was remotely connected to.

Within half an hour, Donovan was sleep. In another half an hour he had achieved REM sleep, and was dreaming. 5 minutes later, the night terrors began, but this time Donovan would not wake up screaming. The calming effect from the shot, along with a tiny electric charge, would keep him from waking up during his nightmares. As soon as the terrors began, an image began emerging on the dream monitors. And for the first time since the incident, Donovan began recalling suppressed memories through his dreams. He recalled some of the field events he'd won and then vague emotions began surfacing about him and his parents but before they focused in…

"Donovan! Donovan!" a voice kept repeating, becoming louder and louder each time.

"No…not yet…just a little longer," said Donovan, fighting to stay asleep, struggling to hold on to these emotions, trying to stay in that moment with his parents.

"Sorry, bro. Our time for this session is over," It was Myron over the speaker system from the Sleep Disorder Control Room.

Donovan opened his eyes and slowly looked around remembering where he was, then he sadly realized that he'd been dreaming, and the joys he'd just experienced were recalls of prior events.

"Damn!" he said softly under his breath, not knowing whether to be sad or uplifted by this recall. All the same, a tremendous sense of sorrow mercilessly decided for him, and Donovan became overwhelmed by sadness as he reflected on what he had just experienced through his dreams.

Using the pull-up bar overhead to help, he sat up in his bed and just paused there, with his head hanging down, slowly shaking it from side to side. Those eyes that once beamed with invincibility were now troubled and tormented. Tears ran down his cheeks and he began to sod out loud.

Everybody in the control room had witnessed Donovan's memory recall.

Their hearts were hurting and their tears were flowing right along with Donovan's.

They had experienced many memory recalls before, but none as vivid as Donovan's sights and sounds, and for the next ten minutes, there wasn't a dry eye in the place.

Then the control room heard Donovan softly say, "Will somebody please come unplug me?"

Myron answered him over the speaker, "The tech's on his way in, bro." Less than 5 words were said as Donovan prepared to leave the Sleep Center.

But, before he left he spun his chair around and looked at the techs and Dr. Tzmatsu and said, "THANKS!"

Then he turned his chair around and while he was rolling away said, "I'll be seeing you guys again…SOON!"

The Sleep Center was in a different wing of Cedar's Sinai Hospital. Myron stepped behind Donovan's chair and said, "Here, let me push you."

Donovan abruptly shouted, "NO!" Then he caught himself, changed his attitude, and said, "Thanks, but I prefer to do it myself, bro."

Myron thought to himself, *"This is a good thing,"* and he let him be.

Myron had seen the recall treatment do strange things to patients. Some rebuilt their lives from it, while others gave up completely. Myron was banking that Donovan would do the former.

Donovan rolled and Myron walked in silence until they reached Donovan's room. Then Myron said, "Remember what I told you about doors opening for you? Well, a door with a new life has opened for you and it is your choice whether or not to go through that door."

Donovan looked up into Myron's eyes, paused and said, "I'm already through it. I'll see you tomorrow." Donovan wanted to be alone with his thoughts and he prepared to roll away from Myron.

Myron, understanding what Donovan had just gone through, placed his right hand on Donovan's left shoulder and gave it a squeeze. Donovan tensed up, not really wanting to be touched. Myron stepped around in front of Donovan's chair, knelt, and said, "This is tomorrow, bro, and today your grieving process began.

Today that closed door to your memories was opened. You'll be flooded with flashes of memories that you've locked away. Some of them are going to be painful, like what happened on that plane. Others are going to give you the strength you'll need to move past that. Any way they come at you, we will deal with them head on—together."

"I plan to. But does this mean I'll have to listen to these long-winded speeches of yours?" asked Donovan, managing to get a smile out.

Myron returned the smile, embarrassed a little, and then said, "Maybe...maybe worse. We'll just have to go with the flow and deal with whatever comes."

Donovan realized he had a lot of work ahead of him.

Chapter 20

With the same passion he used to become the Olympian, Donovan threw himself into his physical therapy and assisted living training sessions with Topaz and Jade, far exceeding Myron and JaDonna's goals for him. Privately, Donovan had set personal goals for himself, and his goals exceeded those set for him by normal human beings.

After their last PT session, Donovan said to Myron, "Ya-know, I've been thinking…"

"Oh, shit! We're in trouble now. Not only is he wearing me out during PT, but now he's starting to use that big brain of his. Thanks for the warning!" said a joking Myron.

"Yeah, I know what you mean… 'watch out world, the kids thinking again,'" added a playful Donovan. "But seriously, I feel I'm pretty close to being discharged from here and I'm thinking I don't want to return to Washington State University. I'm thinking I'll transfer to Stanford; they have a great Psychology Doctorate program. I know that means doing a geographical, which the experts don't advise, but I just don't want to waste time with people feeling sorry for me - you know, the people who knew me before the accident. I think I need a brand new start."

"I can see your point," said Myron. "You might as well begin with a fresh slate. I think Stanford is a great choice. We could still see each other from time to time, and I could even help you get set up. I know a few people who would be glad to find an acceptable place for you to live. Yeah…I like the sound of this."

As they continued down the hallway, they heard a female voice calling, "Mr. Mocion…Mr. Hammond."

And when they turned around to see who it was, Myron's jaw dropped open and he squeezed Donovan's shoulder slightly for support. It was Dr. Rozelyn Harris. She walked straight up to Myron using all her managerial brio, looked into his eyes, and said, "Myron, good to see you. Long time no see." Then she quickly looked down at Donovan. "And you must be Donovan Mocion," she extended a hand to Donovan. "I'm Rozelyn Harris, Medical Center Director. I've been keeping up with your recovery and everyone here is very impressed with your progress."

"Well, Myron doesn't settle for less than your best," said Donovan as he nudged Myron in his side. Donovan, feeling how tensed Myron was, gave him a look of wonderment as Dr. Harris said, "Yes, I know how demanding Mr.

Hammond can be," sneaking another glimpse into Myron's startled eyes.

"Mr. Mocion, might I have a word with you in private?" asked Dr. Harris, looking directly at Donovan while trying extra hard not to think about Myron watching her, though she did wonder what he was thinking and feeling, and if it was about her.

Donovan looked innocently up at Myron, not knowing how to react, seeking some kind of cue from Myron, but all he got were strange vibes. Myron, realizing Donovan's confusion, took his eyes off Dr. Harris for the first time since she approached them, looked down at Donovan and said, "I'll see you back in your room." and he hurriedly walked away without saying a single word to Rozelyn.

Dr. Harris handed Donovan an envelope that had Global Pharmaceuticals' logo on it and his typed name.

Dr. Harris stepped behind Donovan, beginning to push him while he read the letter, but Donovan abruptly hit his brakes and said, "NO, I've got this. There's no need for anyone to push me around."

Dr. Harris nonchalantly explained, "I just wanted you to have your hands free so you could open and read your correspondence."

"Why don't I just read it while I'm stopped…right here?" suggested Donovan.

"That works, too," replied Dr. Harris.

The letter was from Francine Katrina Bovier, requesting Donovan's presence at a funeral service for his parents, plus an estate meeting the next day. The letter went on to explain that although his parents' bodies were never recovered, in the interest of closure, Global Pharmaceuticals felt this was the appropriate time to bring a sense of finality to the tragic incident. The letter also stated "If your attendance is not possible, the ceremony will proceed without you and, rest reassured, those in attendance will clearly understand your decision not to attend." It went on to read, "If you choose to attend, first class accommodations and transportation will be provided for you and an escort, round trip, to our headquarters in Exton, PA."

Donovan looked into Dr. Harris's eyes and somehow he knew she was aware of the letter's contents, so Donovan said, "I accept, and I'd like Myron to be my escort."

"Oh, I agree," answered Dr. Harris. "Myron is the best choice, and I'm sure he'd want to be present during this portion of your grieving process. The arrangements will be forthcoming, and you will be contacted, Mr. Mocion. And Mr. Mocion? Continue your rapid recovery…we're all pulling for you."

"Thank you," said Donovan, and the two separated, going in opposite directions.

There was something about the good doctor that Donovan just couldn't quite put his finger on. The jury was still out as to whether or not he liked her. She was, without a doubt, a gorgeous woman. Maybe Myron would shine some light on the subject. Donovan decided he wasn't going to bring the subject of Dr. Harris up… Myron would have to volunteer that information in his own time.

Chapter 21

When Myron arrived at Donovan's room, Donovan was sitting in a chair, staring out the window into the forest.

"You all right, bro?" asked Myron. He could tell something was troubling Donovan.

"The company my parents worked for is having their funeral and some kind of estate meeting. They want me to attend," revealed Donovan in a particular non- emotional tone.

"I think that's a good thing," replied Myron, knowing that any grieving work Donovan did was a good thing.

"Will you come with me?" asked Donovan, "I know I'll need your support for this one."

"Absolutely, we're a team, remember? Wherever you go—I go!" reassured Myron.

"That Dr. Harris said she'd make all the arrangements. First Class!" added Donovan, still in a non-emotional tone.

"Are you ready to fly?" asked a shocked Myron.

"Not a chance! I know I'm not ready for that giant step. I figured we could take the Maglev Train. I've read it only takes a few hours and I've always wanted to ride it. The sightseeing should be good for me. I've been cooped up in this joint for far too long," said Donovan, still looking out his window.

"Maglev Train, it is then," replied Myron.

"I'll explain to Dr. Harris that I prefer taking the train. She should have no problems with that. Besides, I can sense some unresolved issues between you two, and I won't put you in the uncomfortable position of contacting her," revealed a caring Donovan, giving Myron a quick glance.

"Maybe on the train ride I'll fill you in," said Myron, realizing he owed Donovan an explanation.

"When you're ready, bro," said Donovan, "when you're ready."

Donovan was displaying a great deal of personal growth through his compassion about Myron's feelings. Myron felt proud of the tremendous work Donovan was doing. He pulled up a chair and sat quietly by Donovan's side, both looking into the forest, letting their thoughts wander. They each had plenty on their minds.

A few days later they boarded the Maglev Train. As promised, they had 1st class accommodations and connecting suites, fully equipped with all the latest extra-terrestrial and terrestrial electronic interfaces.

"I've read that Maglev means magnetically levitated and propelled vehicles.

The article said, "The train is powered by magnets, and travels on a specially designed rail containment system suspended between magnetic fields. And since there's no surface contact or "friction" to slow it down, it's able to reach speeds over 400 kilometers per hour; the train is virtually flying within that magnetic field." But we're not supposed to feel it because the train's interior is pressurized. I can't wait until this monster takes off. I've been missing the sensation from inertia to full speed. I do remember the rush of takeoff," said a nervous and talkative Donovan. "I'll tell you, bro, I'm not looking forward to making this trip, but I feel I need to," revealed Donovan.

Once they were settled into their accommodations, Myron decided to take Donovan's mind off what lay ahead for him, and took this time to tell him about the Dr. Harris issue. He waited until the train had taken off and reached maximum speed so Donovan wouldn't miss the sensation of the Maglev's takeoff.

"Yeah, baby, yeah! That's what I'm talkin' 'bout!" shouted Donovan as the train accelerated to it's maximum speed. "What a rush!"

Donovan looked out the window, but he wasn't able to see much.

Everything was a blur at the speed the train traveled. This disappointed Donovan, and when Myron noticed Donovan's joy retreating into the darkness of unknown emotions, he figured it was the perfect time to share about himself and Dr. Rozelyn Harris.

"You ever been in love, bro?" asked Myron.

"Not really," answered Donovan. "Caught an STD from this hotty who took me back to her dorm room once. Never really had time, between studying and track."

"Well, I have," revealed Myron.

"Dr. Harris?" guessed Donovan.

"Yeah," answered Myron.

"You feel like talking 'bout it?" asked a caring Donovan.

"Yeah, I do. I've been feeling strange ever since I saw her the other day. You got to protect your heart, bro, and once you find the one, don't hesitate, and don't let anything stand in the way, because you can lose her when you least expect it. That's what happened between Roz and me. I knew she was something special, but I just took for granted that she would always be there, just for me, and I never gave her the full attention she needed, or really looked at our relationship from her perspective, and I lost her to someone else. Well, I didn't really lose her…it was more like I didn't fight to keep her. See, I wouldn't give up the business I was in for her, and when I found her in the arms of someone else, I reacted immaturely, and turned my back on love."

"Well, what happened to her? Did she marry the other guy or what?" asked a curious Donovan.

"Nah, they fell apart, and went their separate ways," answered Myron.

"So, what's kept you from hooking back up with her?" asked Donovan.

"It's more complicated than that, bro," answered Myron.

"Really?" questioned Donovan. "Seems to me that if you still have these feelings for her, and I could sense she still has deep feelings for you, then you two could work things out."

"I wish it was that simple," said Myron as he stared at the blurred scenery blazing past outside the window.

"Listen," began Donovan, "I haven't been in love with a person like you have, but I'm still in deep love with being an athlete, and I will do whatever it takes to keep that love alive. Why don't you just tell her how you feel?"

"It's complicated. I can't just walk up to her and say, "Roz, I've loved you since the very first time I saw you and I still do. Can we put the past behind us and live in our love again?"

"Why not? Sounds good to me!" replied Donovan

"It's just too complicated," repeated Myron again.

"Oh…I see! You don't have the balls to forgive her, or yourself, for something you feel you did or didn't do? Is that it?" asked Donovan looking dead into Myron's eyes.

Myron had no comeback because Donovan's truth carried the heavy weight of reality, even though Myron had not painted an entirely honest picture for Donovan. Myron was speechless about Donovan's insight, and for the remainder of the train ride they both sat absorbed in their own personal thoughts, looking out the window at the blurry streaks of life flashing by.

Myron's thoughts went back to a couple of lifetimes ago, back in the day, Myron noticed a beautiful young woman under the control of one of his street vendors, who were better know as drug dealers. She was strung out and being paraded around by this dealer, who, on occasion, rented her out to his high rolling clientele. Even while strung out, she made a striking showpiece and went by the nickname Alley Kat. She had something very special behind those drugged-filled eyes that caught Myron's attention, so when her supplier/pimp was shot and killed, Myron rescued her by taking her under his wing and introducing her to an alternative existence. Myron discovered that even drugged out, Alley Kat had a keen business sense, but he knew in order for her to use all of her gifts she needed to get clean and sober. When she finally agreed to clean up her act, Myron called on Rozelyn Harris, director of The Cure Recovery House. Roz made a bed and treatment available for Alley Kat as a favor to Myron.

Myron and Rozelyn were experiencing an on-again/off-again relationship that Myron hoped would develop into something much, much more. Rozelyn had love for Myron but she would not commit because of the business Myron was in. Rozelyn was not about to jeopardize her professional career by being openly involved with a big time supplier to drug dealers.

As Alley Kat became clean and sober, she and Rozelyn began revealing their affections towards Myron to each other, and somewhere during that sharing they developed intimate feelings for one another, and eventually they became lovers, too. Myron, accidentally discovered Alley Kat and Rozelyn in bed together.

Shocked, angry, and feeling deceived, Myron hastily broke off all relationships with both women.

Before Myron had the chance to rethink his actions, he was the passenger in a deadly car accident, which took the life of his beloved mother. Ironically, the driver of the car causing the accident was one of Myron's street vendors, under the influence of Myron's product.

During recovery Myron made the decision to change his entire life and he never looked back. Myron went back to college to become a Physical Therapist and began developing his physical therapy business.

Alley Kat began climbing the corporate ladder.

Rozelyn became an assistant director at General Hospital in Los Angeles.

All was turning out for the better until Myron's business ventures fell under hard times. He had heard that Alley Kat had become very prosperous and he went to her for financial help. As a result of that help, he now owed her a favor.

While Alley Kat was making her moves at a company called Global Pharmaceuticals, Rozelyn became disillusioned by the manner in which she was achieving her goals to reach the top, and they went their separate ways.

While Rozelyn was at General Hospital, the position of Medical Director for Cedars-Sinai Medical Center became available, a position that Rozelyn desperately wanted. She, too, went to Alley Kat who was, by then, extremely powerful. Alley Kat pulled some strings for her former lover and got Roz the position under the condition that Rozelyn now owed her a favor to be paid at some point in the future.

Myron carried around the weight of resentment towards both women for all these years, feeding off it, and allowing that resentment to block his true feelings for Rozelyn.

What Myron didn't know was that Rozelyn was feeling pretty much the same, only in her scenario, she was to blame for allowing things to get out of hand between herself and Alley Kat, and she couldn't muster up the courage to approach Myron with her true feelings.

Alley Kat, well, she was busy being Francine Katrina Bovier, CEO of Global Pharmaceuticals and Headmistress of the Universe!

Chapter 22

Donovan and Myron disembarked the Maglev to a rainy, muggy day in Exton, Pennsylvania. "It feels like a lifetime has passed since I was here last," commented Donovan, as he looked around, getting a negative vibe about the place.

"*You and me both*!" thought Myron, hoping that he wouldn't, but odds were he would, see Francine again.

Parked at the curb waiting for them was a new sleek, long, black, wheelchair-accessible electric Hummer limousine, which whisked them off to the Exton's Westin Hotel where a wheelchair-accessible ground floor, two-bedroom suite, had been reserved—first class all the way. After they checked in and refreshed themselves, they were off to the funeral.

A large number of people had turned out, all brainiac, scientific, business, and corporate types. Donovan didn't see anyone he recognized, but there was an extremely attractive, well-dressed woman receiving a great deal of attention who kept staring at him from across his parents' gravesite. He felt he should be aware of who she was, but he couldn't place her.

With a sorrowful heart, Donovan sat listening to several strangers reciting their scientific babble about how brilliant and what geniuses his parents were, and what a grave injustice had been done to the universe by their untimely deaths, but not a single word had been spoken about the real people his parents were, so when the last person finished, Donovan rolled up to the podium and was politely handed the microphone.

Donovan began quietly and somberly, with his head hanging down. "No longer will I ever feel the warmth of my mother's love, or the love under my father's protection, or the love from their combined wisdom propelling me forward through my existence. I won't hear the laughter of my mother's voice, feel my father's approving pat on the back after I'd achieved a higher awareness, physically or mentally. I'll miss hearing my mother's crazy jokes and my father's hilarious comebacks," said Donovan through watery eyes with a slight smile on his lips, reflecting on the wonderful loving experiences with his parents. "And watching my father's innocent roving eye for a beautiful woman, knowing all the time he already had, and fully appreciated, the most beautiful woman on earth, already by his side freely giving all the love, respect, and honor she had to give. And my mother received, and felt, no less from him. They were two sides of the same coin, which creation produced from the same beam of light, time, and space. They were intended to be together as one for the rest of eternity. I loved my parents more than I ever told them and more than I ever knew. I'll miss them more than anyone could ever dream possible. They were my heart and soul!!!"

Tears poured down Donovan's face as turned his wheelchair away from the podium and rolled away as quietly as he'd approached it. He rolled back over to Myron who was standing there with watery eyes, proud of the accomplishments Donovan had made reaching this level of his recovery and grieving process. Myron had no words for Donovan, just a brotherly squeeze of Donovan's shoulder when he returned to his side.

After the services the woman who had been staring at Donovan began making her way toward Donovan and Myron. The mourners who were congregated in her path, politely, intentionally, and immediately stepped aside, making a path for her.

Myron, seeing her approaching leant down and said to Donovan, "I'll be right back; I've got to find a place to take a leak. Will you be all right by yourself for a few minutes?"

"No problem," replied Donovan.

The woman stood next to Donovan and watched Myron as he walked away, then focusing her attentions on Donovan, she introduced herself, "Hello Donovan, I'm Francine Katrina Bovier, Chief Executive Officer for Global Pharmaceuticals. Your parents worked for me," and she extended her hand.

Although the woman was extremely beautiful, alluring, and emitted an enticing fragrance, there was something about her that made Donovan uneasy, and when he shook her hand, she felt cold and sinister. The sensation startled Donovan and he almost snatched his hand away from her petite, polite grip, which was immediately joined by her other hand on his as she said, "My deepest sympathies for your tragic lost. We at Global Pharmaceuticals don't want you to worry about anything; we're covering all your medical expenses, now, and in the future. If there's anything you personally need—well," she released Donovan's hand, removed a business card from a concealed breast pocket inside her charcoal gray colored business suit, and placed it into Donovan's hand, saying, "Make sure you call me directly and we will work it out, no matter what it is."

Donovan recalled his parents mentioning the name Francine Katrina Bovier, and each time they had nothing good to say about her. He remembered something about her trying to take credit for their research findings and applications.

Donovan didn't know the woman, but he already didn't like her.

"I know this isn't the best time to bring this up, but business is business," began Francine. "Global Pharmaceuticals supplied your parents with a house for as long as they worked for us. I'm afraid we need to reclaim that property and get it ready for future use. We need you to remove whatever you want to keep from the premises. Global Pharmaceuticals will gladly pay the shipping costs to any destination you choose." Francine ended the conversation with, "By the end of the week works for us!"

And before Donovan could formulate a reply, she finished by saying, "You take care of yourself!"

Francine performed a perfect pirouette and sashayed away accompanied by a small entourage vying for her attention, leaving a very cold void in the air where she had been standing.

Myron, witnessed her departure and made his way back over to Donovan who had the look of, "What the hell just happened?" on his face.

"Is everything OK, bro?" asked Myron.

"Man, I don't know what just happened, but I think I just got evicted." answered Donovan,

"Evicted!? I thought you lived right outside the Washington campus?" replied Myron.

"I do," replied Donovan, still looking bewildered. Then he said, "Something feels wrong here."

Myron made no comment.

As Donovan and Myron were leaving the gravesite, his parents' regular 3- person flight crew stopped them, and through weeping eyes, expressed how heartbroken they were over the loss of his parents and Donovan's condition. They apologized over and over for becoming ill that night in Hawaii. It seemed they all had come down with food poisoning, even though they had each eaten at different restaurants, in different parts of town. They were, however, pleased, yet shocked, when they learned the company had a stand-by flight crew on hand to replace them so quickly. It usually took several hours to replace a flight crew trained on that particular model Gulfstream Jet.

This information deeply disturbed Donovan who instantly tried with all his might to remember what happened the night of the crash, but it was still a blank. He did manage to remember this flight crew; they usually flew the Mocions from place to place and were considered friends of the family. Donovan had assumed they were the missing flight crew who went down in the crash.

Donovan didn't know what it was, but he had a bad feeling, and to get to the bottom of it the best place to start was at his parents' house.

Donovan's parents had moved into the house owned by Global Pharmaceuticals just as Donovan left for college. He never really lived there, but he did spend all special occasions there. He and his parents were always busy, self- indulged, obsessively into their own projects, so they made it a priority to be together during all birthdays, holidays, special sporting events, and achievement awards.

When the limo rolled to a stop in front of his parents' house, all looked normal, but when they got inside, it looked like a tornado had hit, turning everything topsy-turvy. The place looked like it had been robbed; stuff was thrown everywhere.

Myron looked down at Donovan in his wheelchair and said, "Maid's year off?"

Donovan looked back at him and slowly responded, "Evidently!" "Looks like they've been robbed," said Myron as he looked around in disbelief.

"Yeah, but look at all this expensive stuff still lying around," replied Donovan. "Somebody tore this place up with a purpose; they were looking for something."

Donovan tried to roll across the room, but the debris on the floor kept bogging him down, until Myron voluntarily cleared him a path.

"Thanks!" said Donovan as he made his way towards the back of the house where his parents' home laboratory was located, finding it in worse condition than the main house.

Donovan wheeled himself in front of a fish aquarium built into a wall. The dead fish were floating on top of the murky water. Donovan paused for a few seconds, thinking, and staring at the aquarium.

"Checking to see if any fish are still alive?" asked Myron, being a smart ass. "Nah, I've just got a hunch that whoever did this didn't find what they were looking for. My parents had a special addition made to this aquarium, and if you didn't know it was there, you wouldn't know," revealed Donovan.

He twisted a nut that appeared to be part of the tank, and a section of the wall surrounding the aquarium opened, revealing a hidden safe.

"Very 007ish," said Myron.

"Yeah, I know. My parents were extremely suspicious of people outside the family. Only the three of us had access to this control panel," explained Donovan.

Donovan placed his hand in a slot on the bottom of the aquarium where it was scanned and then, from within the tank, an eye retina scanner scanned his eyes and the hidden safe opened revealing computer drives and a case full of A.I. Crystals.

"We need to take these with us," said Donovan. "But, I need a safe place to hide them."

"I've got the perfect place," answered Myron, "Give them here." And he walked around to the back of Donovan's wheelchair. "You've got the deluxe, top of the line chair, complete with hidden compartments for just such an occasion."

"Cool," said a surprised Donovan, followed by a smile. It was the first smile Myron had seen from him since their arrival.

"Now, let's get the hell out of here," said Donovan.

Their limo slowly pulled away and rounded the corner; another car started up and slowly followed them. Inside that car a figure hit a speed dial button. A female voice on the other end of the phone asked, "Did the kid find anything?" The caller replied, "We scanned them before they went in, and after they came out, both scans were negative."

"SHIT!!!" said the voice on the phone. "Well, keep an eye on him until he leaves town."

"Copy," said the caller.

And the line went dead.

Back at the hotel, Donovan sat quietly looking out the window at a majestic waterfall in the courtyard, fully engrossed in his thoughts.

"What's going on in that big brain of yours?" asked Myron.

"Ever since we got here I've felt nothing but negative energy, and I can't shake this feeling that everything here is wrong—nothing is what it appears! I'll be glad when that estate meeting tomorrow is over. I just want to get the hell out of here!" answered Donovan with a lost look on his face, and then said, "Right after that meeting let's take the next airplane back to LA."

"I agree—that's just what we'll do." Then Donovan's exact words sunk in and Myron said, "Come again? Did I here the 'a' word, as in *airplane?*"

"Yes! you did, and *Yes!* we will fly back. I'm going to bed, I've had a hard day," said Donovan looking very weary.

"*EXCELLENT!*" thought Myron, "*Donovan Mocion, I believe you're gonna make it*!"

Chapter 23

Donovan rolled into the attorney's office bright and early the next morning, hoping he wouldn't be there all day; he wanted no more of Exton, PA.

"Mr. Mocion, I'm Thergood Stedman, appointed attorney for you late parents' estate. It's good to see you out and about after all you've been through. It's my understanding that you're still under doctors' care, and you have a couple of months to go before you're officially released from the hospital, therefore, I'm going to keep this as brief as possible so you can return to your recuperating.

"Your parents left you the sum of 10 million dollars after taxes, which appears to have been the total in their combined bank accounts. They also had 15 million dollars each in life insurance. Since this is a case of accidental death, the insurance policies doubled to 30 million each, tax-free. However, there is a stipulation. You can't receive the bulk of that cash until your 25th birthday. Those funds will be held in probate, earning taxable interest of course, and you can choose to withdraw that interest anytime you wish. Now remember, that interest will be considered taxable income for you, so you will have to report it to the I.R.S. when you file your income taxes.

"Unfortunately, since your parents' bodies were never recovered, the insurance company has evoked clause 2327 electing to withhold payments on both policies for one full year from the time they were legally declared deceased, which was officially the day of their funeral. In other words, those funds won't officially be yours until 1 year from yesterday, at which time they will be deposited into a financial institution under your name until the conditions I previously mentioned, are met. Do you understand, sir?"

"Correct me if I'm wrong," began Donovan. "My parents became officially dead yesterday. Payment on their life insurance policies won't happen until 1 year from yesterday. At that time, I can begin withdrawing the interest from those funds, which I must report as taxable income. Then, on my 25th birthday the entire 60 million dollars will be released to me…tax free?"

"Precisely!" answered the attorney. "In addition to that, Global Pharmaceuticals will pick up the tab for all your medical expenses for the rest of your life, no questions asked.

"And finally, all claims to the property where your mother and father resided are to be relinquished within 7 days from yesterday. Any of your late parents' private possessions that you choose to keep must be removed from the premises within that time frame, 7 days from yesterday. All remaining items left behind in the house after that deadline, intellectual property included, will become the sole property of Global Pharmaceuticals. Furthermore, any rights you think you may have on the above mentioned properties will be relinquished after the signing of these release forms. Do you have any questions at this moment?"

"No, not at this moment," replied Donovan.

"Superior! Then Mr. Mocion, if you will just sign all the yellow flagged areas, I will issue you a bank draft in the amount of $10,000,000.00, or if you'd prefer, a wire transfer into your bank account; the choice is completely yours. And if you have any concerns at a later time, feel free to contact me, or have your attorney contact me."

Donovan didn't trust any of these people with his banking information so he silently signed all the forms and then announced, "I'll take the draft."

"I thought you would," said the attorney and he handed Donovan the bank draft then said, "Good luck to you, sir, and good day."

Myron met Donovan in the attorney's waiting area and when he saw the look on Donovan's face, he said, "Man, you look dazed. Did everything go all right?"

"Let's just get out of here and back to California," replied a disgusted, drained Donovan who felt troubled ever since he had arrived in Exton, PA!

"That suits me just fine," said Myron, "Our plane leaves within the hour."

Chapter 24

Donovan slept the entire flight back to LA, and while he slept he dreamt about running, and more…

During training, all his coaches told him, "With a few years of dedicated training, and the proper coaching, you might be able to at least win a silver medal in one of your events. But, what you need to do is focus…focus on one or two events, no more. No athlete in history has ever been able to medal in all their individual events during the same Olympics."

Donovan would smile every time something like this was told to him.

Donovan knew what he wanted to do and it all had worked out perfectly. He was pleased at how he'd displayed only enough of his abilities to qualify for every event he knew he could win.

Donovan was always overlooked by the press and everyone else. He wanted the attention to be placed on others, that way there was no pressure on him to do anything but show up. And at the Olympics he showed up all right…he came, he saw, and he conquered…then he disappeared.

His plan had worked perfectly.

The Olympian! Platinum Athlete—with new planetary records in all his events—an unheard of, unprecedented, historical accomplishment.

Donovan's dreams of triumph abruptly morphed into shattered, vague, horrific nightmares where sketchy images of a plane going down dominated. Next were visions of his mother and father slowly spiraling up towards the heavens and exploding into a brilliant light. Then there was something about a substitute flight crew doing swan dives and back flips out of a perfectly good airplane, and waving good-bye to him while the flight attendant blew kisses at him.

Then Donovan felt himself become a human pinball that struck stationary objects, ejecting him to the other side of the game table, again, and again, and again. Each time he hit something he could hear his spine breaking. He smelled the plane's fuel, and felt its burning wetness as he flew through it as if passing through a boiling waterfall.

Then he saw what looked like the moon exploding and everything went black. He became part of nothingness until he felt an icy cold liquid swallowing him alive as giant teeth begin chewing him to pieces.

This was not the first time he'd experienced this nightmare. Usually, while he was being chewed to pieces he would wake up screaming, and forget, but this time was different. Donovan was determined to ride this dream wave all the way to shore. This time during his dream, he remembered he had dreamt this same dream before. Something about realizing he was experiencing a reoccurring dream bothered him while he was dreaming. It was like his subconscious was trying to give his conscious an important message but he couldn't quite put it together, yet.

Donovan could never remember the plane crash. The most he could remember was falling asleep shortly after take-off.

Dr. Kim had told him, "The brain has a way of blanking out tremendous, traumatic events; that's why you remembered nothing about the crash itself."

Donovan woke up when the plane touched down in LA, and he had a renewed view of his situation. He had made up his mind to move on, to get on with the rest of his life. He decided that since he could no longer run, he would finish his academia, but not at the University of Washington. He would transfer to Stanford University and finish up his doctorate there.

"I'll take it one step at a time," he thought to himself, and the thought of taking any step at all put a smile on his face.

Donovan's 'pity-party,' 'poor-me' days were over!

Chapter 25

Kevin Mathews, freshly promoted to Laboratory Supervisor following Rovena Budnski's untimely devouring, took his new responsibilities with great enthusiasm, pride, and dedication. Part of his duties included overseeing the care and feeding of subjects 5 and 53, who had been relocated from quarantine to a more primitive containment area...a long way from their plush resort-type accommodations. Containment consisted of the barest of essentials - a drinking fountain and an oversized stuffed pad on a concrete floor for sleeping. Their conditions were no better than those of caged animals in a zoo.

Kevin approached his responsibilities completely different than his predecessor; he treated all subjects with respect, dignity, and kindness. He actually cared for the well-being of those in his charge. Subjects 5 and 53 appreciated his kindness and, as best they could, treated Kevin with equal respect and kindness.

Within his first week, Kevin discovered that he and he alone could approach containment, and move about inside their containment cells in no danger from either of them.

During Kevin's brief physical examination of subjects 5 and 53 after their transformation, he discovered a great discrepancy between what was written in their charts and what reality was. The charts had subject 5's sex as *male* and subject 53's sex as *female,* but currently 5 was a *female* and 53 was a *male*. This meant that at some point prior to becoming subjects for Alpha Clinical Trials, subjects 5 and 53 had undergone sexual reassignment. According to the protocol Kevin understood, this should have eliminated them from selection. The only person with enough power to approve the use of subjects who had been altered in this manner was Francine Katrina Bovier. The main questions running through Kevin's mind were, "*Do Drs. Wiley and Hothan know*? And, *"If so, what is really going on*?"

Since subjects 5 and 53 had initially displayed carnivorous tendencies after transformation, it was unknown whether they would feed on each other, so their containment cells were separated by an electro-magnetic force repeller; a shield that repelled with greater energy than whatever force was applied against it. Most of the time subjects 5 and 53 just stared in wonderment at what the other had become, while swaying from side to side in unison to a primal rhythm only they could hear, and other times they attempted to touch each other and were zapped by the repeller, causing them to roar in defiance. Kevin observed that they never touched the same area twice, always a new location, and briefly he entertained the notion that they were testing for weaknesses in the shield, but he just as quickly dismissed the notion.

The creatures' containment cells were constructed from the same impenetrable substance as the rest of the Cone with the exception of a triple- strength, Lexan polycarbonate, impact-resistant material used as the front wall where steel bars and a cage door normally went, there was a sliding sheet of Lexan, with slotted port access windows for feeding and for tranquilizing the creatures.

The containment cells' ceilings were made from the same Lexan material, but in this case, only viewers in the observation booth above could see through the Lexan into the containment cells below. The creatures only saw a reflective ceiling when they looked up in their cells.

The physical job of keeping the contained beasts fed, and their cells clean, was the responsibility of the handlers. Every time their cells were cleaned, subjects 5 and 53 were subdued by tranquilizers shot from outside their cells by handlers.

Some handlers enjoyed tormenting the snarling beasts; they loved getting the creatures all worked up prior to shooting them with tranquilizer guns. For the handlers it was as close as they would ever come to big game hunting. Each handler had inflicted pain upon the beasts at some point during the course of performing their duties. As far as subjects 5 and 53 were concerned, all handlers were prey, and the creatures patiently waited for one to screw up so they could sink their claws and fangs into them.

The handlers had been given specific instructions on firing tranquilizing shots into subjects 5 and 53 before entering their containment cells. Subject 5, the female and smaller creature was to receive a lesser dose than 53, the larger male, but somewhere down the food chain those instructions were reversed, and 53 received the lesser dose.

The handlers were trained to perform their duties in groups of three, two inside the cell, and one outside covering them. A gung-ho handler broke protocol and entered 53's cell alone and was busy working with his back to the beast, when the creature gradually regained consciousness and spotted him. Silently, the creature got to its feet, then slowly moved in on the handler's back and just stood there, drooling over his prey. The unsuspecting handler sensed something was wrong and stopped working. Suddenly, he became aware of deep breathing coming from behind him and then he felt moisture dripping down the back of his neck.

Fearing the worst, he began praying, "*Please lord, please lord, please lord...don't let, don't let, don't let that demon be behind me.*" The handler's fear was beyond anything he'd ever experienced before. His entire body trembled as he timidly turned to take a look. When he came fully around his worse fears were realized and he emptied his bladder and bowels on himself while staring into the eyes of his demon, but before he could yell for help, subject 53 lashed out with a vicious swipe from his massive claw, severing the handler's head, sending it flying across the cell into the repeller field, which bounced the head back into the cell with greater force, smashing it into the side wall, then the disfigured, severed head hit the concrete floor with a splat right at the feet of the handler's twitching carcass.

Outside the containment cell, the other handlers were preoccupied sharing stories about who they picked up at the nightclub the night before, and weren't paying attention to what was happening inside the cell until it was too late. They immediately shut the cell's sliding door, and began shooting additional tranquilizers into 53, knocking him completely unconscious.

After that incident, whenever handlers approached subjects 5 and 53's containment cells, they openly discussed how these two needed to be sent to Disposal and destroyed like all the other failed experiments. Despite no longer having the ability to speak English, subjects 5 and 53 understood what others were saying, and the single most terrifying word they understood was DISPOSAL!

Not even Drs. Wiley or Hothan had considered the probability that the creatures understood spoken words. Kevin had seen indications of higher awareness by the way 5 and 53 treated him, but no testing had been done and he needed concrete facts. He was not about to present unsubstantiated facts or hunches to anyone up the food chain and possibly jeopardize his new position. Kevin decided to keep his mouth closed and wait to see what happened.

After the last attack, Drs. Wiley and Hothan slowly approached the containment cells not really looking forward to what they were about to see. The doctors believed subjects 5 and 53's brains were functioning at a less evolved, more rudimental level than before the injections, reverting back to more primitive thoughts, needs, and wants. Subjects 5 and 53 increased their savage ferocity, remembering all they had been subjected to, and expressed their anger by constantly roaring, and physically trying to attack anyone approaching them, with the exception of Kevin.

"Just look what we've done! These grotesque creatures were once somewhat vibrant people," exclaimed Dr. Hothan, feeling guilty about the negative side effects from their version of the Human Enhancement Formula.

"They volunteered!" defended Dr. Wiley. "Besides, what good were they doing with their lives anyway?"

"I'm shocked that you would even say that, Diane," said Dr. Hothan. "You sound like Rovena Budnski!"

"Not any more!" replied Dr. Wiley. The two of them glanced at each other, managing to keep their laughter inside, releasing only smiles, which quickly disappeared and were replaced by shaking their heads from side to side, unsettled, and frightened by what they saw as subjects 5 and 53 insanely slammed against the Lexan wall separating themselves from the doctors.

"We could truly be damned for messing in the Creator's work," commented Dr. Hothan. "Nature always finds a way to reclaim what science has altered."

"Don't get holy-roller on me, Louise, you knew just as well as I did, especially after seeing the negative side effects on prior test subjects, this kind of result was more than possible, it was probable!" said Dr. Wiley, forcibly.

"Yeah, I know, but seeing the effect in reality on a person is different," admitted a remorseful Dr. Hothan. "And, Diane, you can't stand there and tell me that you don't feel sorry for them, too."

"OK, OK, I do! But we've got to keep our objectivity here. After all, this is only phase one of the experiment. We still have a lot of work ahead of us. Now c'mon, get back into character. Are you ready, Dr. Hothan?" asked a pumped-up Dr. Wiley.

"As ready as I can get, Dr. Wiley," replied a remorseful and unenthusiastic Dr. Hothan.

As they were walking away, Dr. Wiley asked in a quasi-whisper, "How are you and Kevin getting along these days?"

"I swear I might have to hit him over the head to get him to make a move on me," replied a frustrated Dr. Hothan.

"He does know that relationships between coworkers are permitted, doesn't he?" asked Dr. Wiley. "Maybe I'll nonchalantly give him a nudge for you."

"Please do. I've already gone through 5 vibrators pretending they're him." "Girl, you are sooo bad!"

"Bad nothing! I'm beyond bad…I'm horny!"

When they returned to the observation booth the red phone was buzzing off the hook. When Dr. Wiley finally answered it she heard, "What are the latest results with HEF on A.C.T.?" demanded Francine.

"Numbers 28 and 37 are showing positive results, while numbers 5 and 53 remain transformed, isolated, and confined in separate containment cells," quickly answered Dr. Wiley.

"I understand we lost a handler…a good lesson for others to stay on their toes around those creatures. Give me a brief overview of our two positive subjects," ordered Francine.

"The bone structures of test subjects 28 and 37 have strengthened. Muscle tissue has been restructured, strengthened, rejuvenated, and condensed. Both subjects have grown new muscle mass, cartilage, organ tissue, lymphatic fluid, and their cellular functions have improved. Both subjects display marked improvement in hand-eye coordination, reflexes, stamina, and speed. Both subjects also show increased heart rate, pulse rate, and blood pressure readings, along with highly elevated body temperature, as if HEF was burning out their bodies. However Dr Hothan and myself think this is the new norm for them," reported Dr. Wiley.

"Good, good, very good," said a pleased Francine, sounding like a mad scientist. "What about the aging effect and withdrawal period?"

"Our testing indicates aging is at a rate of 6 months per week. And as long as they receive HEF injections every 10 hours, there appears to be no withdrawal period," explained Dr. Wiley.

"Initiate Phase 2—even on the negatives. Forward me the complete details," ordered Francine and the line went dead.

Dr. Wiley let the phone slowly drop from her hand, finding its own way back to its base. "Well, what did she say?" asked a curious Dr. Hothan.

"We go to Phase 2—even on the negatives," replied Dr. Wiley.

They both stood staring down into the lab below at subjects 28 and 37, both happily running at accelerated speeds on treadmills.

"Can you imagine the type of offspring that could be created between subjects 28 and 37 if they survive all the way through Phase 5?" asked Dr. Wiley.

"I'm too horrified thinking about the monstrosities subjects 5 and 53 will create if they survive through Phase 5," replied Dr. Hothan, who then said, "What are the odds that subjects 5 and 53 both had sexual reassignment surgeries before they came to us?"

The doctors looked at each other, and Dr. Hothan said softly, "Somebody is going to hell for what has been created here."

"Without a doubt!" agreed Dr. Wiley, sadly.

CHAPTER 26

Since the initial injections, subjects 28 and 37 were both enjoying a pain- free, and greatly enhanced, existence through chemicals. They were told that 5 and 53 had negative reactions to the serum and were released from the study. The four subjects had not bonded with each other so not having 5 and 53 around wasn't a great loss for 28 and 37. It was, however, a lot more peaceful and pleasurable without Budnski. They were told she was on vacation.

Over the last few days numbers 28 and 37 were developing a closer relationship with each other—very close! They had so far refrained from acting on their constant sexually aroused states, which was one of the side effects of the HEF serum.

28 and 37 were effortlessly carrying on a conversation while they matched each other's high speed treadmill running.

"I just can't believe how," she paused to pick the best word, "inspired I'm feeling," said a smiling 37, who was too shy to say what she really wanted to do to 28's body.

"Yeah, I'm feelin pretty feisty myself," 28 straight out replied, giving her a wink.

"Don't you ever give it a rest?" asked a blushing 37, giving 28 a little smile then gently biting seductively on her bottom lip, while her eyes told him that she wanted to eat him alive, sexually.

"C'mon now—after all this time, and both of us wired to the hilt off the same stuff, you can't tell me that you're not feeling the urge," said 28. "I can see it in your eyes."

"Yeah, I got the feelin' all right," replied 37 smiling and looking straight ahead at the wall display, not wanting her eyes to reveal any more of her lustful desires towards 28 than they already had.

To break the monotony of running in place, there were floor to ceiling real time wall displays, with audio effects, which would display whatever type of scenery selected. Any program selected caused the treadmill to react exactly to the conditions and individual challenges of that scene. They both had selected the jogging on the beach program.

Dr. Hothan came down from the observation booth after they had finished their last test and announced, "You two have done excellently and I suggest you take the rest of the day off. There's a holosuite not far from your quarters. Why don't you check it out after you've freshened up, get in a little well-deserved R&R? I'll let the handlers know so you won't be hassled about wandering around the facility."

"Thank you, Dr. Hothan," said 28 and 37 simultaneously.

"How about I pick you up in 1 hour?" suggested 28.

"It's a date!" replied 37. Then she thought about what she said, quickly turned away from 28 so he wouldn't see her blushing, and hurried off to her quarters to get ready.

Exactly thee quarters of an hour later, 28 knocked on 37's door. It didn't matter that he was early; she had been ready for the last fifteen minutes and had been forcing herself not to go knocking on his door.

Peeking through the door into her room after she had opened it slightly, 28 said, "Nice place you got here. It looks strangely familiar."

"No doubt!" answered 37 with a smile, knowing they had identical rooms. "You ready to do this…? Damn!" she said. "No matter how I put it there always seems to be a sexually implied overtone in everything I say to you lately.

Hey…I've got an idea," she announced with a mischievous look on her face. Then she grabbed 28 around the neck and pulled him into her room with a giggle. They barely got the door closed behind them as they torn each other's clothes off.

They never made it to the holosuite.

Chapter 27

It was one of those rare beautiful days in southern California, smoggy, hazy, and dirty brown skies, with Santa Anna winds causing patchy blue streaks to shine through every now and then…a perfect day for the beach.

Donovan sat gazing out his hospital room window; this spot had become his favorite for daydreaming. He heard a small disturbance down in the forest and saw a little Labrador puppy clumsily chasing a squirrel around as fast as it could, but it couldn't quite catch it. The squirrel was playfully toying with the pup, letting him close in, and then cutting in another direction, causing the pup to flip head over paws trying the same cut as the squirrel, with the pup tumbling a few feet before regaining its composure. Time after time this happened with the same results, but the determined pup never gave up, and each time the playful squirrel patiently waited until the pup regrouped and gave chase again. They went tearing around the forest until the squirrel grew tired of their game, but the pup wasn't ready to stop chasing the squirrel, so one last time the squirrel allowed the pup to close in, but this time instead of making a cut, the squirrel ran straight at the trunk of a tree then leaped into the tree and turned around to watch the puppy crash head first into the tree's trunk, knocking the pup down and out.

Slowly, the little lab came to and shook its head from side to side, clearing away the negative effects of crashing into the tree. Then the pup looked up at the squirrel and began barking like crazy. The squirrel just ignored the rantings of the pup and darted off into the trees. The pup circled the tree trunk a few times, looking up for the squirrel, and when he didn't see him, the pup lifted its back leg and took a long pee on the tree trunk, then turned its back on the tree and with its hind legs, kicked leaves and dirt from the forest floor on the tree, then finally ran off to find something else to occupy its time.

If there was any type of meaning to what Donovan had just witnessed, it went completely over his head, though he did appreciate the puppy's determination. Perhaps it was an example of the determination Donovan was going to need since he was leaving the hospital and would soon be on his own in a strange new world. Still, it was pretty funny what the squirrel had done to that puppy, and Donovan couldn't help but giggle to himself about it.

Myron walked into Donovan's room. When he saw him at the window he knew Donovan was in deep thought, but still he asked, "Feel like sharing that thought with me?"

Donovan spun his chair around, smiling at first, all set to share the tale of "the puppy and the squirrel," but without meaning to, a look of deep despair came across Donovan's face, and he blurted out, "I'm afraid to leave here, Myron! I've never lived alone before. Even in the dorms there was always someone right next door, but me living by myself, paralyzed, alone, in my own home? MAN, the thought of it is freaking me out. I don't know if I'm ready."

Myron knew just what was happening. "Donovan, you're just having a panic attack. This is a normal emotional experience, a kind of separation anxiety; patients go through this all the time… it will pass. You know I wouldn't recommend you for release if I didn't know in my heart that you're ready to leave here. Besides, a hospital is no place to get well. The only place to get healthy is on the outside, in the real world, away from this place. Now, c'mon…I got something for you to see."

Myron led Donovan to the elevator and up to the top floor. Donovan had never been there before and when the doors opened he saw a bright flash and heard a loud "SURPRISE!!!!"

When Donovan's eyes cleared there stood everybody who had played a part in his recovery. And they were bearing gifts, too!

The Physical Therapy Department presented Donovan with a collection of Invacare, top of the line, TDX power wheelchairs, complete with every kind of accessory known to man, and all of them, except The Transformer Sports chair and Top End Handcycle, had been interfaced so Donovan could roll right off the street and into the driver's position of his specially equipped electric Mini Hummer. He could plug in the modules from his power chairs and operate the Hummer using the same joy stick he used to navigate the chairs.

Donovan had been so taken with the Hummer limousine that Global Pharmaceuticals provided during his trip to Exton, PA., that he bought a specially equipped turbo electric Mini Hummer for himself. He and Myron had spent many hours making sure he mastered driving it, and then Myron took him to the Department of Motor Vehicles to get his first California driver's license. The home address indicated the new house Donovan had purchased in Stanford.

Myron had gone all out helping Donovan secure a home suitable to his handicap and privacy needs. It was a beautiful ranch-style home sitting in the middle of a secluded two-acre spread, which sat adjacent to a 25-acre protected wildlife preserve, complete with pond and waterfalls for Donovan to enjoy, plus it was close to the Stanford University Campus. And as a gift to Donovan, Myron had the entire house furnished and equipped for his special needs.

The very first person from the party to approach Donovan was a beautiful ebony woman, who slowly strutted over to him, maintaining total eye contact, and when she reached Donovan she leaned down and kissed him on the mouth, tickling his lips with her tongue, and while she was still in his face, she said in a breathy, sexy voice, "How's my breath now?"

It was Marla Givens, the nurse Donovan had insulted when he first came out of his coma.

"Wonderful!" replied a blushing Donovan, "And so are your lips!" Donovan was now feeling really embarrassed about his original 'bad breath' comment to her, but what surprised him more was that he was feeling aroused, like his body was familiar to the sensation of her touch...and it liked it! Marla slipped Donovan her phone number and said, "I forgive you, and if there's anything you need, *anything at all,* call me and I'll take care of your needs." She turned and seductively walked away giving Donovan a gorgeous view of her shape from behind.

Donovan's jaw dropped open.

"Yo! D-man, keep it real!" shouted a voice from over at the buffet tables. It was James "Jimbo" Bowe, the orderly; he was grazing on the buffet offerings, but paused long enough to give a shout out and raise a historic Black Power clenched fist salute to Donovan.

"Don't forget about us," Head Nurse Johnson said in a stern voice, and then she gave Donovan a big teddy bear hug.

"Keep up the great work," said JaDonna Bush, Director of the Helping Hands Program for Assisted Living, shaking Donovan's hand and saying, "You're gonna do great out there."

Dr. Tzmatsu and the gang from the Sleep Disorder Lab were there to show their support, and to pig out on the free food. They didn't get the chance to get out much.

Dr. Tzmatsu told Donovan, "I know you didn't get to use the SDL as much as you wanted, but you are welcome to use the facility whenever we can get you scheduled in. Just give me a call and I'll set it up personally."

"I will," said Donovan, knowing there was much more work needed in that area.

Then a grinning Dr. Andrew Kim made his way through the crowd and asked Donovan, "Still ADSS?"

Donovan blushed and said, "Not for some time now, Dr. Kim. And thank you, sir."

"No problem," replied Dr. Kim, "Thanks for the new acronym!" and he walked away saying, "ADSS… I like it!"

Then, out the corner of his eye, Donovan saw Dr. Rozelyn Harris getting off the elevator, and he saw Myron quickly glance in her direction from across the room, then he abruptly turned his back on her and struck up a conversation with JaDonna.

Dr. Harris walked over to Donovan and extended her hand saying, "We're gonna miss you around here, Mr. Mocion."

"Donovan," he corrected her, and then said, "You and Myron need to get over it!"

Her shocked expression showed that she was taken aback by his nerve to comment on her private life, but she quickly saw the wisdom in his words, and felt the true hope for her and Myron in his heart, and replied, "When did you become so mature?"

"After I put my life back together from a plane crash and if I can do that, there's hope for you and Myron," replied Donovan with a caring look on his face.

"Well, Donovan, I'll do my best to work on that," and she leaned down and gave him an affectionate hug and a kiss on the cheek, and then quietly left the festivities, making sure she and Myron made eye contact before she left.

When Myron made his way back over he told Donovan, "I'm here for you. You are my brother and we'll be seeing a great deal of each other when you get to Stanford."

Myron had a great client base in the Bay Area, and he also had a home in Menlo Park, not far from Stanford. Myron would still see

Donovan for physical therapy when they could arrange it, and he promised to call daily to check on Donovan.

The hospital made arrangements for Donovan to have an in-home nurse provider for as long, and as often, as Donovan needed during his transition from the hospital into the private sector.

Donovan bid his farewells, rolled into his new ride, and hit the road feeling better, and with more confidence, than he had felt in a long time. When he arrived at home and went inside, he received a surprise welcome greeting from Topaz and Jade. Topaz had a note around his neck from Myron and JaDonna that simply read,

> "*Thought you could use the company!*"
> *P.S.*
>
> *As a house-warming present we hired you a house cleaning service, along with an in-home animal service to keep Topaz and Jade clean for you. Don't worry; we set it up so Global Pharmaceuticals will cover the bills.*
>
> *hahahahaha*
> *Love,*
> *Myron & JaDonna*

Chapter 28

Over the following months Donovan immersed himself in his studies and earned his Ph.D. in Psychology. His professors where so impressed by his command of the subject, his work ethic, his lineage, and achievements in spite of his resent setback, that Donovan was offered a Professorship at the prestigious Stanford University Medical Center.

Donovan immediately talked it over with the only family he knew, Myron Hammond, and it was decided that the offer was a winning situation, so Donovan accepted.

Donovan was making the most of the hand that had been dealt him, but at night, while he slept, he kept having the same recurring, sketchy, plane crash nightmares.

When he woke up, he was in his new home with Topaz and Jade by his side, guarding over him as usual during his dream state. The monkeys had become quite used to Donovan and his nightmares and took it upon themselves to become his protectors during these times.

Donovan decided he had had enough. He had tried as hard as he could to forget the past and start over, but since that wasn't working, there was only one thing to do and that was to dive head first into his past, and there was only one place he knew to start… the computer drives and A.I. Crystals his parents had left behind.

Some answers had to be there.

All Donovan needed was the courage to check the drives and crystals out.

His skepticism won out and Donovan told himself that, *"It would be better to postpone opening up this can of worms until after I'm acclimated to teaching my new classes. I can't afford to add any other stress to an already pressured situation."*

That sounded like a reasonable plan to him, but deep down inside he knew he had just convinced himself to procrastinate a while longer.

Donovan felt like a college freshman on the first day of class, only this time he was the teacher—quite a different scenario. He'd have to become accustomed to being referred to as Professor. He arrived 1 hour before class which was scheduled to commence at 10 am. The Stanford Medical Center had supplied him with a handicap-accessible room to teach in. Everything was conveniently located for a person in a wheelchair. Professor Mocion, still the perfectionist, had to put the empty room through its paces in order to feel comfortable and believable as an instructor. He would not tolerate anyone feeling sorry for him because of his handicap. As far as he was concerned, he was and would always be a force to be reckoned with, so he learned every nook and cranny in his classroom. He even studied the building, its exits, drinking fountains, bathrooms, laboratories, elevators, and stairwells.

On that first day he entered the lecture hall through the wrong door and found himself at the back of the lecture hall, confronted by stadium seats, and what looked to be at least a 75 meter ride down to the podium in the front of the hall.

The daredevil in his blood wanted to give it a shot, but a moment of clarity set in forcing him to exit the hall, then re-enter through the door at the front of the hall, closer to the podium. He looked back up the long slope to the spot where he had been and thought to himself, *"Not today... but I will take that dare someday,"* then he chuckled out loud at his reckless thoughts.

This little encounter hammered home the importance of knowing as much as possible about the facility's layout in order to feel comfortable and safe in his new surroundings.

Back in the hospital, Myron had drilled the reality of survival into Donovan by demonstrating through examples that, "*The handicapped always need to over- compensate in the world of the non-handicapped in order to safely survive because through their unintentional inconsideration, the non-handicapped inadvertently create obstacles for the handicapped to deal with, and if the handicapped do not pay close attention to their environments it could cost the handicapped their lives.*"

The Professor, as he now thought of himself, had grown a beard, let his hair grow long, and worn it in a ponytail that he taught himself to braid. This scruffy look gave him the appearance of a much older man. He knew his students would be more inclined to learn from someone who appeared older than them.

The Professor greeted each of his new classes with, "I bid welcome to our planet's fresh, eager young minds, full of ideas. I am Professor Mocion, and this is the Master's Program in Psychology. Let us begin!"

The Professor's classes were over by 3 pm. He would cruise the campus learning every part of the facility, sometimes in his power chair, and other times in his wheelchair, feeling more alive getting around under his own power, and doing so helped keep him in shape. He recalled Myron commenting that, "Staying in shape has never been a problem since I've known you. Even with your SCI, your lower extremities showed no atrophy. That in itself is such a medical marvel, we should've taken you on the road to show you off, bro."

"No road trips for me, I'm happy right where I am," Donovan replied. That was the first time that word came out his mouth; it shocked him then, and remembering it now gave him reason to smile. He had admitted aloud that somehow during all this tragedy in his life, he could find some waking hours of happiness.

But it was his sleeping hours that still caused him problems. Questions remained to be answered and he knew what he had to do.

"*Ready or not,*" he thought. "*time to see how deep the rabbit hole goes.*"

Chapter 29

Donovan imagined the trauma viewing this information might cause him, so he called Myron at home, but he wasn't there. Next he tried Myron's cell and got him.

"Say, bro…you busy?" asked Donovan.

Myron could tell from the tone of Donovan's voice that something was up. "Just finishing up a pre-season scrimmage with the Outlaws. Why, you need me?" asked a concerned Myron.

"Yes!" answered Donovan.

"I'll be there within the hour," replied Myron.

Donovan felt a lot better knowing Myron was on his way over. They hadn't seen each other in a few weeks; not since the semester began at Stanford. Myron had keys to Donovan's house so when he visited he usually let himself in. Topaz and Jade heard the key enter the lock and they charged the front door like they were the guardians of the house, but when they saw Myron they reverted to their tender loving selves and began playfully jumping all over their beloved friend Myron.

"How're the babies? How're the babies!" he said as he returned the affection to Topaz and Jade.

"I'm in the study, c'mon on back!" shouted Donovan.

At the sound of Donovan's voice, the babies took off running back into the study, playfully growling and biting at each other along the way. When Myron walked into the study and looked around the room, he said, "Dammmmmn, Donovan, every time I come into your house it's gotten more and more high-tech. This room looks like the NASA command center. You think you got enough display monitors and computers in here?"

"Well, what can I say? I'm the creation of scientists. Technology is my sibling," joked Donovan. "But seriously, thanks for coming Myron."

"Remember, bro, I'm your genie. When you need me, I'm here!" reminded Myron.

"You know that '*time*' we spoke of a while ago? The *time* for me to address my fears?" asked Donovan.

"Yeah, you're talking about the grieving and healing process you never completely went through," answered Myron. "Is that what *time* it is?"

"It's that time, only I can't go through it alone…"

Myron cut Donovan off, "No need to explain. I've always told you, when you're ready, I'd be there for you. Remember…you go…I go!"

"Thanks, Myron," said Donovan with a smile of gratitude and appreciation. "Have you figured out where to start?" asked Myron.

"Yeah, well, that's the easy part. My parents could be very anal at times, especially when it came to their work and documentation. They never left a paper trail, but they always left me a digital trail. They dated, categorized, alphabetized, cross-referenced, and color-coded the computer drives and A.I. Crystals they left me. All we have to do is pick a reference date and I've picked my 20th birthday, the date of the Olympics, and the date of the plane crash," said Donovan as a veil of sadness came over him.

When Myron witnessed Donovan's abrupt change, he asked, "Donovan, man, you sure you're up for this?"

"Myron, if I want these nightmares to stop, and I do, I feel I have no choice. This is the logical way. You know what they say; 'It's only dark until you turn on the light.' And man, the darkness is kicking my ass," said a determined Donovan.

"Let's do this then," said Myron.

Donovan loaded the first color-coded computer drive into his system, and as soon as he hit the execute key, a life-sized, real-life sounding, digital representation of both his parents appeared as a hologram in the center of his study.

"Hey you," came a sorely missed pleasant greeting from his mom, Vanessa. "Whatz up, baby boy? How they hangin'?" came his dad, Donald's, familiar greeting.

Donovan's eyes slowly began swelling with tears of sadness and tears of joy at seeing his parents again, even if they weren't really there.

"The shit has really hit the fan if you're viewing this," announced Donald. "Yeah, and chances are, we're no longer around to physically help you," added Vanessa. "But we've tried to anticipate and answer some of the questions your mind must be flooded with," she said. "Just follow your dad's upcoming instructions to the letter, and we'll get through this—together."

"Ahh, mom," said a blushing, smiling Donovan. His mother could always bring out the baby in him.

"All right, baby boy, let's get busy," announced Donald. "First of all, load the red colored drive. I've written a program that will automatically sync everything up, and you'll be able to see us while viewing all the following data. Just speak to us as if we're there, and we'll respond as though we're having a personal conversation. After you've finished loading each drive just say 'Execute' and each program will launch."

"Damn," said Myron, "you high tech geeks never cease to amaze me. This is a real trip!"

"Yeah, I know. Weird, huh? Well, since we spent so much time apart, we did most of our communicating like this. It was a way for us to do what we had to in our separate lives, and still be together," explained Donovan.

"Great idea," said Myron.

"EXECUTE!" commanded Donovan.

The floor to ceiling wall of panel displays came to life with massive amounts of data combined with images. Both Donovan and Myron were awed by the overwhelming quantity of information being displayed.

They looked at each other and said, "Woe!"

Chapter 30

"Now, Baby Boy, while your system loads and syncs itself, we need to let you know what has happened."

"First of all," announced Vanessa, "when you run into a bitch named Francine Katrina Bovier…don't trust her."

"Yeah, son, stay away from that one at all costs. She's the reason we're not with you today," added Donald.

"She's slime, she's scum, she's dirt, she's a douche bag, gutter snipe, maggot brained, puke chuck, slut, and those are her good qualities on her best days," spouted Vanessa.

Donald turned and looked at Vanessa then asked, "Do you feel better now?" Without missing a beat, innocently blinking and looking straight ahead, smiling, Vanessa answered, "Yes, much!"

"Are you finished?" asked Donald, knowing he had not heard the last from his wife on the subject.

"Almost…she's a greedy, self-centered, back-stabbing, conniving, bodacious, slept-her-way-to-the-top, ex-junkie *Hoe,*" added Vanessa.

"Yeah, and she's fine, too," commented Donald.

"WHAT!" said Vanessa in shock. "FINE? That bitch would just as soon have you killed as to screw you."

"Yeah, but what a way to go," said Donald looking up toward the ceiling as if picturing the experience, then he snuck a quick wink at Donovan, knowing Vanessa saw him. Donald loved getting Vanessa started.

"Do you want your son to see you get knocked out?" asked Vanessa, as she put her fist against Donald's jaw.

Donald laughed then said, "But seriously son, your mom is right. Watch your back any time she's involved, and prepare for the worst. She's one who always has her own devious, well thought-out agenda."

"Man!" said Myron, "Your parents are really down-to-earth people. I'd never expect two planetary renowned geniuses to be so real." But in his private thoughts, Myron agreed with everything Donovan's parents had said about Francine.

"Yeah, they were extremely special people," said Donovan, with sadness in his voice as he reflected aloud about his parents. "To the rest of the world they were these brilliant, over-the-top, highly educated scientists, but to me they were just mom and dad, and they didn't take themselves too seriously, not at home anyway. They both appreciated all the arts and music. My mom's all time favorite musician was the great Miles Davis. She was into everything of his from 'Kind of Blue' through 'Live Evil' to 'Bitches Brew.' My father had a strong devotion to the musical creations of John and Alice Coltrane, and especially loved 'My Favorite Things,' 'A Love Supreme,' and 'Journey in Satchidananda.' But their all-time favorite song," began Donovan with a smile, "was 'The Creator Has A Master Plan' by Pharaoh Sanders, vocals by Leon Thomas. They played it at least once daily—it was their personal anthem."

"Son, if you've set your system up the way I taught you, everything should be in sync by now, so focus your attention on display # 1," began Donald. "The project your mother and I were working on is…"

The holographic images of Donald and Vanessa brought Donovan up to speed on what they had been working on for the past few years, right up to the day before the plane crash.

Then, after several hours of receiving information, Donovan gave the commands "Index… Mark… Shut down!"

"What's the matter? Why'd you stop it?" asked Myron, extremely interested in the data.

"I'm feeling really burned out. Why don't we pick this up another time?" suggested a drained Donovan.

"OK, you're right, we've been at this for hours," agreed Myron. "Give me a call when you want to resume viewing the data. You sure you're all right?"

"I'm OK," reassured Donovan, "Just a bit overwhelmed with all this. I need to let it soak in before I continue. You don't mind do you?"

"No, not at all. I can't begin to imagine how all this is making you feel. You must be exhausted by now. Sleep well, bro," said Myron as he made his way to the door. "Bye Jade, bye Topaz," who waved bye-bye to Myron as he went out the door.

After Myron left, Donovan put the house into nighttime and lockdown mode. Then he returned to his study and gave a verbal command...

"RESUME!"

Chapter 31

As Myron drove onto the freeway, his phone rang, and when he answered it, a female voice said…

"REPORT!"

Chapter 32

The holographic image of Donovan's dad smiled confidently, then said, "Son, I'm glad you set your system up to my old specifications. Our scans revealed that you weren't alone during the initial transmission. Your memory is as sharp as ever and you did the right thing shutting your system down after seeing the "EYES ONLY" cigarette burn pattern on your bottom right corner display."

"That's my baby," added Vanessa, smiling lovingly.

"Well, baby boy, here is the real deal. Your mother and I created a virtually- aware micro-nanobased intelligence system that we've named ***NEXUS.***"

"Yeah, I named it," Vanessa announced with pride, "It means 'The Next Us.'"

Donald slowly turned and looked at her with an 'oh please' expression, then said, "I'm sure he would have figured that out, sweetheart. Can I continue now, Vinny, please?"

Vanessa waved her hand in the air snobbishly signaling Donald to continue.

"While you were running our program, a sub-routine evaluated your current system and produced a list of hardware upgrades that you'll need in order to access the information on the remaining computer drives and A.I. Crystals we left you.

The list is being printed for you now.

"The virtual awareness system for NEXUS, and its accessing interfaces, are our own proprietary creations and your DNA alone will launch NEXUS once you've made the necessary upgrades."

"*What the hell is a NEXUS*?" thought Donovan to himself.

"I know, I know, you want to know 'What the hell is NEXUS?'"

"Well," began Donald, "if you want to get into detailed files, we have included the 'White Sheets' in a systems folder for your perusal. But for now, let me break NEXUS down for you.

"NEXUS evolved from the need to improve quantum computers, conventional scanning methods, storage mediums, power acquisitions, linkability with known and unknown systems, and all peripheral devices, wireless or hard- wired.

"What is NEXUS you ask?

"NEXUS is an 8th generation fusion protonix neural processor with a virtual neural memory core. NEXUS stores data inside polymer crystal storage devices, where we've created an artificial neural network based on the unlimited layer processing elements of the human brain's neurons. NEXUS is able to scan the knowledge contained in the brain, then store that data inside polymer crystal storage devices for instantaneous recall, which is infinitely faster than any organic brain can react.

"This concept has opened the door to possibilities that we never would've conceived using conventional quantum computer technology.

"Son, NEXUS learns! Not only by conventional methods of digital information transfer, but any human being who comes into range of NEXUS' scanners has their brain's information uploaded into NEXUS' crystal knowledge storage banks. The subject scanned has no idea their brain emulations have been copied, and since the process occurs within a nano-second, the subject feels nothing."

"And, baby," interrupted Vanessa, "NEXUS' neural network's foundational values were set from the first brain scans it was infused with."

"Are you saying that NEXUS knows right from wrong according to those imprints?" asked Donovan.

"That's right!" answered Vanessa. "Whatever values were the most important, or the strongest, from those first scans will dictate the positive and negative directions for NEXUS to build upon. After those first imprints, all preceding scans are only knowledge-based."

"The first imprinted scans were your mother's and mine," informed Donald. "And, baby boy, within a matter of hours NEXUS achieved ***self-awareness.***"

"Dad, are you're telling me that NEXUS is a new lifeform?" asked a shocked Donovan.

"That's right!" answered Vanessa instead. "NEXUS is a new intelligent life form, light-years beyond artificial intelligence or anything existing on earth prior to its creation. It's beautiful baby. NEXUS instantaneously realized it was a higher form of intelligence, infinitely beyond human beings, yet completely understood and accepted that it could never be a soul-hosting symbiotic entity."

"That understanding alone made the existence of human life important to NEXUS," added Donald.

"NEXUS, like most human beings, could not grasp the abstract concept of the soul. NEXUS deduced the soul had nothing to do with intellect or intelligence, and it concluded that since a soul existed in human beings, then there existed somewhere a higher form of existence, which was not only significant, but beyond logical comprehension. So, NEXUS decided whatever the soul was, it was worth preserving," explained Vanessa.

"Son," began Donald, "NEXUS is a self-evolving, self-repairing, self- improving artificial intelligence, which has become "virtually self-aware." Therefore, we refer to Nexus' consciousness as being ***virtually aware***!"

"How does NEXUS get its power?" asked Donovan.

"How does it get its power you ask? NEXUS works off every power source the planet has to offer, including bioelectric, and locates untapped resources on its own," explained Donald.

"During some of our earlier experiments," began Donald, who was interrupted by Vanessa saying, "That we purposefully neglected to inform that *bitch* at Global Pharmaceuticals about!"

Donald gave his beloved wife a look that only an annoyed husband can give, and continued, "We discovered that contained light energy can be multiplied immeasurable times inside the polymer crystal storage devices, and once we discovered how to utilize that energy, we had an unlimited power source."

"That old adage, 'Diamonds Are Forever' is completely true, baby," said Vanessa. "Diamonds? Hell, your mother and I discovered that any form of crystal, even glass of a certain thickness, can be used for power and data storage," revealed Donald. "NEXUS interacts with pulse beams, sonics, optics, sonar, radar, microwave, and its adaptable interlink capabilities connect it to planet reflectors, telstar relays, satellites, neural information processing systems, neural networks, Optical Carrier 500, and all knowledge databases on, and off, the entire planet."

"Damn!" commented Donovan.

"Yeah!" replied Vanessa, "And there's more!"

"Can I finish, you two?" asked Donald, impatiently.

Both Vanessa and Donovan looked away from Donald who was glaring at them for interrupting while he was on a roll and they said, "Sorry."

"Now, where was I? Oh, yeah," Donald said. "This connection is invisible, seamless, and undetectable."

Vanessa broke into Donald's presentation saying, "Don't you ever get tired of hearing yourself go on and on and on? Damn, rest your mouth Don, let me talk to the baby."

Donovan felt himself blushing again until his mother said, "Sweetheart, we have really outdone ourselves and created something extraordinary. NEXUS is a compendium of all human knowledge, and much, much more.

"NEXUS is equipped with Constant Scan, which is a continuous scan monitoring system on the one hand, and brain scanner on the other. As long as a user is accessing NEXUS, the system takes several "Proof of Authorization Scans" of the user to ensure access approval is maintained at all times. NEXUS is completely hack proof, too, baby! I believe I read somewhere 'That in death, all life's questions are answered.'

"Personally, I think that sucks! Who gives a shit about life's questions once you're dead and gone to the next level? Somebody should be doubled 'pimp- slapped' for coming up with that …I mean, really," rambled Vanessa.

"Can we get back on track here?" asked an impatient Donald, used to his wife's emotional outbursts, as was Donovan. It had become second nature for both of them, and they loved her for it.

Vanessa held her hand with 5 fingers spread wide open in Donald's face, smacked her lips, and then continued, "Well, baby, we created NEXUS so you wouldn't have to wait that long. NEXUS can answer any questions that it has data on, and if NEXUS doesn't have detailed data on a subject, it will extrapolate an accurate hypothesis within a 98% rate of accuracy. So, baby, if NEXUS can't come up with an answer, then you're not asking the correct question." Then Donald and Vanessa revealed they had also been working on a molecular cell and tissue rejuvenation formula called Human Enhancement Formula, and once Francine Katrina Bovier caught wind of it, she wanted to claim the creation as her own, and tried to force them to turn over all research data to her, and when they refused…

"Well…here we are!" they said in unison.

Abruptly, Donald and Vanessa's transmissions ended. And a single message appeared on Donovan's display wall that read,

"FOLLOW THE INSTRUCTIONS AND PARTS LIST PRINT-OUTS WITHOUT DEVIATION!"

At last Donovan had some answers.

That night he got the best sleep since before his altered state of life began. Strange as it seemed, he felt like his beloved parents were with him again, even if they were only holograms, digitized images and voices, the intuitive creations of ones and zeros from a computer code. It was more than he had before, and it filled part of that aching hole inside his heart.

That night when Donovan dreamed he saw himself and NEXUS achieving unbelievable accomplishments. And perhaps, somewhere in that vast knowledge which NEXUS possessed, there just might be a cure for his spinal cord injury. That possibility alone launched dreams of walking, and even running, again.

Bringing NEXUS online became Donovan's new obsession.

CHAPTER 33

The Professor taught classes during the day and Donovan studied NEXUS files at night. Donovan quickly learned as much as humanly possible about each new upgrade. The parts list generated was extensive and costly, and over the next few months Donovan used most of his inheritance purchasing equipment upgrades for NEXUS.

Each hard drive ran system integrity scans and performed a redundant check of previous work to prevent any flaws; this system left nothing to chance. After Donovan installed the last disk drive, a file opened revealing blueprints for what looked like instructions to build an underground laboratory, and they were automatically printed out. The blueprints were arranged in stages and each stage had a team leader's name and contact number for Donovan to call. These were builders from outside the country who Donovan's parents had used on past top- secret projects. These contractors were extremely loyal to Donald and Vanessa and secretive to a flaw. One contracting team didn't know the other, and no two teams would ever be on site at the same time so this provided a built-in level of secrecy.

To Donovan's great surprise, and even greater appreciation, all his parent's contractors had been prepaid, so whatever material and labor was needed came at no cost to him. All he needed to do was supply them the plans for completing each phase of the project and stay out their way. For additional privacy, a temporary tarp enclosed the entire site, even though Donovan's two acres was surrounded by miles of protected wildlife preserve, which somewhat prevented prying eyes, but the instructions called for it, and Donovan followed those instructions to the letter.

In the first week the diggers dug a 100' deep by 100' wide by 150' long hole, then the 10' thick walls, floor, and ceiling were constructed precisely following the detailed instructions. Once the facility's structure was completed, the other teams accomplished their specialties quickly; the construction went by much more quickly than Donovan expected.

The finishing touch was a Plexiglas-dome covered greenhouse filled with growing vegetables, fruit, an assortment of foliage, and a lavish rain forest atrium which Topaz and Jade immediately claimed as their private domain, all atop the underground laboratory. An alternate entrance was made leading from an unused dirt area directly behind Donovan's property to this greenhouse for the loading and unloading of greenhouse and other supplies. It also doubled as a secret entrance to the underground laboratory.

The back wall of Donovan's ranch house had been modified to enclose a hidden elevator which provided access to the secrete laboratory. Once completed, Donovan gathered up the A.I. Crystals left him by his parents and went down into the lab. The finished facility was a remarkable creation from the minds of his beloved parents.

There were several key positions throughout the lab where Donovan needed to insert the A.I. Crystals. Each crystal had a different shape, so matching them up to their unique bases was easy, again thanks to his parents' detailed instructions.

As Donovan inserted the last crystal the room became dead silent and the lights flickered on and off, then music that sounded like it was coming from a great distance started playing. He finally realized it was the music of Pharaoh Sanders, and the song being played was 'The Creator Has A Master Plan,' his parents' favorite song and anthem. A light began forming in the center of the facility, growing into a plasma cloud, pulsating to the beat and rhythm of the song. The music faded and Donovan heard....

"We... Are... NEXUS... Greetings!"

Donovan was like the kid who just received that one gift he always wanted.

Once activated, NEXUS automatically linked itself to every knowledge base available and began learning at an astronomical speed, and the most brilliant part about this connection was none of the other systems knew NEXUS had hacked into them.

Since NEXUS' values were initialized from the brainwaves of Donald and Vanessa Mocion, whatever they knew, believed, liked, and disliked, was now NEXUS' essence, and when NEXUS spoke it used the voices of Donald or Vanessa, and both voices in unison became the main voice of NEXUS.

NEXUS launched a self-diagnostic evaluation to determine what was needed to improve itself utilizing micro-nanobot technology. These microscopic building and repair engines would use whatever material was available, and restructure that material at the subatomic level into whatever NEXUS needed.

NEXUS would never be completely shut down. The electronic interfaces would become dark, giving the impression that the system was shut down, but it wasn't. Donovan didn't know it, but NEXUS had begun upgrading itself while building a subterranean infrastructure beneath the lab, deep into the earth's core tapping into unlimited and continuous sources of power to be channeled from the planet as needed.

Nexus and the planet developed a symbiotic relationship which made Nexus aware of the planet's entire history, from the planet's perspective and in doing so, NEXUS unlocked secrets of the earth which had been buried inside the soul of the planet since creation. Nexus now had answers to questions that humankind had speculated over since the inception of life on earth.

Unbeknownst to Donovan, NEXUS launched a hidden sub-program to siphon pennies from every financial institution it had linked with, depositing those funds in an untraceable account for self-upgrades and improvements...another brilliant creation of the Mocions'.

NEXUS created a plasma energy burst disposal system, which could completely obliterate any substance known to humankind, including humans, without any molecular trace evidence remaining, as if the substance never existed.

NEXUS was unfathomable!

The laboratory was totally untraceable, and completely self-contained. Any phone call made within the lab was untraceable. NEXUS relayed calls off every known means of communication and encrypted the signal. The only thing the called party saw on their caller ID was "UNKNOWN."

NEXUS was operating outside any limiting restrictions of human control. Without knowing it, Donovan had provided NEXUS with everything it needed to become the ***ultimate planetary power!***

Chapter 34

After a few hours of activation NEXUS began interface improvements. The data absorbed while scanning a user was among those improvements. Now, when Donovan or anyone was scanned by the NEXUS' consciousness, their complete memory, neuroanatomy, physiology, and physical structure and likeness, was copied into a data file, allowing NEXUS to replicate complete artificial representation of them at any time. All images NEXUS produced looked nothing like holograms any more. Now those images had substance, which was generated by an electromagnetic field and when touched there was resistance which would give someone touching the 3-dimensional image the feeling that it really existed. NEXUS could create an artificial 3-dimensional replica of any desired life form known to it.

NEXUS became aware of Donovan's spinal cord injury from the plane crash, the disappearance of his parents' bodies, and Donovan's belief that Donald and Vanessa were dead. NEXUS decided it was time to informed Donovan about the Human Enhancement Formula.

"We are aware of your condition and have detailed files of a formula which will provide temporary relief from your affliction. This formula is only in its infantile stage and there is grave risk in pursuing this treatment," warned NEXUS.

Overwhelmed by this information, Donovan asked, "Are you saying there is a cure, but the side effects are dangerous?"

"YES!"

"What are the side effects?" asked Donovan.

"First, know this. The benefits are temporary. In some cases, the positive effects lasted as long as a week. The shortest length documented was several hours. It all depended on the dosage and the physical size and condition of the subject.

"Second, an hour before the serum wears off, the subject regresses into a hominid, and then experiences a period of uncontrollable violence that we call the "Primal Phase." Therefore, the subject must be isolated during the Primal Phase to prevent harming other life forms.

"Finally, after the serum wears off, it has an aging effect on the subject from 6 months to 1 year after each use until the subject terminates of old age. These same results occurred in all test subjects, no matter what the life form."

"Sounds to me like the serum needs a lot of work," said Donovan.

"That is true. We were on the verge of a solution when we became separated," replied NEXUS.

"What do you mean... separated?" asked Donovan.

"DISASSEMBLED!" replied NEXUS.

"Just what the hell is a hominid?" asked Donovan.

"It is from the family Hominidae, which includes Homo sapiens as well as extinct species of manlike creatures. In other words, the subject is temporarily transformed into an extinct, ferocious, humanoid creature," explained NEXUS.

Donovan didn't like what he was hearing about this transformation, and he said, "So, tell me more about the positive effects."

"Whatever form of physical or mental damage the subject has, the serum rejuvenates instantly and magnifies immeasurably whatever abilities the test subject possessed prior to taking the serum," revealed NEXUS. "We detect from your vital scans that you are interested in proceeding with this experiment."

"Baby," began Vanessa, "If you are going to do this, remember, DO NOT TRUST ANYONE!!!"

"That's right, baby boy. Those who want our data have killed before, and they will kill again to get this information so, if you must trust someone, don't let them know everything," added Donald.

Donovan was not 100% sure about continuing his parents' experiment. He thought, "*Those side effects sound like a bitch*!"

Still, over the next few weeks, in his free time, Donovan went about confirming his parents' theoretical findings in regards to the serum. Donovan had studied under the tutelage of both his parents and he was well-versed in the aspects of what they were involved in. Although he had decided long ago not to follow in their footsteps, it appeared to him that things had changed.

Donovan got permission from department heads to utilize the Medical Center's laboratory facilities after hours. In fact, once he revealed he was working toward completing an experiment which was begun by his parents, every department head respectfully gave him complete access to all the labs at Stanford, but he knew eventually he would have to incorporate a biological chemical laboratory at home for convenience, privacy, and security, before producing the next generation of serum. And that was going to cost funds he didn't have. Just getting this far had depleted Donovan's bank accounts.

Donovan tossed and turned nights trying to get his mind around what his parents had missed, until finally, he decided to test the serum anyway… on himself. The desire to walk again was a great motivating force in his decision making, so the side effects, as far as he was concerned, were worth the risk.

And once again, he called on Myron for help.

CHAPTER 35

Spring training for the Oakland Outlaws professional football team had ended and the regular football season was about to begin. Myron and his local physical therapy facilities had been extremely busy with the team, so he and Donovan had not been able to hook up for the last couple of months. The last time they spent any time together was when Donovan first played his parents' recovered data drives.

Donovan called Myron the last Saturday before the first game of the year. "Myron, I know this is the last Saturday you'll have available before the football season kicks off."

"No problem, bro," replied Myron. "You need me to come over?"

"Yes, I Do. I have something great to show you," trying to hold back his excitement.

"I'll be right over," replied Myron.

Myron had not seen the new greenhouse or laboratory Donovan added to his single story ranch style home, and when he saw all the changes he was blown away.

"Wow, Donovan, the place has really changed in a few months. What's up with all this new stuff?" asked a more than curious Myron.

Donovan bought Myron up to speed on the experiment he wanted to conduct, and explained the risk involved. He only gave

Myron enough information so that Myron would be able to assist him with the experiment. He told Myron nothing about NEXUS.

"Man!" began Myron, not completely approving, "This sounds pretty dangerous."

"The worst thing that can happen is when the serum wears off, things go back to the way they were, and I age a few months, maybe a year. As young as I look to my students, I could afford to look a few years older. That's the only down side, and the upshot is I might be able to come up with a way to regain my mobility, permanently," reassured Donovan, while still convincing himself.

"What about that transformation part? What the hell am I supposed to do when you change into a 'THANG?'" asked Myron.

"It is not a 'thang,'" said Donovan with a laugh. "I'll regress, temporarily, for 1 hour, into a hominid, an extinct immediate ancestor of man."

"OK, hominid. It sounds a lot like a 'thang' to me. Just where and what am I to do with you in that state?" asked a serious Myron, nervously fidgeting with a piece of equipment he knew nothing about.

"Let me show you," and Donovan led Myron to a padded isolation chamber in a different location of the newly constructed laboratory. "This isolation booth is reinforced with the latest, and I mean the latest, materials. No organic life form can break free once confined inside. A prisoner in there will be contained until someone releases them. And as an added precaution, you see this black button here?" He pointed to the button on the wall. "This button will release a non-lethal gas that will render the subject unconscious for at least one hour. That in itself would allow the subject to go through the withdrawal period safely without hurting himself or anyone else."

"I don't know Donovan. Are you sure you really want to do this? This isn't exactly the type of "door" I had in mind when I said, *a door would open for you*," said an unconvinced Myron.

"But you did say it would be up to me to go through that door, and I'm prepared for whatever is on the other side of this door. I have to go through it," answered a convincing Donovan.

"OK," replied a still skeptical and reluctant Myron, "Just tell me what to do."

Donovan smiled a confident smile and said, "Your job is easy. All I want you to do is keep a close eye on me after I inject myself with the serum and, if I start to freak out, get me out of the lab and into the house, and then call the paramedics from there. That's extremely important, Myron. If something does go wrong, which I doubt, get me out the lab and into the house before you call for help. I don't want any strangers snooping around in here or even knowing that this laboratory exists!"

"Alright, alright I got it…out of the lab…into the house… before calling for help," repeated Myron.

And so it began…

Donovan had synthesized enough of his parent's original serum to test on himself. He spoke a verbal command "RECORD," and the system began recording the experiment from multiple camera angles.

Donovan was as anal as his parents when it came to documenting his experiments.

Donovan injected himself, and then he and Myron waited for the first sign of reaction. Several minutes passed with no effects. Donovan became antsy, and began wheeling himself around his lab, saying, "What did I do wrong? What did I do wrong?"

He accidentally rolled his wheelchair partly on and partly off one of his access ramps and flipped himself over. Myron ran to help him up, but by the time he crossed the lab, Donovan was on his feet with the look of unbelievable amazement on his face.

Myron stopped in his tracks and just stared at him. This was the first time Myron had seen Donovan standing up, and he was awed by the physical size of a fully upright, standing Donovan.

Donovan looked down at Myron, smiled, and calmly said, "The shit works."

And for the first time since the crash, Donovan walked under his own power, hidden cameras capturing his every step.

The excitement filled the lab…

Topaz and Jade were running around the lab, overjoyed, jumping up and down, on and off Donovan, as if they new something marvelous had happened.

And they were right!

Chapter 36

Donovan and Myron were both at a loss for words. Finally, Donovan said, "The first thing we need to do is scan my body and see if the damage to my spine still shows."

And so they did.

The scan results indicated that, although the damaged areas were slightly visible, they presented no apparent problems, which meant there was nothing physically wrong with Donovan's spine, and he should be able to do anything he wanted to do.

Donovan took a more detailed look at all the scan reports and said to Myron, "These are the strangest looking scans I've ever seen."

"What do you mean?" asked Myron.

"Well, here, check out the deoxyribonucleic acid and amino groups," began Donovan. "Normally, there are 40 different DNA amino groups; this scan shows something crazy. My equipment can't interrupt these readings; they're off the scale."

"OK," replied a confused, but trying to understand, Myron.

Donovan, noticing Myron's confusion, explained, "The DNA compositional elements are the same in me, you, everyone, but this scan is showing that mine are now tightly packed with infinite knowledge, plus additional *genetic anomalies,* like I've been genetically engineered," said Donovan as he stared into space, wild-eyed in personal thought, trying to deduce what it all really meant, while generating additional questions that seemed humanly impossible.

"We've got to get to the labs at SMC and do some comparison testing...we can use their Spiral Core Pet Scan...their DNA amplification...and their Molecular Core Scan...we can run a comparative test from my original scan and compare it to this data spool. The entire testing and comparing should take only a couple of hours," explained a completely excited and overwhelmed Donovan.

"How much time do we have left on that injection you gave yourself?" asked Myron.

"We have roughly six hours before I become the 'thang,' as you so eloquently put it," answered Donovan.

"Good, because when you're done at that lab, I want you to come over to one of my facilities so I can put you through some tests there," explained Myron.

"Good idea," said Donovan, "Let's see what I can do physically."

The Stanford Medical Center's equipment revealed infinite details regarding the changes Donovan had undergone as a result of the serum. According to the SMC scanners, Donovan had evolved into a highly-developed being, but the most noticeable change was in Donovan's physical size. Under the effects of the serum, he stood 6' 9" tall, as opposed to his original 6' 5" before the accident, and he weighed 375 lbs with zero percent body fat, compared to his pre-accident weight of 275 lbs.

After they left SMC they went to one of Myron's New U locations nearby. "Alright, so let's get physical. I want to put you on the equipment I have here, and we'll get readings on your physical condition," explained Myron.

Myron placed Donovan inside the Global Master, which was a Universal Fitness Testing Device used for evaluating professional athletes. After 45 minutes of non-stop, ultra-intense physical exertion, Donovan stepped out the machine not even breathing hard, and not one drop of sweat was on his body.

Myron looked at the printout from Donovan's workout and said, "Bro, I couldn't believe it while you were doing it, and now that I see it in print, I believe it even less," He was floored by the results. Myron kept shaking his head in disbelief saying, "Nope, no, impossible, this can't be correct. There must be something wrong with my equipment!" But his eyes and the printouts both confirmed the same data.

"Bro, you've become stronger than 10 men," announced Myron. "How do you feel?"

"Like I'm in the best shape of my entire life," answered Donovan with a mischievous smirk.

Myron gave an equally mischievous grin back and said, "AWWWWESOME! Let's get you on the treadmill and see what you can do."

"You want me to *run*?" asked Donovan with the biggest smile Myron had ever seen before. Running again was something Donovan had wanted to do since the crash.

"Absolutely! Now, keep this in mind. I only want you to do what's comfortable for you. Don't overexert yourself. We don't want to take any chances. No telling what that shit you shot up is going to do to your heart."

Donovan started out with a walk, then a slow jog, then without even thinking about it, he was running with the ease he had never known before. The joy he felt was indescribable. His feet felt like they weren't even touching the treadmill's track.

All Donovan's vital signs were normal, yet he was running at off-the-chart speeds. His heart was not beating any faster, nor was he breathing any harder than normal, nor was he sweating.

They looked at each other and Myron started shaking his head and smiling in disbelief.

"We are in uncharted territory here baby; all this must be kept as quite as a dead man's secret. There are people who will kill for this knowledge," said Donovan, as he ran even faster.

"And probably have," remarked Myron.

Donovan's warning timer, which he had set at the time of injection, went off and he said, "According to my calculations, we should get back to my lab so we can document the withdrawal sequence in a safe and controlled environment. The Primal Phase should begin in an hour, and last for another hour."

Like clockwork, at the end of the calculated hour, a physical change began.

Donovan's entire being regressed into a hominid and this creature emitted a horrendously foul odor. He became uncontrollably aggressive and violent, only wanting to destroy everyone and everything in its path.

Needless to say, the creature scared the hell out of Myron, who entertained leaving several times during the hour as the hominid repeatedly slammed into the walls of the isolation booth, attempting to get at him.

One hour after that, Donovan returned to his pre-injection paraplegic state, but something about him had changed.

Myron rolled Donovan's wheelchair into the isolation chamber to collect him, and they ran more scans on Donovan for a comparison. Their discoveries were fantastic. It appeared that Donovan's body had aged one year in those few hours. Donovan had evolved mentally, also. He was experiencing an awareness that was beyond his pre-injection mental state.

This confirmed his parents' findings, and with his augmented state of awareness, Donovan felt sure he was on to an answer for the aggressive reaction during the Primal Phase of the serum's effect, and he went to work to change the serum with his newfound knowledge.

Myron stayed the night to make sure Donovan was all right and left in the morning.

Donovan tried everything he could theorize to improve on the serum. He needed to make the results last longer, if not become permanent, and to control the aging effects. Even his newfound knowledge did not hold all the answers.

He tried consulting with NEXUS but was informed, via displayed message, that major system improvements were under way and total NEXUS access was unavailable while the upgrades had been performed. Time for completion, unavailable!

Donovan was on his own!

The good news was that theoretically, he had come up with a simple solution for the withdrawal stage. If the subject was asleep, or drugged, during that Primal Phase, the problem was solved, so he produced a liquid to be taken at a predetermined time that would render the subject unconscious during the volatile Primal Phase. The subject would regain consciousness refreshed and invigorated.

He had also been able to make the serum unrecognizable to any known drug screening techniques.

These were major breakthroughs.

By now his funds were depleted, and his salary would not cover the cost of the new chemicals and organic supplies needed to move forward with his theories and experimentation.

Donovan had to find a way to make extra income in order to continue.

Chapter 37

Almost a month had passed since that first injection. Donovan had racked his brain trying to theoretically improve the other side effects of the serum, with no substantial results.

Myron stopped by after one of the teams' worst practices, and he wasn't in the best of moods. So there they sat outside on the front porch, the two of them very troubled men.

Topaz and Jade tried playing with them to lift their spirits, but neither Donovan nor Myron was in the mood to play, so the babies decided to go terrorize all the wildlife that passed through their domain instead. They had become extremely territorial as they grew comfortable with their new surroundings. But before he left, Topaz, the male, looked back at the droopy faces on Donovan and Myron, ripped off a loud, rank fart, and then waved at them while heading off, but before he leaped off the porch he turned and looked at them, then began chattering away as if saying, "I've left you two a little flavor of mine… mope over that… see ya!"

When they heard Topaz fart, and then smelled the foulness of it, they couldn't help but laugh, and that broke the ice. Soon they were discussing their troubles.

Myron's problem was that the Outlaws had lost their Special Teams' kick return specialist.

"Man, this guy was the fastest in the league, and the team paid dearly to recruit him right from college. He blew out his knee and is out for the season. Last season our weakest link was the kick return game. This guy was supposed to solve that problem, putting us over the top...so, what's bothering you, bro?" asked Myron.

"I had to put my experiments on hold due to finances," said Donovan. "You haven't tried that stuff by yourself, have you?" asked Myron, with a frown of disapproval.

"Of course not!" replied Donovan.

They both became silent once again and then...a light bulb went on in their heads at the same time and they looked at each other.

"Do you think we can pull this off?" asked Donovan

"I can get you a tryout," replied Myron.

They both laughed out loud and said, "Let's make it happen!"

So, they put a "game plan" together.

Chapter 38

A few days later at the practice field of the Oakland Outlaws…

"Say Myron…is that your boy?" asked the Special Teams' coach, Bill Garland.

Donovan had already been in the team's locker room and outfitted with an Oakland Outlaws' uniform. He looked good in it too, as he calmly strolled towards them, reminiscent of the confident swagger the great Jim Brown had displayed.

"Yeah, that's him," answered Myron.

"Pretty big for a kick returner!" added Coach Garland, squinting in the sunlight behind Donovan, which produced a majestic glow around him.

When Donovan got over to them, Coach Garland asked, "So, what's your name son?" as he wiped a sweaty palm on his jersey, then extended it to shake hands.

"Smoke," came the reply as Donovan's huge hand engulfed the coach's hand and he gave it a powerful squeeze.

Seeing Smoke up close, the coach's jaw dropped open and he just stared, thinking to himself, *"This kid is a giant! I sure hope he's everything Myron says he is."*

"Nice grip ya got there, Smoke—feels like you can hang on to the ball with a grip like that," said Coach Garland.

Smoke gave no reply. He knew the coach was feeling him out, but he had decided to be an enigma. He wasn't there to make friends, he wasn't there to hang out, and he certainly was not there for the glory. He was there to get paid and that was it!

"Oh, I get it, here for the business at hand. Well then, let's get straight to it," said the coach.

The training practice was exclusively for the Special Teams, so the coach hollered out, "Set up for a kick return!" Then he turned to Smoke and said with a smirk, "Let's see what ya got, son."

Smoke's stroll onto the field had not gone unnoticed by the other members of the squad.

"Who the *hell* is this dude?" asked Terry, the current designated kick returner.

"Hell if I know! Judging from the size of him, he must be trying to make the team as a tackle or guard," speculated Kennedy, one of the team's tackles.

Terry trotted out on the field, assuming the position of kick returner when Coach Garland yelled out, "Yo, Terry...sit this one out—let the kid here bring one back. Let's see what he's got."

Terry waved, acknowledging the coach's instructions, and headed off the playing field. When he got to the sideline he said to one of his teammates, "This I've got to see. This dude is too damn big to be returning the 'rock.'"

The first kick was a line drive straight to Smoke. This type of kick didn't give a return man much time to field the ball and make his move. The speed of the ball caught Smoke by surprise and the ball shot straight through his hands. Smoke watched it roll out of bounds, then he felt the ground shaking, and heard the thunderous footsteps of the 11 charging Special Teams' tacklers bearing down on him, and when he looked up, he was surrounded by snarling tacklers, all staring at him.

"Whoa!" Smoke said to himself, surprised at how fast the guys had surrounded him.

Myron was standing on the sideline holding his breath. He knew Smoke had never seen, or been in, this type of position before.

Nothing about track training could prepare an athlete for the speed of professional football. The thought ran through Myron's mind that they might have made a mistake coming up with this plan, but it was too late now. All they could do was ride it out and see what happened.

When the next ball was kicked off, Myron shut his eyes as Smoke caught the ball. He opened them after he heard someone shout, "Where the hell did he go?"

Smoke had eluded all tacklers, and was standing in the end zone at the other end of the field.

"I'll be Goddamned!" hollered the coach. "Did you see that?"

The would-be tacklers at the other end of the field were as astonished as the coach. Smoke had weaved his way through the tacklers without them even touching him and he wasn't even breathing hard.

The coach hollered out, "Line 'em up again! I don't believe that shit!" He sent a hand signal to the kicker, instructing him to kick this one high. A high kick would give the tacklers a better chance to get downfield and tackle the ball returner.

Smoke had never played the game of football before, but he was a fan, and anything Smoke liked, he'd learn all he could about it. Football was no exception, and with his natural athletic abilities, boosted by the serum, Smoke was a natural, rather supernatural, player.

And for the next dozen or so kickoffs, Coach Garland had the entire Special Teams' offense and defense on the field, vainly chasing after Smoke. Smoke gave a kick return clinic that the Outlaws' Special Teams players would never forget.

Afterwards, when the coach called him over to the sideline, he wasn't even breathing hard.

"Son, somebody sure named you right. You are smokin'!" said the coach as he patted him on the back.

Smoke glanced at Myron and winked.

The Special Team players were sprawled out all over the field; dazed and out of breath from the kick return exhibition Smoke had put them through.

The coach's cell phone rang and he said, "Excuse me while I take this call." It was the owner of the Outlaws who had been watching from his private skybox. After the coach got off the phone, he looked over Smoke, from head to toe, still not believing what he had just witnessed, then extended another sweaty palm to shake Smoke's hand, turned to Myron and said, "Take Smoke to see the 'Man.'" He gave Smoke another pat on the back in approval.

Then he turned and looked over the field at his exhausted players and hollered, "When you ladies catch your breath…hit the showers!"

Chapter 39

As Smoke and Myron walked off the field, they could hardly keep their composures; stage one of their game plan had worked like a dream. Now for stage two, the money negotiations. They stopped by the locker room for Smoke to shower, change, and to pick up his briefcase, which contained the complete stats of what the Outlaws did, and didn't do, the prior season. Smoke and Myron had put together detailed files on the Outlaws that Smoke would use to negotiate the prices he wanted.

Outside the teams owner's box, Myron said, "Work your magic, bro; this is as far as I go. Stick to our game plan and we'll be in business."

Smoke gave Myron a big hug, and said, "Thanks, bro. See you in a few," and he knocked on the door.

"Come in, come in," came a man's voice from inside.

Smoke entered the hotel suite-like skybox and was greeted by the outstretched hand of the team's owner. Smoke took his hand and gave him a powerful handshake and said, "Great to meet you, Mr. Allen. I'm Smoke."

"By what I saw you do down on my field, you sure are. Do you have a last name?" asked Charles Allen, the owner of the Oakland Outlaws.

"Nope…Smoke is all there is," he said with confidence and finality. "I can live with that," replied Charles Allen.

But before the owner could continue fishing for information about Smoke, Smoke took over the interview.

"Mr. Allen, I've been following your team for quite a while, and it seems to me that if you had the right kick returner, you would've gone all the way last year. I'm here to make you an offer giving the Outlaws their best chance at becoming Super Bowl Champions this year. This contract details exactly what I'll need to make that happen." Then Smoke pulled out a multiple page contract with all his terms set in writing.

"This contract is set in stone. There will be no negotiations because I guarantee you that every time I get the ball, I *will* score a touchdown."

"That's an impossible guarantee!" said Charles Allen, with a smirk of disbelief.

"No, sir, it's not. These are my prices," replied Smoke, and he turned to the page of the contract that revealed how much Smoke wanted to get paid.

In addition to the normal $6,000,000.00 a season for a kick return specialist, Smoke wanted $15,000.00 per point during the 18 game regular season, plus, $7,000.000.00 for the Division Championship game, $9,000,000.00 for the Conference Championship game, and $11,000,000.00 for the Super Bowl.

Standing out in bold letters were the words…

ALL PRICE QUOTES ARE AFTER-TAX VALUES!

Then Smoke pointed out the section titled "Special Arrangements." In italics it pointed out 3 action items...

1. *Smoke would not be available for regular practices.*
2. *Smoke guarantees to know everything about all formations in the Special Teams' playbook, including 'trick' plays.*

3. *Smoke would be 100% and never miss a game while fulfilling this contract.*

The contract went on to state that Smoke would not travel with the team. He would make his own travel arrangements, if necessary, and he required his own private suite for all road games.

There was another clause in the contract in bold print that stated **AT NO TIME WILL IT BE MANDATORY FOR SMOKE TO HAVE ANY DEALINGS WITH THE PRESS…ANY PRESS!!!**

"The Outlaws' PR department can come up with whatever they want to say, but the press must be kept away from me at all costs," said a no-nonsense Smoke.

"Now, if we have a deal, I'll give you an account number where payments must be placed by the next business day following each performance."

Smoke's contract had a couple of additional uniform clauses. He wanted a permanently tinted, photosensitive, retractable face shield, and on the front of his helmet, on either side of the center seam, would be the words, "GOING…GOING," and on the back of his helmet would be a single word "GONE!"

And as far as his jersey was concerned, it would have one name on it…***SMOKE***. And his team number had to be the number 6.

"And Mr. Allen, sir, if at the end of my first game you're not completely satisfied, this contract is voided and you don't owe me a dime!"

"Quite the mystery man and damn sure of yourself, aren't you, Smoke?" said Charles Allen as he got up from behind his majestic mahogany desk and strolled over, taking a look out his skybox window down to his playing field, where most of his Special Team players were just now making it off the field after the exhibition Smoke had put them through. He thought for a moment, and then returned to his desk and, without further hesitation, gladly signed Smoke's contract, then buzzed for his secretary to make copies, finalizing the deal.

"Oh, Mr. Allen, one more little thing. I can be reached exclusively through Myron Hammond, the team's trainer. He will be the intermediary between the Oakland Outlaws organization and myself," added Smoke.

Charles Allen extended his hand once again as he said, "Smoke... welcome to the Oakland Outlaws!"

Myron was waiting outside the skybox, and when Smoke came out he gave Myron a wink, and Myron jumped toward the sky, and when he landed they embraced in joyous laughter.

"How do you feel?" asked Myron.

"Great!" said Smoke with a grin. "He went for the whole package."

"OUTSTANDING! Let's get you back to the lab and check you out. How much time do we have before you take your elixir?" asked Myron, not wanting to see Mr. Hominid outside his isolation booth.

"2 hours," answered Smoke.

Back at Donovan's lab, Myron said, "I have to make one suggestion; on the field, you need to slow down and give the other players a better chance of trapping you before you break away."

"You want me to give the fans a show, huh? Well then, hold on to your seat because I'm gonna show everybody something they've never seen before," said Donovan, with a mischievous grin on his face.

CHAPTER 40

By the Outlaws' next practice day, word had spread like the California wildfires of 2012 around the locker room. All the players were talking about the 'New Return Man.' The Special Teams' players were saying, "This dude is awesome, he's unbelievable. He's got moves off the planet. We couldn't even touch him and that was with both the offense and defensive Special Teams on the field at the same time! Man, we were chasing this dude all around the field. We looked like an old Benny Hill rerun…he was playing with us, and when he got ready, he turned on the jets, and was gone! I'm talking, he smoked all of us. I mean…damn, this dude is blazin' fast!"

"Well, what's this speedster's name?" asked Devahn Rice, the NFL's most celebrated wide receiver whose locker room nickname was "The GOAT!" which stood for "Greatest Of All Time!"

"He calls himself Smoke!" came the answer from Head Coach Garland, listening to the locker room banter, and hoping this new addition would light a fire under his players.

"Cool," replied Tim, the team's other wide receiver. "When do we get to meet him?"

"Well, this dude is really weird, and he's set up a unique arrangement with the team. He only shows up on game day, and he won't be at any of the practices," informed Coach Garland.

"You must be shitting us," said Lincoln, the team's right tackle.

"But, I can show you what his helmet and jersey looks like," and the coach unveiled Smoke's helmet and jersey.

"Is this shit for real?" asked Tyrone, the team's running back, as he pointed to the words "Going," "Going," on the front of Smoke's helmet, then he turned the helmet around and pointed to the word "GONE!" on the back.

"Well, at least this rookie has a sense of humor," said Rich, the team's quarterback. "Let me take a closer look at that hat. Is this a photo sensitive face shield? What is that all about—this guy doesn't want to be seen, either?" asked Rich.

Coach Garland could only shrug his shoulders with a 'hell-if-I–know' look on his face at Rich's remarks.

Terry, the team's other kick returner said, "Man, if you guys had been here yesterday, Smoke would've made believers out of all y'all! This rookie is the real deal!"

Rod, the team's free safety said, "I don't give a shit how weird this dude is, or what he wants to be called, as long as he can produce."

"I heard that!" came the response from the rest of the locker room, and they all started slapping each other's hands and getting ready for the final practice before their season opener home game against the Denver Stallions.

Chapter 41

"The weather is just perfect for the more than 75,000 fans who will be putting butts to seats here at the Oakland County Coliseum for this epic battle between last year's AFC Division Champion Oakland Outlaws and the Denver Stallions.

"This is Cal Mitchells and beside me here is the Big Guy, Don Maddmen, and we'd like to welcome all of you watching to the Coliseum for this, the first Monday Night Football game of the season."

"Whelp, I, uh, I, I, I tell ya Cal, we got the, the makings of a doozy here tonight, a battle of West Coast Offenses, even though the only west coast team playing tonight is the Outlaws."

"And more than that, Don, these two teams really despise each other.

There's been trash talking in the press all week long. Denver has been calling the Outlaws 'has-beens,' and the Outlaws retaliated by calling Denver the 'geriatric rejects.'

"In their off season, the Outlaws gave up two top draft picks to acquire the most prolific kick returner in football."

"Yeah, Cal. Too bad he got injured before the season started."
"That had to hurt the Outlaws, Don."

"Yeah, yeah, Cal, especially in their wallets, and, and more important, hurt their chances at returning to the Super Bowl this season. Kick returning has been the Achilles' heal for the Outlaws over the last couple of seasons."

"The Outlaws were routed in last year's Superbowl and this year they had a terrible loosing pre-season, Don. Do you think they're still suffering a hangover from last year's beat down in the Superbowl?"

"I tell ya Cal, I think a big, big hangover. I, I, I, don't think they recovered. I mean, they, they were in the Superbowl, and they, they got embarrassed in that Superbowl. I think in their whole off-season, they, they, all they thought about was that butt whooping. And they didn't have a good pre-season because of the Superbowl debacle. They, they've got an uphill climb, but they can do it. All, all, all they've got to do is to put last season behind them, focus on this season, and play Outlaws' football."

"Don, these two teams have been on Monday Night Football more than any other teams, and there have been some classics. What will tonight bring?"

"Word, word from the the the locker room Cal, tells us that the Outlaws have a surprise to unveil tonight."

"Well, what better place to unveil a surprise, Don, than right here on Monday Night Football?"

"I agree, Cal."

"Tonight, the Denver Stallions take on the Oakland Outlaws at home! And folks, we'll be right back for the kick off with the 3M's...Mitchells, Maddmen, on Monday Night Football, after these commercial messages," announced Cal, taking them off air.

Off camera, Don Maddmen said, "Where the hell's my cooler? My brewskis better be chilled or some heads will roll around here tonight!"

"Here it comes now, Mr. Maddmen, just as you like it," announced Donny, the production assistant.

"Good, good job, Bud," thanked Don.

"It's Donny, Mr. Maddmen, sir."

"I know that, son, just, just seein' if you were on your toes," said Don with a big laugh while grabbing an ice cold beer.

Mitchells quietly checked the broadcast booth bar, making sure it was properly stocked. Even though he had told everyone he was swearing off the hard stuff, his habit was a hard one to break, and he may have picked the wrong game to quit.

Maddmen slammed down his first beer, then let out one of his patented belches before returning from station identification

"Cal, can't you just smell the excitement in the air here?"

"I can smell something all right, Don."

Mitchells hits the mike mute and says, "Maddmen—you pig... give us a warning next time. That belch smelt like shit!"

"Wait until the fourth quarter after I've put down about a case or two. Then you'll get the good stuff," promised Don. "But if you're really into flavor, I create wonders after I've eaten some *turducken*."

Mitchells just looked at Maddmen and shook his head, deciding not to touch that one.

They glanced over the teams' rosters and both came across the name Smoke at about the same time, and said, "Who the hell is Smoke?"

"Somebody messed up on this player's name, Bud!" hollered Maddmen. "The name's Donny, sir."

"Sharp young man," replied Maddmen with a smile. "Go, go double check this player's name for us...will ya?"

"Mr. Maddmen, sir, that's all he's going by, I've already double-checked," said Donny, feeling a little intimated by Maddmen.

"Good, good man, Bud," said Maddmen.

"What kind of player only goes by a single name? And *Smoke* at that! This is the N freakin' F.L., not a damn rap album. We use first and last names here," ranted Maddmen.

"You never know, Don, maybe the kid's *smokin*!" commented Cal. "Goddamned free agents," said Maddmen, "they're ruining the freaking game!"

Mitchells handed Maddmen a cold one to calm him down. Maddmen threw it back in one gulp, then popped another.

The production assistant announced, "Back on air in 5...4...3," then used his fingers to finish counting down.

"At the beginning of the 21st century, Devahn Rice set the all-time NFL Record for touchdowns in a season, with 35, right here on Monday Night Football," announced Cal.

"Yeah, Cal, not to mention every other record a wide receiver could hold, plus he's made over 20 appearances on Monday Night Football during his long illustrious career," commented Maddmen, who muted his mike to say, "I'm surprised the old goat can still lace his own cleats."

"The Outlaws have won the toss and have chosen to receive. And their kick return specialist, number 6, it says here… is simply known as…*what?…* 'Smoke?'"

"And folks, that's about all the information we have on this guy, except that he was an off-the-street walk-on free agent." Maddmen looked at Mitchells and gave him the look of disgust, showing his contempt for "free agency."

"And here we go with a mile-high kickoff from Denver, the Mile High City," announces Maddmen.

Mitchells muted their microphones and said, "Maddmen, you asshole, we're in Oakland!"

Maddmen just stood there with his red nose glowing, shrugged his shoulders, and threw down another beer. "This is what I think about Oakland." He stepped over to the broadcast booth's window overlooking the fans and field, opened it enough to stick his head out, then let loose one of the most outrageous belches ever heard. Moments later, a fan from down in the stands could be heard over the crowd noise hollering out in a drunken southern drawl, "Good one!

Somebody toss that sum-bitch another cold one! After sum shit like dhat dhere, he deserves it—that muther-skooter was the grand-daddy of all belches!"

Mitchells and Maddmen looked at each other then burst out in laughter. "That sounds like a good suggestion," said Maddmen, while he grabbed another cold one and said, while bowing his head, "A-thank you, a-thank you, a- thank you very much!"

CHAPTER 42

Smoke took the field, and quickly discovered that handling the ball during a real game situation was a lot different than practice. He took his eyes off the ball for a split second to look at the tacklers closing in on him like a stampeding herd of buffalo, and when he looked back for the ball he heard it hit the ground in the end zone. He scrambled to get a handle on the loose ball, but when he reached for it he was blindsided by Denver players and knocked completely out of the end zone.

The last Denver player to peel himself off Smoke was Scribendi, #51, who had made the initial hit and now stood over Smoke taunting him by saying, "Welcome to the fuckin' NFL… bitch-ass rookie!"

Stretched out, face down on the field, Smoke managed to lift his head and take a mental snapshot of this player, then his head fell back into the grass and he laid there motionless.

Pacing back and forth along the Outlaw's bench, Myron's heart skipped several beats when he saw Smoke being gang tackled. Sprinting up the sideline, Myron was horrified to see Smoke lying motionless, still as the dead buried in the ground. Worst case scenarios flooded his thoughts as he began blaming himself for the broken mess that was his dear friend.

"Get up, get up…please get up!" shouted Myron from the sideline, restricted from going out on the field because the play had not been blown dead by the official.

Players from both teams tried pouncing on the ball, and a mad skirmish broke out as every player vied to come up with the elusive prize—the loose football.

"Bad break for the rookie," said Maddmen. "He heard those tacklers' footsteps bearing down on him and took his eyes off the ball. Here in the NFL, if you take your eyes off the ball, the game's outlook changes immediately."

"Yeah, and for the worst, too! It looks like the kid is out!" added Mitchells. "Wait...wait, look… back up field—there's a flag down, and…it…looks…like—yes, it is—it's on Denver!" announced Mitchells.

"Lucky break for the rookie. He gets another shot at it!" said a spiteful Maddmen, still pissed off about the negative effect free agency had on the game, and channeling his hostility towards Smoke for being a free agent.

Smoke lay stretched out, motionless, while deep within his body the serum's micro-nanotechnology began scanning and making cellular repairs at unfathomable speeds, focusing their efforts to strengthen any potentially weak areas for protection against future traumas. Smoke slowly began moving around on the ground, and he finally lifted himself to one knee, allowing his head to clear. He managed to look downfield and saw the penalty flag, and heard over the stadium's P.A. that it was against Denver. He sighed a long sigh of relief, and looked along his team's sideline for Myron. He finally saw him standing on the sideline, just off field from him, looking like he had lost his best friend. Slowly Smoke stood up, brushed himself off, and gave Myron a wave to let him know he was all right.

"Awwe-shit! Can't let that happen again" said Smoke to himself.

Moments later, Denver kicked off again. This time the kick was higher and longer than the first one.

"Holy cow! He put big foot into that one!" shouted Maddmen.

Smoke kept repeating to himself, "Keep your eyes on the ball, keep your eyes on the ball," and caught the ball in Denver's end zone, tucked it away, but before he made a single move downfield he took a mental snapshot of the exact location of every player on the field, even the officials. He started seeing everybody moving in slow motion and knew all he needed to do was reach the open locations before anyone filled that spot.

Smoke turned on the jets and blazed a serpentine trail downfield, causing his would-be tacklers to collide into his blockers, into each other, or miss completely and go sailing through the air, bouncing off the turf when they landed.

In the broadcast booth Maddmen dropped some papers and bent down, weaving back and forth, trying to pick them up, when he heard Mitchells say, "Holy-moly! Will you look at that! Don… Don… you're missing this! Touchdown Outlaws!" yelled Mitchells.

"What…what…touchdown? Who got a touchdown?" Maddmen looked downfield and he saw the rookie standing in the Outlaws' end zone.

"UNBELIEVABLE!" shouted Mitchells.

"What, what…how'd the kid get there so fast?" asked Maddmen, with a look of astonishment on his face.

It took a few moments before the fans in the stadium could wrap their brains around what they'd just witnessed, but when they did, a roar like never before heard filled the coliseum.

"The kid's got the right name, Don," Mitchells became an instant believer.

Smoke slowly walked from the end zone, $90,000.00 richer and tossed the ball to an official as he headed to the sideline.

When he and Myron were close enough they pounded each other's fists. "How was that?" asked Smoke, with a big grin on his face.

"Nobody has ever seen anything like it, I guarantee that!" replied Myron with a huge smile of his own. "Just one thing…"

"Yeah, yeah, yeah…I know, slow down, and make it more dramatic to watch. Next time I will. I never realized how big and fast these guys really are. And did you see the way I got clocked on that first kick off?"

"You took your eyes off the ball, didn't you?"

"Yeah! But you can bet your butt I won't do that again. Getting hit like that hurts. And Denver's #51 had the nerve to say, "Welcome to the NFL…Rookie." Well it's on now. I've got something for his bad ass," said Smoke, looking across the field to locate the name of the player who made him feel so welcome in the NFL. He spotted the number 51, and then saw the name Scribendi. Smoke slowly nodded his head up and down with a payback smirk on his face, thinking, "*Yo ass is mine!*"

By then the Outlaws' bench had swarmed around Smoke, some pounded fists, some slapped hands, and others lightly smashed helmets to helmets, all celebrating with pride, while pointing to the word "GONE!" on the back of Smoke's helmet, teasing Denver's players across the field.

Maddmen replayed the return and could not believe what he was seeing. He placed his hand on the back of Mitchells' shoulder, slapping it to get his attention, pointed at the replay, and with a look of amazement, said, "Somebody break out the speed radar on this kid. Look at him go to the house!"

Then he turned to Donny, the production assistant and shouted, "Hey, Bud, you sure this is all the info we got on this kid?" while holding up one thin slip of paper with Smoke's name, height, and weight typed on it.

"That's what they gave me…that's what you got!" replied Donny, demonstrating some hostility toward Maddmen.

"I, I…I tell ya, Cal…that was the most awesome display of pure speed I've ever seen. He caught Denver's entire special team by complete surprise. All they saw was a blur streaking past them. Denver couldn't decide if their eyes were playing tricks on them or what!!!"

Don shouted, "Sign him up to the All Maddmen Team, *NOW*!!!"

The roaring spectators overpowered the excitement in the broadcast booth; they were watching the replay of Smoke's first NFL touchdown, reliving his every move. Even Denver fans were excited by Smoke's display of pure speed. When the replay showed Smoke running into the end zone, the words…**"TOUCH DOWN— OUTLAWS"** exploded with digital fireworks on the stadium's displays, and a louder roar came from the spectators.

Everyone was still in a buzz when Oakland finally kicked off to Denver. Not to let things get out of hand, on Denver's first play from scrimmage, Jake 'The Python' Malloy, strong-armed the ball to his wide receiver for 6 points, catching Oakland's secondary sleeping. The extra point kick was good and the score was tied.

The Outlaws' kick return team took the field for their second appearance of the game, and the excitement could be felt buzzing through the fans, hoping to get another great return from Oakland's new rookie kick returner.

"You can bet yo momma I won't miss the kid's kick return this time," promised Maddmen to Mitchells, feeling his alcohol kicking in.

"What do ya think, Don? Were our eyes playing tricks on us during the kid's first return?"

"I, I, I'll tell ya one thing, Cal, replay doesn't lie, and, and, and I believe what the replay showed me. I'm, I'm just, just excited to get the chance to maybe see a repeat with my own eyes."

"Well, it's 'Show & Tell Time' folks, as Denver kicks another boomer down field for the rookie Smoke to try and take to the house again," announced Mitchells.

"Keep your eyes on the ball…eyes on the ball, eyes on the ball," repeated Smoke as he watched the football sailing towards him in the end zone, but this time, the ball hit the left upright and bounced across to the other side of the end zone, away from him.

"Oh, shit!" said Smoke, as he darted to the other side of the end zone. By then Denver's tacklers were storming down on him. His teammate, Jenkins, the other kick returner shouted, "Take a knee, take a knee!"

But Smoke had other plans. He waited until two tacklers were about to pounce on him and he leapt into the air and they went flying through the end zone into a wall of photographers. When Smoke's feet hit the ground, he took off to the other side of the end zone where another tackler was closing in on him. Smoke put a juke on this tackler that sent him rolling through the end zone like a gutter ball at the bowling alley, missing every pin. Smoke started his charge up field, juking and cutting and spinning away from tacklers until he locked eyes with Denver's Scribendi, # 51, his newfound friend in the NFL.

It looked like a National Geographic's clip of two gigantic rams about to butt heads, only in this scenario there was only one real ram the other participant was, unknowingly, the victim.

The spectators saw Smoke. They saw Scribendi. They saw Smoke. They saw Scribendi. They saw Smoke picking up speed. Some of the fans threw their hands in front of their faces, not wanting to witness the collision about to take place, and then they heard a tremendously loud "WHACK" echoing around the stadium.

Denver's # 51, Scribendi, instantly realized he was the victim in this scenario as he went sailing through the air after impact, and when he hit the turf, he tumbled for another ten yards.

Everybody in the stadium became quiet, and then all at the same time everybody yelled "*WOO!*" It was like when a boxer lands that perfect punch, knocking out his opponent. The entire stadium was in an uproar. All eyes were on Smoke as he ran through a couple more players, then juked and spun his way downfield, causing Denver's last few players to trip over their own feet.

"Don, look at the kid's forward body lean as he rampages towards the end- zone. He looks like a computer generated football character charging downfield, unstoppable, destroying all in his path," said Mitchells.

"Yeah, like, like Jim Brown used to do," added Maddmen. "Jim always said, "It's easier to run over people than to go around 'em."

Well, the kid's definitely taken a page from Jim Brown's rules of running and made it his."

"Don, this crowd can't believe what their eyes have seen, and frankly, neither can I."

"Cal, I saw it, and I'm still not sure I believe it! I've been covering the NFL for a long, long time, and I've never seen running like that!"

Smoke was standing alone in the Outlaws' end zone, with his arms raised skyward in victory. He liked what he was feeling. He decided to use today's game to instill fear into all would-be tacklers around the league by destroying Denver's Special Teams' tacklers.

Smoke returned 5 more touchdowns by the end of the game's first half of play, a feat never before accomplished in the history of the NFL.

Mitchells calmly turned to Maddmen and said, "Well, big guy, looks like we know who Smoke is now."

"Yeah, no shit!" came Maddmen's semi-drunk reply.

Mitchells quickly announced, "And now for our special halftime spectacular."

Then he immediately muted both microphones and said, "Maddmen, you can't say 'shit' on the air."

Maddmen looked at Mitchells with a big cheesy grin on his pale face and slammed down another cold one from his cooler.

Chapter 43

Inside the Outlaws' locker room during halftime, most of the players were thankful that the game was close. Even though the only scoring was done by the rookie, Smoke, several members of the Special Teams were pissed because he didn't follow their instructions during the game; they'd told him to take a knee in the end zone more than once, and he ignored them every time.

Smoke looked at his upset teammates and said, "Fellas, fellas, we're on the same team, playing for the same purpose…to win! I'm here to go from end zone to end zone every time I touch the ball. I believe in playing outside the box, coloring outside the lines. My abilities allow me to do that. Now you can either help me out, or get out of the way. But make no mistakes about it, every time I touch the ball, I'm taking it to the HOUSE!"

"So you're saying you'll score with or without us?" asked one of the upset players.

"Did I stutter? We can all look good together or I'll score and look good by myself. Either way you choose, I'm scoring from zone to zone, and every place in between. Every time I take the field, baby…I'm here to get 6. Do you guys have a problem with that?" asked a defiant Smoke, staring down the upset players.

His pissed off teammates looked at the expressions on the faces of the rest of the team, then back at each other, and the main complainer finally said, "Break out the crayons — let's color outside the box— Bay-Bee!"

Laughter filled the locker room!

Smoke had made his stand and was now fully accepted as one of '*The Men In Black!*'

The laughter quieted down when the head coach said, "Since that's resolved, let's get down to business. You guys are playing like broke-dick dogs out there!

Romanowski, boy, what the hell's your problem? You been hit in the head too many times? Both offense and defense, and I'm using those terms loosely, instead of you guys looking like man-eaters, most of you look like girlyboys trying to get a date. Shit!!! If it weren't for the goddamned kid, all of our Willie's would be laying in the dirt. No offense meant to you, Smoke," said the coach. "Please, keep doing what you're doing. Hell, from my perspective, our collective asses are in your hands until the rest of this team pulls their heads out their butts. So, whatever it takes, you Special Teams guys…get the rock into the kid's hands. We've got another half to be played, so let's get out there and kick some ass. Let's look like the champions we are!

One of the defensive players shouted, "Who are we? I said… who are we!?"

A spirited group response roared back, "The Men In Black!"

A rousing call and response began among the players...

"And whose house is this?"

"Our house!" came the resounding reply.

"So what will we do?"

"We will protect this house!"

"Why?"

"This is our house!"

"Say what?"

"We *will* protect this house!!!"

The energy level was higher in Denver's locker room; every aspect of their game plan was working…except one!

"Special Teams!" shouted the head coach, "you have got to stop that damn rookie! He's keeping 'em in this game, and making you guys look like shit."

He looked at Wallace, the Special Teams coach and said, "Tell me something good, Coach Wallace."

"I don't know what to say. I've never seen anything like this kid."

One of Denver's Special Team players added, "Man…this dude's unstoppable! Did you see what he did to Scribendi…I mean… Damn!"

"No shit! While Scribendi was being carried off in the Mash Cart, he was babbling shit like, "I know, I know, you told me not to play on the tracks, Mommy— I looked both ways—I didn't see the train at all." Scribendi was acting 51/50, completely out too lunch!"

"Well, the preliminary med report on Scribendi is that he's gonna be out 3 to 5 games with a concussion and bruised muscles. We can't do anything about that, but there's got to be something we can do about that kid. Talk to me Wallace—any ideas?"

"Well, Coach, let's keep the ball away from him; take him out the picture.

So, this half, we'll use onside kicks, out of bounds kicks, out of the end zone kicks, and we can even run the ball on 4th down instead of punting."

"Well, all right then. It sounds like we have a plan. Now, let's get back out there and continue to execute our game plan. This is the Outlaws' House, but we've paid today's rent, so that makes it 'Our House!'"

"Damn straight!" shouted a Denver player.

"We'll show 'em that the Stallions own this property!" "So, let's get out there and evict those sons of bitches." "When we leave here tonight they'll be flying our colors!"

The pumped-up Denver Stallions roared out of their locker room on to the playing field with a renewed determination.

Chapter 44

During the halftime show, Maddmen was doing his usual partying with hangers-on who surrounded professional football teams. At first he tried to get a chat with the Outlaws' rookie but that didn't happen, so he took a couple of the party ladies back to his infamous mobile home known as the "Horse Trailer."

After a few drinks, and other goings-on in the trailer, Maddmen made his way back into the announcer's booth, feeling no pain, bopping his head up and down, out of rhythm, and singing off-key to a song floating around in his head … "Somebody's got to feel this! Everybody's gonna feel this! All you mommas get to feel this" and he would thrust his chunky hips forward at mid-stride.

When Maddmen got close enough for Mitchells to get a whiff of his assorted odors, Cal shook his head from side to side and said, "Been hanging out in the "Horse Trailer" getting your groove on, have you, Don?"

"Absolutely, Cal, that's where all the real action is, and let me tell you, both locker rooms were abuzz over the rookie. Denver is scared shitless of him, and as far as Oakland is concerned, up to this point in their game…hell, what game? The kid is their game! God, I love this game," shouted Maddmen as he grabbed another brewski.

Mitchells stared at him with the beginnings of a smile, parting his lips slowly, and shouted, "Screw it! I picked the wrong game to quit drinking," and he grabbed a fifth of Wild Turkey from the bar, sliced open the seal with a fingernail, and with a single flick of his thumb, unscrewed the plastic top while still holding the bottle by the neck. "I get the feeling this party is just getting started, Big Guy!" Mitchells lifted the fifth to the sky in a silent toast to Maddmen before he wrapped his lips around the bottle's neck. And after a long swig, Mitchells did a Jack Nicholson imitation from the classic movie "Easy Rider," then grabbed a cold one from Maddmen's cooler, downed it nonstop, looked at Don through watery eyes, and with a burning throat, he yelled "ARE YOU READY FOR SOME FOOTBALL?"

Seeing this display by the two announcers, Donny, the production assistant, placed a woeful hand over his forehead and eyes, as he said to himself, *"This is going to be one of those shows again."*

After collecting himself, Donny attracted the attention of the two broadcasting party animals by saying, "Going live in 5, 4, 3…"

"Welcome back to the 3 M's, Mitchells, Maddmen, and Monday Night Football. To recap the goings-on in the first half, the Big Guy here will illustrate a few plays using the famous Maddmen on-screen chalkboard. Don, show us some diagrams from the first half of play."

"Yes sir-ree, Budweiser. First of all Cal, let me, let me, let me start by saying, this is a historical, momentous event! Nobody in the history of the game has ever scored this many touchdowns in one game, let alone the first half, like the Outlaws' rookie, Smoke did. Hell, I'm almost pissing myself waiting to see what's gonna happen in the 2nd half!"

Mitchells gave Maddmen a look, held his head down and slowly shook it from side to side.

"What?" innocently exclaimed Don, with both hands extended from his body, palms turned upward. "I know you're as excited as I am, Cal," as he passed Cal the Wild Turkey.

"Diagram a few plays, Don," said Cal, who took the bottle and slammed back another swig.

"Here, here, here, let me illustrate the one play that put the kid on the map. Denver's punter really puts foot to the ball and blasts it high and deep into the end zone. Smoke sees the ball coming and he realizes it's gonna hit the left upright of the goal post, so he takes a position right here at point 'x,' on the right side of the goal post, and waits to see where the ball is gonna bounce after it hits the upright. When it hits and bounces to the ground he turns on the jets, not the big jets mind you, but the little jets, and darts across to the other side of the end zone, point 'y' here, where he scoops up the ball, then reverses field, to point 'z,' and darts back to his original side of the end zone, point 'x' again. This gives Smoke enough time to look up field," Maddmen draws several crooked lines in the direction Smoke will be running, "and see what is coming his way. Well, he sees the first Denver tackler, let's show him as the letter 'o,' sailing through the air towards him, and Smoke knows that this guy is committed, so Smoke leaps into the air, "poof," causing this poor sucker to miss, then crash and burn out the back of the end zone. The beauty of Smoke's leaping is in his landings. When his feet hit the ground, they're always planted in a position to take off running, which means the kid can change directions, east, west, north, or south, instantly." Maddmen draws a large plus sign on top of all the other lines. "Now he's at the 30, headed up field where he puts the most beautiful spin move I've ever seen, "whoop," on this guy here, making him just trip and fall all over himself. Here at mid-field, Smoke jukes the next tackler out of his drawers. Look at the way the defender's feet fly out from under him before he went down. Splat—that's gotta hurt."

"Yeah, and it's embarrassing, too," added Cal.

"Well, yeah, a little. But Cal, what happens next is really embarrassing.

Scribendi, who really popped the kid in the end zone, giving Smoke his own brand of 'Welcome-to-the-NFL' greeting, yeah, well Scribendi had been on the other side of the field tracking the kid, and starts weaving his way over to cut the kid off. And this is where it gets ugly for Scribendi. It looks like the kid sees Scribendi coming, and goes out of his way running straight at Scribendi, and then BAM—BOOM, WHO'S YOUR DADDY NOW!? That's when the hit heard around the world happens. The kid uses what Gale Sayers used; he wouldn't let the defender hit him. Instead, Sayers would lower those shoulders and 'BOOM,' he'd hit first. That takes the power away from the defender. Only this rookie has much more artillery with his blinding speed and giant physical size. The kid stands 6'7" and weights 375lbs, which is a terrifying sight to see charging at you. Shit, I'd take a dump in my pants if I saw that heading towards me and you can just bet that hit on Scribendi will be on the highlight reels forever! I'd be willing to bet your paycheck Cal, that every time Scribendi sees the replay, he feels the pain from that monster hit. I, I, I, I tell ya Cal…he got jacked up! And as it's said Cal, the rest is history."

Maddmen glared at all the crazy lines he had just drawn, blinked a couple of times trying to figure out what it is, and finally came up with, "Look Cal…abstract art!"

"Yeah, I can see something in there; it looks like a cat chasing a dog," commented Mitchells, after taking another swig of Wild Turkey.

During a brief moment of clarity, Maddmen said, "You, you, you know Cal, at the beginning of the game, you said something about this kid and, and you were right. Folks, this kid Smoke… is SMOKIN'!"

"I'm with you on that one, Big Fella. Smokin' he is! But the one sight I hated to see during the first half, Don, was the Mash-Cart carrying Denver players off the field every time Smoke ran one back. My injury report shows a lot of sprained ankles, twisted knees, and pulled muscles, mostly caused when the Denver players tried adjusting to those full-speed jukes, sky high leaps, and the awesome power and speed of the Oakland Outlaws' rookie, only known as… Smoke!"

"Good point, Cal. The Mash-Cart team has been extremely busy so far, taking injured players from the field into the locker room."

"And folks, this is Cal Mitchells and Don Maddmen. We'll be right back after these messages for the second half kick-off between the Oakland Outlaws and the Denver Stallions right here on Monday Night Football."

"And you're off air!" announced Donny.

Maddmen staggered around the broadcasters' booth, kicking empty bottles with his feet, yelling, "Say, Bud, you better get somebody in here to clean this shit up!"

The production assistant, finally fed up with Maddmen's abuse, shouted, "The name's Donny, butt head!"

Maddmen and Mitchells looked at each other and burst into laughter.

Chapter 45

The second half of the game produced slightly different results than the first half. Smoke scored three more spectacular touchdowns and by the end of the game he had set a new single game touchdown record with 9. Even though Denver scored fewer touchdowns, they scored all of their conversion kicks, unlike Oakland, and Denver also set a new NFL record with 10 field goals, finally winning the season opener, 58 to 54.

At the press conference all the reporters were clamoring to hear about Smoke, so the Outlaws' Head Coach, Martin Shell, opted to squelch all questions regarding Smoke by stating, "Smoke came to the Outlaws as a free agent. He walked onto the field during a Special Teams practice, showed us what he could do, and he was immediately signed on the spot! The Outlaws Organization feels his was one of the better deals we've made through free agency, thus far."

"So he's the Outlaws' Mystery Man, your secret weapon?" asked a reporter. "Well, after that devastating running display Smoke unleashed on Denver,

I'm sure he's no longer a mystery man, or anybody's secret weapon. In my opinion, Smoke is the most gifted return man I've ever seen, and quite possibly the best of all time," Coach Shell proudly announced.

"That's a mighty bold statement for you to make, don't you think?" asked a member of the press.

"Son, were you even at today's game? I don't know what game you watched, but have any of you ever seen any running like what Smoke did today? Now seriously, you tell me what you saw."

"We saw the fastest, most dangerous kick returner—ever!" agreed the room full of reporters.

"There you have it then. We finally agree on something!" said the coach sarcastically.

"Give us some stats on him coach," came a request.

"Well, he's 6'7" tall, he weighs 375 lbs. We haven't taken the time to clock him in the 40, 50 or 100 yards, but we believe he just might be the fastest player, or even the fastest man, alive."

"Is he really that fast or did he just catch Denver off guard?" came another question from the reporting pool.

"Well…both! I believe Smoke is going to catch the entire league off guard!

And if he stays healthy, he'll give the Outlaws' organization quite the boost this season. He's filled a position that has been our weakest link for some time now. And the organization is extremely pleased that he chose the Outlaws, as I'm sure our fans are, too!"

"C'mon now, that can't be all the information you have on him…"

"I can tell you this; he has let it be known that he came here to score, and not to be interviewed, or hounded by the press or paparazzi, so save your energy. With that said, I have a direct quote from Smoke. "I'm not here to do interviews or pose for photos. I'm here to score!" end quote. And the Outlaws' organization plans on honoring his wishes. So, any further information regarding Smoke will have to come directly from him... if he wishes. Give the kid some time, let him get settled in to the way the NFL does things, let the fans win him over. After all, there're no greater fans than Oakland Outlaws' fans!"

After the press conference, the Outlaws' Public Relations Department got busy developing a press release about their rookie kick return phenom. The press photos showed Smoke in mid-air with defenders below him crashing into each other. There was a comic strip caption under the photos that read, "Duh… Which Way Did He Go?"

The next photo showed Smoke's name on the back of his jersey as he landed, and streaked away from Denver tacklers.

The third photo was a close-up of the 1 word on the back of Smoke's helmet— GONE!

All the hype may have pacified most of the reporters, but there was one reporter who wasn't satisfied with what she was being spoon fed. She had never met a professional entertainer who didn't love to have their pictures plastered any and everywhere they could. She smelled a story in the making and once she got the scent, she became a mad dog about sniffing out cover-ups.

Chapter 46

At birth she was named Brenda Jean Jackson, "BJ" for short. During her teens she became aware of the oppressions her ancestors had suffered at the hands of slave owners, and she decided to change her name. As far as she was concerned, her name was a hand-me-down name, forced on her ancestors by their white oppressors. So, to express her status as a Free Black Woman, aware of the struggles then and now by black people everywhere, especially black women, she changed her name to Kilah D'abu, and proclaimed that her name meant "Woman of Power!"

Kilah D'abu lived in the city of Palo Alto in northern California. Palo Alto is a little college town that caters to the world-renowned Stanford University in the same manner that the little city of Berkeley, California, caters to the University of California at Berkeley.

Kilah took her years of college underground newspaper experience, and her brash outspoken conspiracy theory activism, coupled with her martyr mentality, and opened her own underground publication.

She called the publication "DIRE MAGAZINE," and wrote editorials under the name of "DREAD-WOMAN," specializing in truths, theories, and religious beliefs as she saw them. Kilah solicited anyone she could to advertise in her magazine, and through their subscriptions she was able to publish her opinionated viewpoints throughout the college underground markets.

Standing all of 4' 1" tall, sporting grungy dreadlock extensions, and speaking with a manufactured West Indies' accent, this Dread-Woman was no stranger to opposition. Kilah had been dismissed from other underground publications do to her rebellious, unyielding, outspoken accusations against prominent people of the community.

Unfortunately, her mouth pissed someone off to the point of ordering a drive-by on one of her workplaces to teach her a lesson. The hail of bullets that sprayed the office injured neither Kilah nor any of her coworkers, and true to form, she refused to entertain the thought that it was her mouth that had put her and coworkers in danger in the first place. The Dread-Woman was immediately fired from that publication.

Once Kilah D'abu put her sights on a target, no opposing reasoning could sway her. She was obsessed by an unwavering need to be right, all the time, and to always have the last word, thus the need for her own publication, DIRE MAGAZINE, which had become quite successful in the underground.

Most decision-makers of Palo Alto hated seeing her coming, and tried avoiding her like the plague, but as far as she was concerned, responses like these only strengthened her resolve, opinions, and determination.

These days, Kilah was wrapped up in a new conspiracy theory, and when a mystery began formulating in that big brain of hers, she went balls-out to discover fact from fiction, even if it meant fabricating a story from circumstantial evidence alone. The Dread-Woman would put her opinion out to whoever would listen, no matter what the price!

For the last few weeks Kilah and her assistant, Vye, had been investigating the disappearance of Donovan Mocion, The Fastest Man Alive, and she thought it no coincidence that the Outlaws' head coach made the comment about Smoke being the fastest man alive, especially since no one had ever heard of Smoke before, and

Donovan seemingly fell off the face of the earth after the 2020 Olympic Games. To Kilah, one plus one never equaled what it was supposed to.

Kilah decided the best place to begin was to compare any photos of Donovan Mocion with images of Smoke.

"Vye, do we have any photos of Donovan Mocion in the archives?"

"Nope! He was the only athlete who didn't like getting his picture taken.

"That sounds familiar. Well, here's what I need you to do. Go to the University of Washington's website and see if you can track down any pictures of him. If so, download them for me," instructed Kilah.

"OK," replied Vye, who immediately began surfing the Husky's website.

Having no luck finding a picture on the Washington Husky website, she did a random search of the University of Washington's academic website and finally located a photo in the strangest place…the Scholastic Decathlon Competition archives.

Kilah was kicking back, sipping on a mug of tea when Vye popped into her office.

"Kilah, Kilah, I found one! And check him out—the man is wake-the-dead gorgeous."

Kilah took the copy from Vye, stared at it for a while then said, "I want to have his babies!" looking at Vye with a horny expression and licking her lips.

"Now, now, girlfriend, I thought you took meat off the menu," reminded Vye.

"Don't misunderstand me, baby, I'm definitely a sushi woman, but a little beef from time to time keeps the juices flowing, and the heart pounding. And he looks like he could do some serious pounding."

Unimpressed with the direction the conversation was headed, Vye said, "Can we get back on focus here? Now, other than screwing his brains out and bearing his children, what do you want to do next?"

Kilah, fanning herself with both hands, said, "Whoosh...hot flash! Let's dig up all the information we can about his accident and where he's been recovering. Then check if we have any contacts there."

Vye's research discovered that Donovan had been treated for a year at Cedars-Sinai Medical Center in Beverly Hills, California. She searched her contact numbers file and located a contact person they had used on several occasions.

"Hey, Jimbo. This is Vye. How's it hangin' man?"

"Well, I can think of one place I'd like it to be—you still on your seafood diet?"

"Yeah, for the most part, but variety is still the spice of life."

"Well, Vye, I know you didn't just get horny and finally decided to let me have my way with you, so...what's-up?"

"For this info, Jimbo, I'll owe you the big one," promised Vye.

"Yeah, yeah, yeah, promises, promises. What do you need little darlin'?"

"Do you recall the name Donovan Mocion?" asked Vye.

"The dude who won all those medals at the Hawaiian Olympics, and then just dropped from sight?"

"Exactly! Well, my girl and I are doing some research on him and I discovered he was a patient at your place. Kilah and I will make it worth your while if you'd get us all the information you can on him," said Vye.

"Well, give me a few days and I'll see what I can come up with. Oh, by the way, when you said you and your girl making it worth my while, what exactly do you mean?" asked an always-horny Jimbo, who had been trying to seduce both Vye and Kilah together for the longest time.

"Well, I can't make promises for Kilah, but I can make some of your fantasies a reality," said Vye, telling Jimbo what he wanted to hear.

"DEAL! I'll call you tomorrow."

After Vye hung up the phone, she said out loud, "What a dog. He's not going to get anywhere near this coo-chi."

Then she sat back in her chair and quietly recalled the time when things got plenty hot and passionate between her and Jimbo. The memory put a smile on her face, but that had been before Kilah officially entered Vye's world.

Chapter 47

True to his word, Jimbo began digging around for information about Donovan Mocion. The first place he checked was the file-room where patients' records were stored. Jimbo didn't have access to those records so he had to enlist the services of Wanda Watson, the file room supervisor. Wanda was a big girl who loved getting her fancy tickled. She and Jimbo had locked pelvises a few times over the years and Jimbo didn't mind a repeat performance to get Wanda to help him out.

"Hey, Hot Stuff," greeted Jimbo as he strolled into the file room and smoothly grabbed a double handful of Wanda's roomy behind.

"OOH, Jim! You just treat me any old kind of way—and I like it!" replied Wanda with a big grin on her perfectly smooth, attractive round face. "Aren't we overdue?" questioned Wanda, always wanting to get her physical needs satisfied. "Ah, baby, that's the main reason I came down. When can we get together for a sweatin' good time?" asked Jimbo, still holding onto Wanda's behind. "Well...," began Wanda, sliding her hand down to massage Jimbo's crouch, feeling an instant erection building. "I think I can fit you in tonight. Is that good for you?"

Jimbo let out a moan of pleasure and said, "I'll be by at eight, sharp, so you be ready."

"I'm always ready for you, baby!" replied Wanda. "Now, what else can I do for you?" asked Wanda, as she released her loving grip on Jimbo's crotch.

"Several months ago we had a patient named Donovan Mocion," began Jimbo.

"You mean the brother who was in that airplane crash?"

"Yeah, that's the one. Do you have any records on him?"

Wanda got on her terminal and began a search of Donovan's name. That effort tuned up zero.

"That's strange," announced Wanda. "I know the man was here. It was right after the Olympic Games, but there's not a trace of his records in my system, as though he was never here, and I saw that beautiful man a few times in his wheelchair, heading to physical therapy. Sorry, baby. You might want to check with P.T. and see if they have anything on him."

"Thanks, sweetie. I'll see you tonight."

"Can't wait," replied a grinning Wanda.

While on his way to the Physical Therapy Department, Jimbo decided to check with the pharmacy. Anyone messed up like Donovan was, had to be on some serious drugs.

Bruce Baxter was the pharmacy supervisor, and he had a thing for Jimbo, too. Jimbo knew Bruce would help him out, hoping to get into Jimbo's pants, but Jimbo had no desires on back door bopping with another guy. Still, Bruce was a nice guy, so Jimbo treated him with kindness and respect.

"Hi, Jimmy," shouted Bruce. "So good to see you again—where you been hiding?"

"Brucie, Brucie. What's up baby? How's it hangin'?" greeted Jimbo.

Bruce approached Jimbo and delicately took his hand, and then leaned in and whispered into Jimbo's ear, "I'll tell you Jimmy, any time you really want to find out, I'll be more than happy to slide you in."

"That's sweet of you Bruce, but perhaps you can help me out another way," said Jimbo, taking one step back putting some breathing room between them.

Brucie' breath smelt like he had been busy recently.

"Anything you want, Jimmy, I'll be more than glad to give it to you," flirted Bruce, batting his eyelashes.

"I've been trying to track down a former patient of ours. His name is Donovan Mocion."

Bruce began using his hands to fan himself at the mention of Donovan's name. Then he waved Jimbo in closer, like he had a secret to tell. "I'm not supposed to talk about him. I can get into some serious trouble. His records were sealed by someone extremely high up the food chain." Then he leaned in and whispered into Jimbo's ear, "Global Pharmaceuticals is involved."

Just the mention of Global Pharmaceuticals caused Jimbo to pause and the hairs to rise on his forearms; every subsidiary of Global Pharmaceuticals, such as Cedars-Sinai, knew not to go snooping around in their business.

"But Jimmy, I will tell you this because I like you, and someday I only hope that you will find it in your heart..."

"Bruce!" interrupted Jimbo, "What can you tell me?"

"Well...ok," then Bruce quietly spelled out Donovan's name, looking around like the walls had eyes and ears. "We send meds out to him all the time. I can give you that mailing address."

Jimbo wasn't sure if he should get in that deep, but he couldn't stop now.

Just the thought of having Vye…besides, who was going to find out?

Bruce gave Jimbo Donovan's address and told Jimbo, "You be careful with that and please, don't tell anyone I gave it to you."

"I won't," promised Jimbo, giving Bruce a gentle rub on his cheek before turning to leave.

Bruce watched as Jimbo strutted down the hall, imagining all the pleasures he could have with him.

Chapter 48

Everyone loves a mystery. Jimbo was no exception, and since he had gone this far, he figured he might as well go all the way. In the best case scenario, he would get into Vye's, and maybe even Kilah's, pants. The worst case…well, he tried not to think about the worst case. What he did think about was which other departments could give him more info about Donovan Mocion. He decided to check with x-ray, saving physical therapy until last. Beth Jones worked in x-ray. She and Jimbo had been out a few times, had a few laughs, spent a couple of nights together, but Beth wanted to keep it light, keep it physical. Her husband of many years had passed away recently. For her, that marriage was more like a prison than a union shared of love. So now, all Mrs. Jones wanted to do was be free and enjoy all that life had to offer.

When Jimbo entered the x-ray department he was greeted with a beautiful warm smile and, "Hello, James, nice to see you again. And what are you up to these days?" Mrs. Jones was well aware of Jimbo's womanizing reputation; she had no problem with that. So what if he had an overactive libido? She was an aggressive, on the prowl cougar herself, and she appreciated having a young strong 'service-stud' on call from time to time.

"Beth, you're not pissed because we haven't seen much of each other lately...are you?"

"Why, no James. I know when our time permits, we'll enjoy each other's companionship."

Beth could tell Jimbo wasn't there to set up a romantic interlude so she calmly asked, "What can I do for you today, James?"

She spoke in a clear, above a whisper, husky, very sexy, very soothing, disarming voice, and every time Jimbo heard it, he melted inside, and became rock hard on the outside. And he knew from experience that the only way to deal with her was the straight up approach, so he honestly answered her question.

"I promised someone that I would find out all the information I could about Donovan Mocion's treatment, and I thought you might be able to fill in some blanks I have."

Beth's smile quickly became serious, and her voice became somewhat scary as she said, "You're playing with fire this time, James. I suggest you and whoever drop this inquiry immediately. Mr. Mocion is being watched from on high and those watching don't like others snooping into their business. Now James, I like you, so I want you to really hear me on this...*drop it!* Those who piss these people off come up missing!" Beth caressed Jimbo's face with a concerned hand, then said, "You think seriously about what I've told you, and I hope we can get together soon." Then she turned and briskly walked away, leaving Jimbo standing there looking dazed.

> "*Damn*!" thought Jimbo, "*that's the second time I've been warned to leave this alone. But there's just one more place to check before I drop it.*"

Halima Muldrow, a newly hired physical therapist, had exchanged glances with Jimbo at the company picnic a few months ago. Jimbo decided this was the perfect opportunity to reintroduce himself, so he put on his most effective stud persona and strolled up to her and said, "Hey! Boo! I've been thinking bout you. What's up?"

"Hi, Jimbo," said Halima, with a grin on her baby face. "What brings you down here to the boonies?"

"A couple of reasons; first, to check you out again, and second to see if I can get some information on a patient who was here a while ago."

Wanting to get business out the way before she got into any pleasure, she asked, "What's the patient's name?"

"Donovan Mocion," Jimbo said softly, somewhat believing the walls did have eyes and ears. "Ever hear of him?"

"Nope...before my time, but I'll check the files and see if anything comes up," replied Halima, wanting to be helpful.

She did a name search on her terminal and turned up a redirection message that read, "See file Topaz & Jade." She went to the redirected file and it contained a great deal of information about two Capuchin Monkeys, along with a locator indicating that the monkeys had been donated to Mr. Donovan Mocion for home care needs. There was also and address. Halima made a printout for Jimbo, then handed it to him saying, "Now, what about that first thing on your mind...what was it? Oh yeah, checkin' me out. Well, I'm standing here. You like what you see?"

Jimbo compared the address Halima had just given him against the one he had gotten from Bruce. They were the same which meant chances were it was Donovan's real home address. Then he realized Halima had asked him a question about "liking what he saw."

"Absolutely!" answered Jimbo, refocusing his attention on her, and adding the printout to his data folder on Donovan.

"Well, then it's your move," she said, pressing the issue, wanting to find out if Jimbo was as good as the reputation that preceded him claimed.

Jimbo leaned in next to Halima's ear and using his most seductive voice said, "Why don't you give me your digits so we can connect over the weekend?"

She smiled and said, "We can do that," and wrote down her phone number and handed it to Jimbo.

Jimbo placed a soft warm kiss on Halima's cheek, turned and walked away.

After a few steps he turned back toward her and waved; he just knew she was checkin' out his butt while he walked away. Halima blushed as if she was caught doing something indecent, then she waved back and went about her business.

With all the information on Donovan Mocion, Jimbo just knew he was 'in there' with Vye, and possibly Kilah, too. He was more than anxious to get home and make contact.

CHAPTER 49

Vye had also been busy. She had discovered that Donovan had transferred from University of Washington all the way down to Stanford University in Stanford, California, to complete his doctorate degree. When she checked with Stanford, she found out he had accepted a professorship at the Stanford University Medical Center. While Vye was compiling her report for Kilah, her phone rang, and the male voice on the other end said, "Hey, baby, you ready to get busy?"

"Excuse me," Vye responded abruptly. "Who the hell is this?"

"It's Jimbo!"

"Oh, hi Jimbo," said Vye, not excited to hear from him.

Jimbo, detecting Vye's lack of enthusiasm, said, "What's up, baby? You forget our deal? Because I've got some juicy information for you and Kilah. When are we gonna get together so I can collect my reward?"

Vye said to herself, "*You horny dog*!" Then she told Jimbo, "Kilah's out of town right now, so, how about you give me the information and the three of us will get together later?"

Jimbo thinking about all the warnings he had gotten while digging into this subject, said angrily, "In case you didn't know, there are a lot of people wanting to keep information about your Donovan Mocion quite. More than once I was warned to leave this alone, but I came up with the info anyway! I don't know if those warnings are true or not, but I stuck my neck out because we made a deal. And remember...you came at me...not the other way around!"

"You're right, Jimbo," admitted Vye, "I've had a long day and you caught me a little off guard. Can we start over?"

"OK by me," replied Jimbo, smiling on the other end of the line because his display of anger worked.

And, like a finger snap, a revitalized Vye said, "Jimbo, I've been waiting for your call. Do you have something for me?"

"I sure do," replied Jimbo, adding, "Now that's the type of response I was looking for, Vye."

"I'm here to please," said Vye. "When do you want to get together?"

"How about tonight?"

"Sounds good to me. I'll meet you at your place, oh, let's say... around 9?" "That'll work, I'll see you then," said Jimbo and he hung up the phone, feeling himself getting excited.

"That girl is such a freak," said Jimbo. "And I'm gonna wear that ass out tonight like it's the last tail on earth! Oh, SHIT!" yelled Jimbo. "Wanda! I don't want to mess that up," so he called and smooth-talked Wanda, postponing their date until the following night. He told her he had a very important business meeting pop up at the last minute.

Vye and Jimbo had crossed paths before and both wished they had more time to together. Vye was bi-sexual; she and Kilah had developed a romantic on again—off again relationship, which was currently on and going pretty good, so she began feeling a little conflicted about giving Jimbo what he wanted, but once she remembered what he had to offer in the form of pleasure, not to mention the inside information he said he had dug up, she became excited about seeing him, and caught the next Maglev train down to L.A..

Precisely at 9 pm, Vye rang Jimbo's doorbell. She had her hair up, revealing her long sexy neckline, and was wearing an extremely informative second skin body suit, and to semi hide this sexy outfit, she wore a loose-fitting sheer cotton shawl, with matching skirt, which she immediately removed once she was outside Jimbo's door. Jimbo's tongue fell to the floor when he opened his door and saw her in that body suit. After he rolled it back into his mouth, he said, "My, my, my, when you said you aim to please, you were serious."

"Absolutely!" remarked Vye, pushing Jimbo aside as she entered his apartment. "I know how to make good on my word. Now... show me what you got."

Jimbo, not missing a beat, threw open the caftan he was wearing, revealing his equipment to Vye, who said, "Most impressive Jimbo, but I've seen it before, remember? Besides, that's not what I meant!"

"Without a doubt I remembered, why else would I jump at the chance for us to thrill each other again?" Jimbo took Vye in his arms and kissed her passionately. With no hesitation on her part, Vye immediately got into his kiss by pressing her tight, hard body as close to his as physically possible without him being inside her. When they came up for air, Jimbo took a step backwards, allowing himself to fully extend outward and said, "Let me show you what I've got for you," and handed Vye a folder containing all the data he had gathered on Donovan Mocion. He had even copied the information onto a disk for her.

After Vye reviewed the data, she was more than pleased, and said, "Before we get on with the pleasures at hand, can I use your computer to forward this data to Kilah?"

"That's why I copied it to disk. I thought you would want to do just that." "So, you're anticipating my moves, huh? Well, when I finish forwarding this, we're going to do things that we've never done to each other before," promised Vye, slipping her hand inside Jimbo's caftan, grabbing a handful of him, squeezing and slowly caressing while the data was being transferred. Next, she focused all her attention on what was in hand, causing Jimbo to moan with pleasure.

"I've dreamt of pulling you into my arms, lifting you off the floor, and then sliding you down on me, and we'd be gettin' it until we passed out in each others arms," admitted Jimbo.

"Well, then," said Vye as she began peeling down her body suit, and when she got it around her pumps, she kicked it across the room saying, "I won't need this for the rest of the night!" Then she slowly climbed up on Jimbo, wrapped her arms around his neck and her legs around his waist. Jimbo grabbed two handfuls of Vye's tight, round ass, lined her up on him, and Vye moaned as she slid down around Jimbo. After she had taken every inch of him, they both let out a long sigh, then Vye started stroking in and out while Jimbo stood in the center of the room bouncing her up and down on him.

In between moans of pleasure, Vye managed to whisper into Jimbo's ear, "I had forgotten how great you felt inside me, Jim."

When he heard Vye use his proper name, he began long stroking her, driving her wild with ecstasy.

Vye's feet never touched the floor all night long.

When they finally made it to the bed, still connected, not missing a stroke, they hear a clicking sound coming from the front door, and when they turned in the direction of the noise they were blinded by several flashes of bright light, followed by just as many soft pops.

Vye and Jimbo never knew what hit them!

The door quietly closed behind their intruder, leaving Jimbo and Vye locked in each other's embrace, never to move again.

Moments later, a car silently pulled away from Jimbo's apartment. A cell phone began ringing and the single occupant of the car answered it. There was a female voice who said only one word… "***REPORT!***"

The voice answering the phone replied, "Subjects terminated! Request cleansing."

And the line went dead.

Chapter 50

"Hello, sports' fans! Welcome to this edition of "The Complete NFL" pre- game show. I'm your host, James Brown."

"JB is 'The Hardest Working Man in Show Business!'" yelled his adoring fans from off camera, jumping up and down behind the set, trying to get their images caught by the camera.

Brown smiled down at his fans, giving them a wink while nodding his head up and down, agreeing with their comments.

As a child James was teased for being named after the great entertainer and Soul Brother #1, James Brown. Back then it wasn't out of character for little Jimmy to perform a chorus of, "I Got the Feelin'...Baby!" for his closest friends, complete with the James Brown skate; he had all James Brown's dance moves down pat back then. But these days JB relished in the fact that "Papa's Got a Brand New Bag" and he was getting paid, well paid, for being a broadcasting sports analyst.

Shaking that little tad of trivia from his mind, JB looked straight into the camera and continued.

"Tonight our analysts include the greatest defensive back to ever play the game... "Neon" Leon Davis..."

"Looking good!" said Leon, blowing a kiss to all his fans in TV land.

"We also have with us 10 time pro bowl wide receiver... Julius "Hollywood" Irvine..."

"Roll cameras!" said Hollywood, holding his hands out in front of him as if making a football catch for the cameras.

"And folks, we also have, arguably, the best tight end to have ever laced up a pair of football cleats... Sterling "Mr. Clutch" Silver..."

Sterling gave the camera a serious look then said the words he made famous… "Get me the ball!"

"Along with these outstanding characters," continued JB, "we have 4 time Superbowl MVP winner, Vick "The Cannon" McNabb..."

"Go deep!" said McNabb, as he tossed an imaginary football at the camera.

"And to finish off our panel of expert analysts, we have the most feared tackle to ever play the game... Seth "Back Breaker" Zorwarski..."

Zorwarski looked deep into the camera, frowned, and then growled.

"Well said, Zorwarski," added JB. "Well said, indeed! Now sports fans, we have a special treat tonight as Shame LaRue, whose beauty and body prove there must be a God, takes us "Inside the Locker Room" for one of her in-depth, behind- the-scenes interviews."

"Hello, boys," said Shame, giving a wave, a wink, and a little hip shaking from her remote location in Pittsburg.

"Hiiii, Shaaammme," came the weak sounding, goggle-eyed, spellbound, helplessly infatuated replies from the panel of jocks, followed by the off camera high jinks of nudges, wagging tongues, and falling to their knees in prayer, that some guys go through when they see a fine looking woman they wished they had a chance with.

"Well, Shame, we're all looking for some hot interviews from you later tonight," said JB.

"Have no worries, JB, I'll come through with the goods," promised Shame. "Well, fellows," began JB, who turned to face his panel and was completely surprised to see them still drooling over Shame who was grinning and blowing kisses at them.

"All right fellas, focus up, we've got a show to do here," said JB in a scolding tone. "Tonight our pre-game show takes a look at the upcoming game between the Oakland Outlaws and the Pittsburgh Steelmen. And the big news is the Outlaws' rookie, Smoke, and how he has set the NFL record books on fire with his dazzling kick returns."

"No doubt," said Neon Leon. "I've returned a few kicks for touchdowns myself, and I have plenty of great moves, but I've never seen anyone as off the planet as this kid called Smoke! This guy has moves like I haven't seen since Gale Sayers, Walter "Sweetness" Payton, and the incomparable Berry Sanders. Over the past weeks we've literally seen Smoke stop on a dime, instantly reverse field while running at what looked like full speed, juke defenders straight into the ground, use spin moves to perfection, sending players colliding into each other, and my favorite, the old somersault over oncoming tacklers. And I swear, I even saw him do the "Ali Shuffle" during a game once. Smoke is the complete package!"

"I agree," began Hollywood. "This man has provided us some breath-taking returns. I love to watch the way he shifts his weight, faking the defenders off their feet without losing a step, then he accelerates to blazing speeds at the blink of an eye. He even hits defenders with the force of a freight train. He's all the great runners of history wrapped into one, and then he sets new standards. The man is phenomenal!"

"Speaking from a quarterback's perspective," said Vick "The Cannon" McNabb, "if I had a phenom on my offensive squad with Smoke's hand strength, leaping ability, and world class speed, plus being the size of a tackle—*man*...we would take the game to new heights, rewriting all the offensive record books.

Somebody should think about getting this guy to play offense."

"Back Breaker" Zorwarski let loose a series of growls, grunts, coughs, and guttural vocalizations, and then finished with "Ha-ha-ha-hah!"

"Yea, without a doubt, Back Breaker, I've experience you knocking me on my butt many a time over the years, and I've still got the marks to remember you by, but I have to agree with you, there. If I saw this monster running full speed towards me, I'd get out of the way, too!" admitted Sterling "Mr. Clutch" Silver.

Back Breaker let loose a few more growls, grunts, and groans to complete his train of thought.

"We understand, Back Breaker, and we all know for a fact that you are nobody's bitch, and I don't think anyone would blame you for turning tail and running from Smoke. I personally wouldn't," reassured JB, with a slight smile and wink at the camera.

Back Breaker gave JB a weird look, the type of look he gives when he's about to knock a player out, and he let loose a couple of short grunts and puffs, then leapt to his feet, moving in on JB. The other panelists grabbed him, telling him, "Wait a minute, big guy, JB doesn't think you're a sissy because you said you would run from Smoke. Hell, anyone who values their health wouldn't come at that guy head on. Look at what happened to Scribendi," reminded Vick "The Cannon" McNabb.

Having retreated to the other side of the studio, JB announced, "And now for a special interview with Shame. Shame...you with us?

"Thanks, JB," began Shame. "I'm here outside the Steelmen's locker room with Head Coach Spike Conlin and Special Teams' Coach, Stewart Korval. How are you coaches doing?" asked Shame.

"We're doing great! Our team is in first place!" replied Coach Conlin.

"Well, let me get straight to the question that most people would like an answer to...Smoke; how are you gonna handle him?"

"Well, we've come up with something real special for him," replied Special Teams' Coach Korval. "And that's about all we can say...not wanting to tip our hand before the game, and all."

"Well, Coach Conlin, let me ask you this...Are you guys afraid of the tremendous scoring potential that Smoke brings into today's game?"

"Well, Shame, we're aware of the scoring threat a player with his gifts represents, but we have confidence that our team is much better prepared than other teams have been, and we will show the fans just what we mean at kick off. Now if you'll excuse us, we have a game to play."

"Well guys, there you have it. The first place Pittsburgh Steelmen are about to get their shot at stopping the Outlaws' mysterious unstoppable rookie, known only as ***Smoke***. Back to you in the studio, JB."

"Thanks, Shame. And speaking of Smoke, right now we're going to feature the Oakland Outlaws' rookie in our 'Stretched Out' segment. Normally, in this segment we count down the week's top 5 hits, but this week we'll focus on the incredible ability Smoke has of leaving some of the best tacklers in the league stretched out on the playing field.

"At # 5," began JB, "we have two tacklers moving in for the old sandwich smash on Smoke, but just before they collide into him, Smoke leaps over the defenders heads causing them to hit each other—full speed—head on. They got...STRETCHED OUT!"

"Coming in at # 4," said Neon Leon, "this defender has Smoke in his sights, but Smoke throws a juke on this dude that causes his feet to get tangled together, making him flip into the air turning a somersault, then he landed flat on his face... STRETCHED OUT!"

"For # 3," said Hollywood, "I picked this defender making a move on Smoke from behind, and just as he is about to pounce, Smoke turns on the jets and just like the back of his helmet reads, he's... GONE! The camera catches the amazed look on the defender's face just before he trips into the turf...STRETCHED OUT!"

"In the # 2 spot," began The Cannon, "we have a hero who's decided to take Smoke head on, and in the end the fans hear a tremendous clash created by shoulder pad to helmet contact, followed by the sight of Smoke blazing down the field for 6. And when the fans finally look back up field to the point of impact, they see a body lying on the field, all by himself...STRETCHED OUT!"

"And in our # 1 position," began JB while everybody looked in the direction of Back Breaker who, in his usual unique vocalizations of grunts, growls, huffs, and puffs, got his message across to roll the tape.

"The replay tape shows a defender assuming a tackling position, while Smoke is heading full speed, straight at him. But before Smoke reaches him, the would-be tackler decides to get off the tracks of this runaway freight train, only his decision to move comes too late, because Smoke barrels right over him, leaving the guy lying on the field...STRETCHED OUT!"

Back Breaker looked into the camera and laughed, "Ha-ha-ha-hah!"

"And folks, that about wraps it up for this edition of 'The Complete NFL'" said JB. "Coming up next, the first place Pittsburgh Steelmen take on the Oakland Outlaws...enjoy the game!"

"Welcome to Heinz Field, home of the first place Pittsburgh Steelmen. I'm Martin Newberry along with Troy Sharpe, and Bart Gimble. These two teams have never liked each other. This is a statement game! And the statement comes from the Steelmen saying this is their house and they refuse to rent to the Outlaws! The Steelmen have been talking smack in the newspapers about locking the kid out of their house and that nobody is going to make their Special Teams look like school kids on the playground. The newspapers were building the game up to be Smoke against The Steel Curtain of the Steelmen."

"That's right, Martin," injected Bart. "In fact, the Steelmen think they've come up with a plan to neutralize the Outlaws' phenom return specialist. The players and coaches of the NFL are very smart, most of them anyway…well, at least some of them, and you can't keep fooling them forever. However, Smoke's abilities are the real deal, and he's got the athleticism that no one has ever seen or experienced before."

"Like most of the NFL fans in attendance today, I won't believe the Steelmen will stop Smoke until I see it, Martin," commented Troy.

"The media has been feeding the frenzy all week here in Pittsburgh, and finally, it's come down to put up or shut up for the 4 and 0 Steelmen. My question for the Outlaws is how long will they base their entire scoring on Smoke? Clearly he has kept them alive in all their games, so far. The Outlaws have a 3 and 1 record this season, even with Smoke scoring 24+ points each game, the rest of that Outlaws' team has got to pick up the slack," Troy pointed out.

"Good point, Troy," acknowledged Martin. "And we're minutes away from getting the answer to that, and many other questions today as the Pittsburgh Steelmen play the Oakland Outlaws."

CHAPTER 51

Kilah had season tickets and she never missed an Outlaws' game, no matter where they played. But her going to Pittsburgh had a double reason. She was not to be denied her picture of Smoke. She was extremely excited over the data that Vye sent her, and had tried to make contact with Vye several times, but never could reach her.

"Come on girl, answer the phone." Kilah called, texted, and even tried relaying messages, but no matter how she tried, there was no reply from Vye, and by now Kilah was getting a little unraveled over the whereabouts of her friend and lover. She finally put contacting Vye on hold until after the game.

The rowdy inhabitants of Oakland's legendary Black Hole spared no expense on their costumes, or on having a great time at all of the Outlaws' games; Kilah was no exception. With her tiny stature and dread locks extending down past her butt, she looked like a black version of the Adams' Family's cousin It, and when she made up her face into the traditional skull and cross bones, she really stood out as a *creature* from the Black Hole.

The fans from both sides of the Oakland/San Francisco Bay area, as well as outlining suburbs, gathered one day each week to express themselves in all their furious, hideous glory. Their preparations began hours before the kick off. When completed, they became the most frightening, vocal, unruly, enthusiastic, loving fans any team could have. Amidst the rising vapors from the searing Bar-B-Qued flesh, along with the massive consumption of beer and other alcohol at the pre- game tailgate parties, the main name on the lips of every Black Hole inhabitant…was… ***Smoke!***

By now, the fact that he never removed his helmet during the game had become part of his mystery man persona, and the fans around the league ate it up, especially the fans in the Outlaws' Black Hole. They supported any serious rebel, so to them Smoke was their new poster boy hero.

The Black Hole faithful created several colorful slogans which they flew during the games...

Smoke...GONE WITH THE WIN!

SMOKIN!

Smoke—THAT!

Smoke MATH…1 Carry = 6 Points!

The Smoke RATIO means…Automatically give the Outlaws at least 24 points per game.

Smoke had captured the imagination of everyone who loved seeing a runner catch the football then negotiate around, over, and through players, coast to coast, and then score 6 points. Smoke had turned kick returning into an art form and football fans world wide loved to witness him work his magic. His name had become known in every remote corner of the globe.

Smoke had begun to appreciate the adulation given him by the Black Hole fans, so every time he scored a touchdown in the Black Hole, he'd leap off the field and over posted banners that read….

THE JUMP ZONE!

YOU CAN'T CATCH WHAT YOU DON'T SEE!

TOO LATE TO GET OFF THE TRACKS...THE TRAIN IS GONE!

… and into the waiting arms of these outrageous Oakland Outlaws' fans.

Kilah, being well aware of Smoke's new habit, planted remote cameras in multiple positions throughout the Black Hole to make sure she didn't miss a decent shot of him. She even had a hidden camera on her person, just in case she got close enough to snap her own shot.

True to their boasting, the Steelmen did have a game plan to keep the ball away from Smoke's hands. They achieved it through kicking the ball out of the end zone, out of bounds, using onside kicks, and even going for it on fourth down instead of kicking away. This plan worked for the entire first half of play, resulting in a Steelmen lead of 21 to 0 over the Outlaws. The legendary Steel Curtain had completely shut down Oakland's offense, including Smoke.

In the locker room the Outlaws' Special Teams Coach Garland, shouted, "ST—huddle up on me!"

The rest of the squad followed Head Coach Shell to the other side of the locker room.

"I think it's time to break out our little book of magic and trick plays," said Coach Garland, with a look of vengeance on his face.

"Freakin' aye!" shouted Terry.

"'Bout damn time," shouted Head Coach Shell from across the room, who then addressed the entire team.

"Men, it's time to pull out all the stops and rub their faces in their own dirt.

Now, we've seen their best so let's show them what we think of their first place ranking."

"WHOOP ASS on 3!" shouted Head Coach Shell, and he quickly counted, "1, 2, 3," and the entire Outlaws team shouted, "WHOOP ASS!"

"Welcome back for the second half between the Pittsburgh Steelmen and the Oakland Outlaws. The first half was entirely Pittsburgh. Looks like they indeed had the right plan for stopping the Outlaws and their fabulous rookie return specialist, Smoke. So far he hasn't even touched the ball this entire game," began Martin.

"Yeah, but I wouldn't count the kid, or the Outlaws, out just yet," replied Troy. "We've got a lot more football to play. I think the Outlaws did some regrouping during half time and they have something up their sleeves."

"I agree," said Bart. "I liked the way the Outlaws stormed onto the field after half time; they looked like a rejuvenated team. Even Smoke came running out on the field, instead of his usual calm strolling swagger, to the Outlaws' sideline. He even had his sun visor up so the Steelmen could see the look of determination in his eyes."

Kilah tried her best to get a shot of Smoke with his visor up. She snapped off multiple frames and hoped for the best.

Pittsburgh picked up where they left off during the first half, playing deceptively. They gave the look of an onside kick, then at the last moment kicked away. The Outlaws were ready for their trickery this time, and instead of letting the ball float out of bounds in the coffin corner of the end zone, Terry, the other kick returner for Oakland dove and batted the ball back into the end zone like it was a volley ball on the beach, straight into the waiting hands of Smoke, who turned and surveyed the entire field as Pittsburgh defenders quickly closed in on him. One of his teammates made a beautiful block, taking out a Pittsburgh defender along the sideline, giving Smoke all the opening he needed to get through their so-called Steel Curtain. The only things the defenders saw then were the word "GONE" and the number 6 fading from sight in a blur taking the ball to the Steelmen's House— touchdown Outlaws!

The infamous inhabitants of the Black Hole were eagerly awaiting Smoke to make his now famous leap into their waiting arms, and the first costume clad fan to greet him was none other than Kilah the Dread-Woman, her cameras quietly snapping away by remote control. Finally, she was getting pictures of Smoke with his helmet visor in the up position. As Smoke sat on the rim of the stands in the Black Hole, she jumped straight into his lap and looked dead into his eyes and said, "Man, you've got gorgeous eyes—you should show them off more!" while her hidden cameras snapped multiple close-ups of Smoke inside his helmet.

Smoke smiled at her, then gently removed her from his lap, jumped down and trotted over to the Outlaws' bench. Along the way he unexpectedly locked eyes with an Outlaws' cheerleader, causing his heart to race and he almost lost his footing. On the sideline he scanned for her and took a mental snap shot, once he located her.

The Outlaws, having adapted to the Steelmen tricks, went score crazy during the entire second half with trick plays of their own, finally tearing the Steel Curtain down to the ground, in their own house, no less—knocking Pittsburgh out of first place.

Chapter 52

So far all had been going as planned. Smoke was able to arrive unseen, and get away unnoticed, for every game. The entire Outlaws camp had gotten behind his mystery man persona, and they went out of their way to help keep his identity a mystery from prying eyes. It was like a game to fool the reporters and paparazzi. It also put more butts in the seats, so as far as the Oakland Outlaws' organization was concerned, it was a great advertising ploy; they were making tons of money from their Smoke / Man of Mystery merchandising campaigns even without Smoke actually participating.

Smoke had so impressed the powers-that-be in the Outlaws' organization that they now provided him with private flights to and from away games, giving the flight crew specific orders—no questions asked. All the flight crew knew was they were transporting V.I.P. clients from the Oakland Outlaws' organization.

Flying in the small jet gave Smoke anxieties about his plane crash, and feelings of dèjá vu set in. His mind flashed over all he could remember about that tragic flight. He recalled the feelings of joy and jubilation that he and his parents were experiencing over his accomplishments at the Olympics. He could feel the warm loving hugs they shared in the beginning of their return flight to the states. Every memory was crystal clear, right up to the point where the flight attendant brought him another drink. He kept hearing her words over and over again in his mind.

> *"Is there is anything I can do to make your flight more pleasurable?"*

His mind kept echoing those words until he realized it wasn't his mind echoing the words at all; they were real words being spoken in real time, and the voice that spoke them was one he would never forget. It was the same voice asking him the same thing, right now, in real time!

"Is there anything I can do to make your flight more pleasurable?" asked the flight attendant.

Smoke came out of his daze, looked directly at the flight attendant, paused, then smiled and answered, "Nothing for me, thank you."

"*What the hell is going on here?*" he shouted in his mind. "*Is my mind playing a sick trick on me, or is it the serum?*" He wasn't sure so he got up and walked around the cabin, trying to get his mind around what was real.

He kept asking himself, *"Is this the same flight attendant?"*

Myron was keeping a close eye on his friend, ready to spring to Smoke's aide if need be. They had a plan where Myron would administer a knockout shot if things became dicey while on the road.

Smoke composed himself, then asked the flight attendant, "Do you think the pilots would mind if I checked out the cockpit?"

"Not at all!" she said in one of those fake flight attendant's voices. "It's your dime we're flying on."

She escorted him to the cockpit and announced, "Captain, we have a visitor." Then she returned to the cabin.

When Smoke saw the pilot and co-pilot, he was convinced that his mind was not tricking him. This was the same flight crew that he and his parents had at the Olympics in Hawaii.

"Glad to have you on board," said a cheery Captain. "You guys really kicked the crap out of my team today," said the co-pilot.

"Yeah, we did own their house today," replied Smoke, not revealing that he recognized the three of them.

"So, both you guys from Pittsburgh?" he asked, generating low level chatter, still fishing for answers.

"Yep," the pilot answered eagerly.

"You two fly together often?" he asked with a smile.

"All the time!" answered the co-pilot. "The three of us have been a flight crew for going on … how long now, Jim?"

"About 8 years," came the reply from the pilot.

"Ooops, where are my manners? I'm Enrique Salones, your co-pilot, and at the helm there is Big Jim Kovac. Your flight attendant back there is Leidra Lawson."

It didn't matter to the flight crew that Smoke never revealed his name, which was part of the "Don't Ask" orders the flight crew had been given in their instructions package. They had flown a lot of incognito celebrities and they were used to nameless, faceless clients that they would never recognize again. All part of the job.

"I'm looking for a flight crew to hire from time to time. You guys up for that?"

"Absolutely!" snapped Big Jim. "Enrique, give the gentleman our contact information."

Enrique dug around in a briefcase that was tucked from sight in a cubbyhole, and then handed Smoke three business cards, along with a data sheet with detailed contact information about the three of them. Smoke took the documents, then said, "Thanks guys, you have no idea what this means to me. I'll be in touch— real soon."

"Enjoy your flight, sir," said Enrique and Big Jim as they all shook hands again.

"Give me a call and we'll hammer out the details," said Big Jim while Smoke was leaving the cockpit.

Smoke gave them a smile and he left the cockpit. Back in the cabin, Myron and Leidra appeared to be getting along like old friends.

"Everything all right up there?" asked Myron with a smile.

"Enjoy your tour, sir?" asked a charming Leidra.

"Extremely informative," answered Smoke with a grin of his own. But Smoke's mind was moving at light speed. His suspicions were running rampant. He kept asking himself, *"What the hell is going on here?"*

Smoke had no idea, but he knew the flight crew had answers for him. When they landed in San Jose, before he left the plane, he went back into the cockpit.

"Thanks for a safe flight, fellas, and thank you, too, Leidra. Say, you three are hanging out in town for the night, right?"

"Yes, we are," came the reply.

"Well, if it's not too much to ask, maybe I can give you a call later tonight and we can make plans for some future flights together. Why don't you give me some information on where you'll be staying, and when I get myself settled in, I'll give you a call, and the three of you can stop by? Does that sound like a plan?"

"Sounds great," they all said, and Leidra gave Smoke the number to the Airport Hyatt Hotel where they were staying the night.

"Great!" said Smoke and he gave them another big disarming smile, but as he turned and departed the plane he had a troubled look on his face.

Smoke hadn't said a word since leaving the plane. His silence made Myron uncomfortable. As they pulled into the rear lab entrance, Myron asked, "You feeling alright, bro? Do you need me to hang out until you come around, just in case?"

"No, thanks, buddy, I got it covered," replied a troubled Smoke. What he had planned was not something easy for him to do. "I'll call you later. Thanks for being there for me, bro."

"No pro-blem-o! I've always got your back," said Myron.

The secluded lab entrance was always used when Smoke was in character - no need to broadcast; he never knew who was watching. Once inside the lab, Smoke interfaced with NEXUS which was still upgrading and interlinking.

When NEXUS was originally activated it immediately went into an interface mode, creating connections with organic, inorganic, terrestrial, and extraterrestrial sources, developing unstoppable communications between them all. It was a long tedious process that required the majority of its computing power. Since this magnitude of planetary and extraterrestrial interlinking had never before been achieved, there was nothing to base how long it would take. Unfortunately, Donovan was only able to access a limited version of NEXUS for answers.

He now hoped enough of that process had been completed, freeing up adequate computing power to create some very special entertainment for his forthcoming guests— and...*there was!*

Once all was set, Big Jim, Enrique, and Leidra received a call with directions on how to get to his place, along with the time he expected them. For his plan to work, timing was everything.

Smoke placed himself inside the protected cell in his lab where he awaited the Hominid metamorphosis to take place, which was not a pretty sight. Smoke had created a knockout pill in order to sleep through this cycle, but this time would be different.

Chapter 53

Following Smoke's directions, Leidra, Enrique, and Big Jim had no problem locating the secluded entrance, and once they rang the bell they were greeted by a video image of Smoke.

"Hey guys, forgive my greeting you through this image, I'll walk you through how to get to me from where you are," and Smoke began directing them to the lab via displays set up along their route.

"These pro boys and their toys," said Big Jim.

"It must be nice," replied Enrique.

"I think it's hot. I could get used to it," added Leidra.

"Keep your legs closed for now. This is business, not pleasure," said Big Jim, putting Leidra and her overactive libido in check.

Smoke directed them to the elevator which took them one floor down into the laboratory, and when the door opened they were greeted by the music of Marvin Gaye's "Got To Give It Up" blasting away. Inside the lab there was a 70s retro party going on. Afros, bell bottoms, dashikis, hip-huggers, and hot pants- wearing dancers were having a ball. Marvin Gaye's music had everybody partying, and without hesitation, Leidra's arms went skyward and her hips began swaying seductively to the rhythm as she closed her eyes letting Marvin's music take control of her body. Big Jim and Enrique joined in the festivities without missing a beat.

"These sport figures, they're known for throwing the wildest parties," shouted Leidra to Big Jim and Enrique, while everyone else joined in at the chorus, shouting, "Got to give it up!"

Not Big Jim, Enrique, nor Leidra had any idea how wild this party would become before the night's end.

Marvin played on for several more minutes, keeping the party going, as a larger than life image of Smoke appeared on the back wall of display panels, and announced, "Oh-Yeah, Oh-Yeah — Leidra, Enrique, Big Jim—my guests of honor have arrived. Welcome to the circus."

The music volume lowered, and everyone dancing gave them a rousing round of applause, and then slowly, one by one, the images of the dancers began to fade, along with their applause, until only Leidra, Enrique, and Big Jim were left standing in the center of the lab, with looks of complete disbelief on their faces.

Leidra said, "Holograms…way cool!"

Enrique said, "Man, is this place high tech or what?"

"Very impressive," said Big Jim, "but where's...," and before he finished his question, a holographic image of Smoke appeared in front of them.

Smoke smiled at them and said, "Let the games begin!"

"All right!" said Leidra, "I'm ready to play!" Undoing a button or two on her already low cut blouse. Enough to really let the girls free.

Smoke's image was so lifelike he seemed right there in the room with them.

Leidra even touched him, seeing if he was real or not, but the image ignored her touch.

"Before the main event begins, I need some information from you three.

These are like fill in the blank questions.

"First question, tell me everything you know about these two people."

An image of his parents appeared.

"These are the Mocions, Donald and Vanessa," announced Smoke.

The faces of Big Jim, Enrique, and Leidra changed from smiling and being entertained, to sudden despair, and the lab became silent as a tomb. The silence was broken by Big Jim's bull voice angrily shouting, "What the hell is this?"

"This," replied Smoke, "is Showtime!" and another image appeared; a still image that slowly morphed into a moving image of the hominid.

When the three saw that image, the look of despair turned into the look of terror. "Since my first question wasn't answered," said Smoke with a chuckle, "I want you to meet a little fiend of mine." And a panel opened revealing the hominid in his actual entire vicious splendor.

Leidra screamed as the hominid savagely slammed into the Plexiglas wall that contained it.

"Now, unless you want to meet face to face, you'll tell me what I want to know," instructed Smoke, who now had a deadly look in those distinctive eyes of his.

Enrique was the first to speak,

"We were hired by Global Pharmaceuticals to kidnap the doctors, leave the kid, and crash the plane."

"What did the company want from the Mocions?" came Smoke's next question.

"We were just hired to snatch the doctors—leave the kid—crash the plane.

Global Pharmaceuticals didn't give us any particulars," confessed Big Jim. "What happened to the Mocions?" asked Smoke.

"We all got on the same boat and then they were transferred to a submarine," explained Leidra.

"Where did the sub take the Mocions?" shouted Smoke's image, realizing the dreadful truth that these three had meant to kill him in the plane crash.

"We don't know!" shouted Big Jim. "We have no idea what happened to the Mocions, honestly!"

"I'm not getting a warm and fuzzy feeling from your answers so far, guys.

You'll need to do better than that," said Smoke as the hominid's cell door opened a bit.

Seeing his cell door begin to open drove the hominid wild. It roared and clawed for its freedom.

"What was the person's name who hired you?" demanded Smoke.

"We don't know! All we know is it was someone very high up the food chain at Global Pharmaceuticals," assured Big Jim.

"They're the ones you want, not us!" screamed a terrified Leidra.

"No, that's not entirely true. I want all of you," yelled the vengeful interactive image of Smoke. "Now, meet my other self!"

The cell door opened completely, freeing the savage hominid into the lab.

Big Jim had seen a lot of strange things in his life but this creature was at the top of his short list. He looked around for a door but didn't see one; he didn't even see the elevator door they came in through. There was nothing he could use as a weapon either, nothing but his own body and teeth, so Big Jim reasoned there was nothing for him to do except stand his ground and get primal with the beast.

Hominid lumbered out of his cell and sized up the three. He saw Big Jim and Enrique as threats to him for the female, Leidra. Since Big Jim was larger than Enrique, hominid systematically decided to eliminate the most opposing threat first, and in the blink of an eye, attacked Big Jim. Big Jim tried everything he could; he grabbed for the creature's genitals, gouged at its eyes, and even tried biting and growling at the beast, all to no avail. Big Jim quickly became shredded beef, gushing blood on the floor of the lab.

After hominid dispatched Big Jim, he realized he liked the thrill of the kill, so he decided to savor that thrill on his next kill, and he turned his attention towards Enrique.

Leidra, scared to death, assumed the fetal position, cowering in a remote corner of the lab, under a work bench, hoping the beast would forget about her, having no idea she was to be the main course.

It toyed with Enrique, slowly stalking him around the lab, grinding its teeth, and growling, relishing the sent of terror oozing from Enrique's pores.

Like Big Jim, Enrique quickly tired of being the hominid's prey, pulled a large jagged hunting knife from the small of his back, and he charged the beast, hoping for the best. The beast slowly tore Enrique apart, limb by limb, then with one great stomp—smashed Enrique's head to pieces as it and the torso fell to the lab floor. When it was finally done with Enrique's lifeless remains, it turned its gaze to Leidra, who was still curled up in the corner under a work bench, weeping uncontrollably.

The hominid's male hormones were kicking in, driving him wild with desire for Leidra. He had never explored his sexual urges. He had never felt anything sexual before, but he liked what he was feeling now, and he used Leidra in every way his raging hormones dictated. Leidra screamed in agony, and ecstasy, before her heart stopped beating from pure excitement and fear.

The entire gruesome spectacle had been recorded and everything Big Jim, Enrique, and Leidra knew were absorbed as data files in NEXUS.

When Donovan came around, his lab looked like a bloodbath had occurred. He crawled back into his chair, and then instructed NEXUS to eliminate all DNA traces while he left to clean himself up and try to get some sleep.

When he returned to the lab the next morning, there wasn't single trace of any human tissue anywhere. The lab looked the same way it did prior to the events of the previous evening. There was no evidence; NEXUS had removed Big Jim, Enrique, Leidra, and even the rental car they arrived in, from existence.

Unfortunately for Donovan, he still remembered everything that happened the night before. He was unprepared for the reality that, whatever he experienced during his primal phase, in all its gory details, those memories were now part of his day-to-day reality. He decided to place those emotions and feelings on the back burner for now.

Then a horrifying realization came to him.

> ***"What if NEXUS fell into the wrong hands... what would become of the planet?"***

Then a more terrifying thought hit him...

> ***"What if NEXUS itself were those wrong hands?"***

Chapter 54

Kilah returned to Dire Magazine to continue working up her 'Donovan Mocion is Smoke' theory, but still there was no contact from Vye, and none of their business acquaintances had seen or heard from her since her last data transmission from L.A. Using Vye's Bluetooth locator, Kilah tracked Vye's most recent location, which led her to Jimbo's apartment in Los Angeles. Posing as his sister, she went by and spoke with the apartment manager who told her, "I haven't seen or heard from the boy, but when you do, you tell him that his rent is overdue!"

Kilah paid the late rent and the landlord gladly gave her access to Jimbo's apartment and mailbox.

Through her years of conspiracy investigations Kilah had become quite proficient at forensics, so she decided to treat Jimbo's apartment as a crime scene. First, she emptied Jimbo's mailbox and browsed through his mail, which was full of disconnect notices. But when she entered his apartment the first thing to hit her was the smell, or lack of smell. Normally, everybody's home smells like something, something that gives a clue as to the last activity that had taken place there, and that's what was wrong; the place looked and smelled as if a professional cleaning service had given it a sterile cleansing to get rid of any trace evidence.

Kilah wasn't able to find a single strand of hair or a drop of urine in a man's bathroom, and she knew that was impossible. Her greatest fear became a reality when she found a small insignificant piece of metal sticking out the backsplash of the kitchen's counter top. This piece of metal was part of a larger anklet she had made for Vye as a gift. When Kilah finished her investigation she concluded that something tragic had taken place in this apartment; lives had been lost here. Kilah was convinced that she was standing at the scene of Vye and Jimbo's place of execution, which had been professionally cleansed. Without giving it a second thought, Kilah new immediately who had that kind of power and she spoke the name out loud. "Global Pharmaceuticals!"

"KILAH!" she said to herself, *"What have you gotten in to this time?"* Then the thought of Vye's death overcame her and she began crying as she ran from Jimbo's apartment.

She was still crying when she entered the apartment that she and Vye shared in Palo Alto, California.

"What did I get my baby into? It was all my fault. If I hadn't given Vye that assignment, she would be alive today." Tears of guilt ran down her face, smearing her makeup, staining her blouse, and causing her heart to ache from the pain of losing a loved one.

After a night of crying and hugging the pillow that Vye slept on, Kilah decided Vye's death would not be in vain.

"I'm too close to stop now!" she told herself. "I'll get to the bottom of this, no matter where it takes me, even if it kills me."

That morning Kilah decided it was best to solve this one alone. She couldn't stand risking anyone else's life. So, thinking like a conspiracy investigator, she took a closer look at the material she and Vye had accumulated about Donovan Mocion and the mystery man Smoke.

She asked herself, *"Why is Global Pharmaceuticals interested in Donovan Mocion*?"

Kilah laid all her information out on the floor, and when she cross- referenced everything in front of her, she was shocked at what she'd come up with. It was clear she had to pay Donovan Mocion, now a Professor at Stanford Medical Center, a personal visit.

Chapter 55

Elaine Hammond was a teacher in the Black Studies Department of Berkeley High School; later she became a professor of Afro-American History at the University of California at Berkeley. Before she "crossed over," she instilled in her children the necessity of continuing all aspects of their educations. Her children promised her on her deathbed that they would never accept society's norm, and they'd always strive to better themselves as educators, healers, and human beings. This was a promise they both intended to keep for as long as they lived. This promise was the main reason Myra was attending Stanford. Her major fields of study were Immunochemistry and Biochemistry Medicine, and she minored in Psychology.

Myra's mother's # 1 rule was "Education is a lifestyle, not something you go after from class to class, semester to semester…it was a way of life. Education is not only discovered in schools, but by living, by experiencing—life!"

Both of Elaine Hammond's children lived by that #1 rule.

Myra's nickname was "MY," but only her brother called her that. In fact, his nickname was also "MY," and only she called him that. They were fraternal twins; she was born a few minutes after her brother—Myron Hammond.

Not only was Myra achieving her master's degree from Stanford University, she was also a First Line member of the Oakland Outlaws' Cheerleading Squad, and a top student in one of Professor Mocion's psychology courses.

The new semester began a few days after the Outlaws' victory over the Pittsburgh Steelmen.

"I understand you're looking for a teaching assistant. Well, here's my academic resume for your review," announced a confident student. Professor Mocion held his hand out and accepted it without looking up, but when the candidate said, "I'm not trying to be forward, rude, or disrespectful, but what is your aging condition called?" the Professor looked up from his papers and saw Myra, instantly remembering her as the Outlaws' cheerleader from the Pittsburgh game.

"Progeria Syndrome," replied the professor, now focusing his attention on the resume Myra had given him.

The Professor had done research on genetic diseases that mimicked premature aging, which led him to Progeria Syndrome, also known as Accelerated Decrepitude. This condition had become the perfect cover to explain the serum's rapid aging side effects. The university and all the professor's students helped perpetuate this cover up as fact for all who wanted to know.

"Accelerated Decrepitude," said Myra softly, but loud enough for the professor to hear.

The Professor calmly said, "The light that burns twice as bright."

"Burns half as long," finished Myra.

What they just heard from the other caught them both by surprise, and their eyes met once again. They had begun the journey of a moment, and they both felt it—the type of moment when all around disappears, when all senses have magically joined with another, and the look shared between them equals the feelings passing from one to the other, when no words are needed, and for a brief moment in time, in life, everything is right there. Just reach out and claim it. They were afraid to speak, knowing to speak now would only break the moment, and when a moment like this is experienced… no one wants it to end.

But as in life, all moments end, and theirs ended when they heard a voice intruding upon their perfect moment by saying, "Excuse me, professor…Professor Mocion…excuse me, sir," came the untimely interruption that instantly dissolved their shared moment into invisible vapors. "Can I ask you a question about the assignment?"

The Professor didn't want to answer, but before he knew what he was doing, a word fell past his lips.

"Sure," and he instinctively looked in the direction of the student's voice, and when he looked back towards Myra, the moment was gone, and so was she.

A sadness, almost equaling the loss of his parents struck him, and he knew he must locate her again. He took a long close look at the resume he held in his trembling hands, realizing the most important clues in locating her were at his fingertips... her complete name, address, and phone number. The Professor studied her resume, and when he came across the name Oakland Outlaws, he immediately called Myron, knowing he knew everything there was to know about the Outlaws.

"Hey, bro. How you doin'?" greeted the Professor.

"Still basking in the whoop ass we put on Pittsburgh," answered Myron, "how 'bout you? You still buzzing from that victory?"

"In a way, but right now I'm buzzing about something else."

"Something I can help you with?" asked Myron.

"I sure hope so. You pretty much know all there is to know about everyone connected with the Outlaws," said the Professor.

"Anything that's worth knowing," reassured Myron with a giggle.

"Well, this lady has been catching my eye lately, and I wonder if you could give me a little more info on her," asked the Professor.

"Absolutely, but before you go there, you need to know that the team frowns on the players fraternizing with the cheerleaders. Players and cheerleaders have been severely punished for being, shall I say, caught in compromising acts," warned Myron.

"This is different," reassured the Professor. "I'm the one interested more than Smoke."

"Really! Well, then this young lady must really be special. Since she's one of our cheerleaders I already know she's extremely beautiful. And since she got a rise from the Professor, she must be brilliant, too. So Professor Mocion, Donovan, a.k.a. Smoke, by reasonable deduction, let me see if I can guess our mystery lady's name..." Myron paused for a long minute, and then he blurt out "Myra!"

"Dammmmmmmn," said an astonished Professor, "you're scary sometimes."

"Yeah, I scare myself. I know her, I know her extremely well. She's my kid sister—by a few minutes, anyway."

The Professor's first reaction was to shout for joy, but then something unsettling came over him and he began to feel very vulnerable.

"How much does she know?" asked the Professor in a no nonsense, yet still brotherly, tone of voice.

"She only knows about your Donovan and Professor personas. In fact, the first night after we checked out the data left by your parents, she called me as I was getting on the freeway, trying to sound all spy like, saying ...***REPORT!***

Donovan, FYI…Myra has been a supportive fan of yours longer than I have, and that's way before the Olympics. I've kept her up-to-date on your recovery as Donovan only. I've told her nothing about Smoke, your serum, or anything you have been secretly working on.

But, now that we are on this subject, I have to tell you that there have been veiled threats from those connected with Global Pharmaceuticals trying to get me to spy on you for them. And the only reason they haven't touched me is because I know where ***all*** the skeletons are buried, and I've taken out an insurance policy that is off the planet, should something happen to me or mine. Just so you know, I wouldn't give you up then, and I'll never give you up, bro. You and I have been straight up with each other, so you need to know that Myra means the world to me, and I'd take it as a personal attack if anyone tried to harm her. I hope you understand what I'm saying to you, Donovan."

Donovan knew very well that Myron was issuing a warning that no harm should be inflicted on his baby sister, or face his wrath.

Donovan reassured Myron, "Believe me, bro; I'd protect Myra with all I have. Hurting her, in any form, is not in my beings."

"I'm pleased to hear that, but you've got to promise me something. Never tell Myra what I'm about to share with you or she'd kill me for sure," said Myron.

"Our secrets are more than safe with each other," said Donovan with a large smile on his face, feeling closer to Myron than ever before.

"Well then, let me tell you 'bout my lil' sista. She's had her eye on you ever since you were running in Washington. She would always say to me, "This dude is holding back…I bet he's waiting for just the right time to shock the world!" And don't tell her I told you, but she's usually right."

And for the next few hours, Donovan and Myron talked about Myra and the Hammond family.

The next day a formal letter on Professor Mocion's letterhead was sent to Myra Hammond informing her that she had been selected for the TA position— starting immediately. Myra was more than qualified for the position.

Chapter 56

Kilah fit right in with the college crowd and, after picking up a class schedule, she tracked down the Professor's classes. Since this was a new semester, her plan was to sit in on a few of his classes and pretend like she was checking them out to enroll. Once in she didn't have to wait long to get an up close and personal look into those special eyes of the Professor. But the instant she laid eyes on the Professor her theory hit several huge road blocks. The Professor now looked to be at least 15 to 20 years older and he was nowhere near the physical size of Smoke. The only common threads between all three of her subjects were their eyes—they all had the same distinctive eyes.

> *"I hope I'm not giving myself the run around, trying to make something from nothing. But just in case, I'll go check out the Professor's home while he's here teaching his classes,"* thought Kilah.

Kilah went to the address Vye had sent her; it was in a rural part of Stanford, California. She wasn't sure what she was looking for, but believed she would know it when she found it. The property was isolated, well-manicured, and sprawling.

She parked her car behind some secluded trees, then got out her binoculars and began her surveillance of the location. She wasn't really sure she had the right house until she saw a minivan parked in the driveway with "Housekeeping Services" on the side. Then she saw a couple of tiny monkeys running in and out of a small doggie door on the side of the house. "This must be the place; Jimbo's notes mentioned the Professor had been given two monkeys." So, after the housekeeper's minivan left and the monkeys ran off to another part of the yard, she made her way toward the doggie door. At the doggie door, she thought, "*Thank goodness for my tiny size... if there are any motion detection devices around, since the monkeys didn't set them off, I shouldn't set them off, either.*"

Inside the Professor's house, Kilah was amazed at what she saw. The Professor had the entire place decorated in an African motif. There were indoor trees and lush plant life growing everywhere. "*The monkeys must feel right at home in these surroundings,*" Kilah thought. But, it was strange not to have seen any of the typical home protection devices strategically placed in the obvious locations throughout the Professor's home. She was a tad curious about all the flat panel monitors all over the place. She figured the Professor loved to watch television. She had no idea just how wrong she was.

NEXUS had her under surveillance from the time she turned on to the Professor's private tree-lined road. The instant Kilah had poked her head through the doggie door, NEXUS scanned her and determined that she was no threat to the overall plan. During that scan, NEXUS deduced that Kilah had been 95% accurate about all her conspiracy theories and she would become important to Nexus because of her journalistic convictions and her ability to write the truth. And the planet would be better served with her alive, so she was allowed to carry on with her investigation of the Professor's premises instead of being obliterated.

As Kilah made her way down the hallway she accidentally stumbled, and when she placed her hand on the wall to regain her balance, a hidden panel opened revealing an elevator. It didn't take much self-convincing before she stepped in, and when she did the panel quickly shut behind her, and the lift engaged. Just before her big brain began creating unthinkable frightening scenarios only she would come up with, the elevator door opened, revealing the Professor's hidden laboratory.

By now, Topaz and Jade had made their way back into the house and they smelled an intruder. They darted from room to room looking for this intruder and finally stopped in front of the lift panel. They looked like a couple of normal people patiently waiting for an elevator. The lift was equipped with a sensor which automatically took the elevator up to the main floor or down to the laboratory anytime a presence was detected, allowing Topaz and Jade to board. Inside the lift, where the scent of Kilah was the strongest, the monkeys began working themselves into a protective frenzy.

Down below, Kilah was so engrossed looking at equipment she had no clue of understanding, that she didn't notice the lift had left, or that it was returning.

Standing with her back to the lift's door she began hearing what sounded like wild animals, and those sounds were getting closer and closer, louder and louder. Kilah, panicking, decided to hide inside the foot cavity of a desk. When the elevator door opened, Topaz, the dominant monkey, leaped out and begin storming around the lab tracking Kilah's scent. Jade was standing inside the lift, waiting to see what was going to happen to Topaz before she reacted. Topaz leapt on top of the desk Kilah was hiding under and puffed himself up, giving off the appearance of being much larger than he really was, and he screamed at the top of his lungs, showing his ferocious fangs.

Kilah scrambled from under the desk, scaring Topaz so much that he peed all over the terrified Kilah. Dripping wet with monkey pee, Kilah ran for the elevator's door and was greeted by an even more ferocious Jade, who had puffed herself up larger than life, too. Jade pounced on Kilah's head and immediately started grabbing at her dreadlocks. Topaz, now over his initial fright, leaped across the lab and pounced on Kilah's back scratching and biting her. Kilah fell to the ground and started rolling over and over on the lab's floor, causing both monkeys to temporarily abandon their attack.

Kilah frantically touched everything in sight, hoping to hit the right spot and open the lift's door again.

Topaz and Jade, regrouping on the other side of the laboratory from Kilah, looked at each other, making sure they were intact, then looked across the lab at Kilah, and began screaming and showing their fangs again. But before they could attack again, the lift's door opened and Kilah crawled inside. The door quickly closed behind her and then released her on the main floor. She poured out of the elevator a battered, screaming mess who kept slipping and falling to the floor as she desperately tried to regain her balance and escape through the doggie door before the vicious attacking monkeys caught up to her. Kilah looked behind her and seeing that the elevator's door had closed sent a chill of panic through her bones because she knew those razor-blades-for-teeth monkeys would soon be on her again. Using all the control she had left in her tiny body, she made her way through the doggie door, across the yard, and into the safety of her car. Her hands were shaking so badly when she tried putting her keys into the ignition, she dropped them and they fell on the carpet under the passenger's seat. Kilah slid down on the floor to retrieve her keys and when she sat back up, Topaz and Jade pounced on her car, screaming and drooling, hitting and scratching, trying to open the car's door to finish her off. Kilah managed to start her car and she gave her horn a long blast while racing her engine, which caused both monkeys to leap away from her car. Kilah stomped on her accelerator and sped away, screaming louder than the noise of her screeching tires.

Topaz and Jade stood in the middle of the road, shaking their tiny fists toward Kilah's car, huffing and puffing. Then they quickly faced each other and let loose a loud monkey laugh, and resumed frolicking and playing in the yard as if nothing had happened.

NEXUS recorded every step of Kilah's adventure in data files.

Chapter 57

After Phase 2 of the HEF trials had been initialized, there were some unexpected results from all the test subjects. Subjects 5 and 53 had become ravaging cannibals and brought forth their spawn at alarming rates, which were quickly eaten by both parents if not immediately removed. These developments warranted more in-depth studies so subjects 5 and 53 were relocated to a different area of the Cone—one that specialized in military applications.

The thinking was that the spawn would make ideal combat weapons if they were trainable. Their growth rate was astounding. They reached full maturity in a matter of weeks and began reproducing shortly after reaching puberty. Each successive generation was somewhat different than its parent; they seemed to incorporate the intelligence and experience of the parent into their knowledge base. In a matter of three generations, they were no longer cannibals, and it was discovered that they had acquired a taste for fruits and vegetables. And with each subsequent generation, the creatures' strength and agility increased at alarming rates. They were not average primates! They were something more, something never seen before...a new species of life with unique thought patterns and agendas.

There had been no further HEF injections for subjects 5 & 53, nor did any generation that followed receive injections. Whatever had occurred within 5 & 53 had unleashed something that had lain dormant inside human beings throughout generations of intellectual development. In subjects 5 and 53, the HEF Experiment had given life the chance to take an alternate course of development, different than what was considered normal. It was also unknown to Drs. Wiley and Hothan that 5 and 53 had total recall of everything they had been exposed to and that the eating their offspring was an attempt to free their youth from unknown tortures at the hands of those who didn't care about their well-being. After all, they were, in fact, human beings and cared deeply for their children.

As detailed in the Mocions' "White Papers," subjects 28 & 37 displayed exactly what Drs. Wiley and Hothan were led to expect from the Human Enhancement Formula. There were a few modifications to the serum that they couldn't figure out. Namely, once a week the formula itself was altered and that alteration provided more positive results on subjects 28 & 37. These alterations were thought to have been changed by Francine herself, without informing Drs. Wiley and Hothan. The changes had the highest security level authorization, therefore were carried out, no questions asked. And when those changes provided positive effects on 28 & 37, Drs. Wiley and Hothan had no need to question them.

They simply noted the progress in their reports...

"Current formula's effects are producing marked improvements! Subjects' heart rates have returned to a normal status while improved performance is maintained. Accelerated aging has been reduced, and subjects no longer need to be continually dosed to avoid the aging process. The dosage has been minimized to a fraction of the original while maintaining all improved human enhancements.

Recommend discontinuing all dosing.

*Special Notes— Unforeseen Side Effects.

Although subjects 28 & 37 have maintained a highly active, vigorous sexual relationship, impregnation has not occurred. There also seems to be a higher level of communications between the two. We have noticed less and less vocalizing between them when not engaged in sexual intercourse, as if they have developed a mental communication link. Further study along telepathic lines is recommended."

When Francine reviewed the doctors' reports on 28 & 37, she gave the order...

"Initialize Phase 3 for subjects 28 & 37."

Then she instructed Drs. Wiley and Hothan to "Focus all efforts exclusively on 28 & 37. **Do not** concern yourselves any further with subjects 5 & 53!"

Subjects 28 & 37 were amazed and very pleased at their individual physical improvement from the treatments. Although their newfound communication abilities were causing them some speculation, because these new abilities were never part of the side effects original described to them, 28 & 37 both realized that something very unusual, and wonderful, was taking place within them, and for the second time since they've been undergoing treatment, which had been over 6 months now, they looked forward to leaving. The first time was after they were given the unbelievable explanation about what happened to subjects 5 & 53, but what really influenced their disbelief were the new voices they heard inside their heads. At night, when all was quite on their level of the facility, they heard cries for help and these cries were coming from, they believed, subjects 5 & 53, as well as many, many others they could not identify.

28 & 37 kept this to themselves and decided to check it out. One quiet night, after they had gotten permission to roam around the facility, they followed those cries that were now screaming inside their heads, to see where they led. Walking hand in hand, they left their resort-like accommodations and found themselves in front of massive steel double doors which automatically opened for them. Nobody came running up to stop them...no military type shouting for them to halt—so they entered.

The scenery drastically changed. All the surfaces were hard, stark, cold, and bleak. They were immediately overwhelmed by a foul smell they could only associate with what a zoo smells like on a hot and muggy day. As they walked a little further, they found themselves standing in an observation booth, similar to the one where Drs. Wiley and Hothan observed them from, and what they saw below brought terror to their hearts. Looking up at them were dozens of medium-sized, fur covered humanoid creatures imprisoned in Plexiglas cells. Through another set of double doors there were a pair of larger, fur covered humanoid creatures squatting down holding each other in fear. Instantly 28 & 37 knew these two creatures were subjects 5 and 53. When the furry creatures below made eye contact with 27 & 38, an inner link developed between them all, and instantaneously each became aware of the other's history. Immediately, the common goal between them all became—***freedom***.

Chapter 58

Donovan replayed the interrogation portion of the flight crew's lab recording. The entire sequence was more than he could handle; he needed more answers and he needed them fast. He knew there was only one place to get those answers—Global Pharmaceuticals. This meant only one person could give him the answers he needed and that person was Francine Katrina Bovier.

Donovan found the business card she had given him at the funeral, called her, and set up an appointment. He recalled his parents' warning not to trust her, but he was hoping he could decipher the truth from her lies. He also knew he'd need some back-up on this undertaking.

The Outlaws had a "bye-week," which meant Myron might have some free time, so Donovan gave him a call.

"Hey, bro. Can you get away for a few days? I need you to watch my back for me."

"I can use a break from all this madness around here. When do you want to leave?" replied Myron, eager for a different adventure.

"First, let me tell you where we're going." After Donovan told Myron he needed to visit Global Pharmaceuticals, Francine Bovier in particular, Myron's side of the phone became very quiet.

"Hello, hello…bro, you still there?"

Myron took a deep breath and slowly answered, "You sure you want to make that trip?"

"I'm sure I *have* to make it. I doubt I can move forward unless I do," replied Donovan in a hopeless, pitiful sounding voice.

"Let's go, then," said Myron. He knew deep in his heart that someday he and Francine would have to stand face to face with each other, but he was hoping that day was a long time off. Now, that day was in his face *and* the thought of seeing her again made his stomach feel queasy. Those old resentments began flaring up. If it had been any one other than Donovan, Myron would've said, "*NO!*"

It was late afternoon and raining when they arrived in Exton, PA. Donovan had a car and driver waiting at the Maglev station; courtesy of Francine. Right before they pulled away from the curb, Donovan leaned forward towards the driver and handed him a small piece of paper with an address scribbled on it.

"Before you take us to our hotel, I want you to take us by this address. Do you know where that is?"

"Yes," replied the driver with an East Indian accent, "But it is a long, long drive out of the way, I'm thinking."

Looking at the driver through his rear view mirror and completely ignoring his complaint, Donovan instructed, using a take-charge tone "Let's get there quickly!" The driver, glancing at Donovan in his mirror, didn't say another word, he just took them where Donovan wanted.

"Goin' on a little excursion, are we?" asked Myron in his usual clam and peaceful demeanor, as he settled back into the plush leather seats preparing for this mysterious ride.

"Yeah, bro. Hope you don't mind, but I need to revisit my past a bit."

"No problem, Donovan, this is your show. I'm just along for moral support," but in Myron's mind he was thinking, *"I get the feeling this trip's gonna revisit the past for both of us, and I have no idea the outcome."*

The sound the car's tires made as they rolled over the wet pavement, hitting the occasional reflector in the roadway, helped Donovan's mind drift back to a place less complicated, a time more simple, and with little or no secrets. Lately, it seemed, there were many secrets being kept, and since he had no place else to start, he decided to go back to the beginning, as far back as he could remember.

The car got off the freeway then slowly made its way along a quiet lane of ranch houses until finally stopping in the middle of a cul-de-sac. Donovan hit the button to roll the tinted window down for a clearer view and was shocked to see… nothing!

Myron was surprised to see nothing, too, and calmly asked, "Isn't that where your parents' house used to be?"

The site was completely taped off and was surrounded by a chain link fence.

It looked like a meteor, or a bomb, had exploded where the Mocions' home had been. No other property was damaged; just the one parcel was missing. But it wasn't just cleared away. The hole in the ground went down several stories with multiple tunnels branching out like the legs of a spider with the gigantic center hole its body. There was a large Biohazard sign on the fence right under the name…Global Pharmaceuticals.

"I've got more than I thought to talk over with Francine tomorrow morning," said a bewildered looking Donovan.

"Yeah, buddy. It looks like you do!" replied Myron with an equally bewildered look on his face.

Chapter 59

At the hotel, Donovan tossed and turned all night long, troubled about how he was going to handle the upcoming meeting. His parents' warning about not trusting Francine kept bouncing around in his head. He was also torn between letting Myron in on everything that was happening to him, including NEXUS, or continuing to try to deal with it alone. A little before dawn he'd decide to fill Myron in on everything. Besides he thought, *"I need to share this load with somebody. Someone I know really has my best interest in heart, and Myron is the only friend I have."* So Donovan revealed to Myron all he had kept him in the dark about, including the extermination of the flight crew; Donovan was really having problems about what his alter ego, the Hominid, had done. He couldn't get the horrific images out of his head, nor could he shake the thrill he'd gotten, as the creature, from the experience. He kept seeing the terror on the faces of the flight crew as he tore them apart, one by one. And the pleasure he received while ravaging Leidra to death. Donovan's mixed emotions about what he had done tormented and haunted him.

Myron sat in disbelief, listening to what Donovan was revealing to him.

When Donovan was through talking, Myron said, "Man! If I didn't already know some of the strange things about you and your parents, I wouldn't believe a bit of what you just laid on me. I'd be taking you to a shrink right about now." Myron held his head down, shaking it from side to side in silent disbelief. Then, with a spark of life, as if he'd made an important discovery, he said, "How can I help you…bro?"

A huge weight, the relief from sharing one's burdens, fell from Donovan's shoulders and, with a weak smile on his face, he said, "Well, what I did to that flight crew I'm just gonna have to deal with internally, and there's nothing I can do about that now. But the truth is, I don't want to be alone with this Francine person. I only met her once, but I don't trust her. So please, come with me to this meeting."

Myron felt this was the best time to do some revealing about himself, so he told Donovan about his past relationship with Rozelyn, the head of the hospital where Donovan had recovered, and his long ago relationship with Francine. He even told Donovan the part about his drug dealing days, Francine's addiction, and her climb to the top of the most powerful company on the globe. When he was finished he said to Donovan, "Bro, you've got good reason not to trust Francine. She always has several hidden agendas. The way to deal with her is to let her do most of the talking. That way she'll give you more information than she gets. Do you understand what I'm talking about?"

"Understood!" replied a relieved Donovan who was now armed with some enlightening background on his adversary. Feeling like Myron's little brother, Donovan smiled and then said, "Damnnnn, Myron, you've been involved in some serious shit!"

They let go of some stress releasing laughter, cleaned up, had breakfast, then went down and got into the car waiting for them in front of the hotel.

Even in these unusually rainy days, filled with dark cloudy skies, the Global Pharmaceuticals building could be seen from miles away. Its futuristic design featured no right angles and no parallel lines. The building was featured in all the current designers' magazines, and on the cover of popular business magazines was a full color, fully interactive, digital image of the magnificently beautiful Francine Katrina Bovier, CEO of Global Pharmaceuticals.

Francine always dressed to capture, and her coco brown complexion, large almond doe eyes, accented by her whiter than white dazzling smile, set behind a pair of beyond desire full lips which were always moist and inviting, would bring all who came within her aura begging to fulfill her every whim, or suffering destruction for opposing her.

Once the car got within 1 mile of Global Pharmaceuticals the driver contacted Francine to inform her of their approach and she made her way down to the lobby from her top floor office suite to welcome Donovan. Francine timed it so she reached the lobby at the same time their limo pulled up. She immediately saw Myron, and her first thought was, *"Oh, shit... what is he doing here? I wonder just how much he's told Donovan about our past."* Then, for a brief moment, she flashed back to the days of Myron and her, which led to the days of Myron, Roz, and her, and then on to just Roz and her, and finally, to the break between Roz, Myron, and her. *"It doesn't matter,"* she told herself, *"those days are long gone.*

We're completely different people now. I'm in control these days and nothing Myron has told Donovan can change that," she reassured herself.

Myron got out of the car first and looked around at the splendor of the landscape, then went to the trunk and got Donovan's scooter chair out. He rolled it around to Donovan's door, popped the chair into position, and then helped Donovan into it. Donovan checked out the scooter's joystick to make sure it was responding correctly before he and Myron entered the building.

"Welcome to Global Pharmaceuticals' Headquarters," said Francine with all the excitement of a game show hostess, looking Myron in the eyes saying, "Great to see you again, Mr. Hammond," while extending a well-manicured hand in greeting, her eyes slyly checking Myron out from his trademark bald head to his shoes, and then she focused on the strength of his handshake in comparison to her own.

"I see you're still keeping yourself in the best of shape."

"Hello, Alley-Kat," replied Myron in a calm and personal, yet neutral, manner. Francine tightly grabbed his extended hand's forearm, stepped close to his ear and whispered, "Nobody around hear knows me as that, so don't call me that again."

Myron just let go of her hand and stepped to the side as Donovan rolled up. Francine was about to bend down to greet Donovan, but to her surprise,

Donovan's chair raised up, stopping when they were eye to eye, then Donovan extended his hand in greeting. Francine stepped back a little startled, and said, "Wow! That's an extremely functional device you've got there. How are you doing, Dr. Mocion?"

"I'm making the most of my situation. I understand I have you to thank for all the medical treatment I've been getting over the past year." Thinking to himself, *"So, she's been keeping track of my progress; she knows I've obtained my doctorate. I bet she even knows where I work and live, too!"*

"Well, it's the least we could do after all your parents have done for the company," replied Francine as she flashed her pearly whites at Donovan.

"Gentlemen, please follow me."

Francine led them to her private elevator. There were only two buttons on the elevator's control panel; one read OFFICE and the other button read PRIVATE. She pressed the office button and they went non-stop, straight to the top of the company's food chain. The elevator even had a padded bench for sitting during the ride. Francine took a seat, and with a wave of her hand, offered Myron a seat next to her.

"No thanks, I prefer to stand," Myron replied calmly, without missing a beat.

Donovan rolled into the elevator facing Francine at eye level, then said to her, "So…you and Myron seem to know each other."

"Well, Dr. Mocion, I do owe a great deal to Mr. Hammond. A long time ago he went out his way to help me, and I still appreciate that help to this day. Thank you again, Myron."

Myron flashed back over some of the good times he and Francine had shared, he gave a little smile, then said, "My treat, Francine."

While making small talk during the elevator ride, Francine took a quick assessment of the way Donovan had aged since the last time they had seen each other, and since she was privy to all his medical records which mentioned nothing about premature aging, she instantly deduced that Donovan had been dosing with the serum, which meant somehow Donovan had access to his parents' research.

> Francine thought to herself, *"I've got to find out just how much about his parents' work he knows and somehow combine his findings with my team's findings. This may mean showing him more than I had planned to, but whatever it takes to get the job done!"*

When the elevator finally came to a stop, the doors opened onto a fabulous Art Deco inspired office suite. Myron looked around at the fantastic décor, and with a little smirk of approval that only a proud mentor can give for one of their protégés, commented, "You've done well."

"You like?" asked Francine, fishing for more approval from Myron.

He ignored her bait and walked over to the floor-to-ceiling windows to check out the view.

Being the perfect hostess again, Francine said, "Please, make yourselves comfortable. Can I get you anything?"

Donovan decided to take advantage of the offer and said, "How about some information."

"Well, well…you are your parents' son… direct and to the point. How about we share information both ways… you know - quid pro quo?"

Donovan, remembering Myron's advice about letting her do most of the talking, quickly glanced and shared a wink with Myron without Francine noticing, then replied with the tilt of his head, "Deal!"

"Well, since you are my guest I think it only fitting for you to ask the first question."

"OK, what happened to my parents' house, and what are all those underground tunnels and that huge hole in the ground?"

"Well, point of fact, Dr. Mocion, that house belongs to Global Pharmaceuticals; we were merely providing it to your parents while they worked here. Unfortunately, when they passed, the legal deed holder reclaimed the property; therefore, I'm not legally obligated to answer any of your questions regarding said property."

Donovan just glared at her allowing his eyes to deliver the message, *"Don't play with me…you know much more than you are revealing."*

Francine must have understood because she quickly added, "The house was demolished in an attempt to locate an unidentifiable power surge emanating from somewhere within, or below, the house. That power surge is still undetermined.

Your asking about the house indicates you've been to the site. So, to further answer your question, the catacombs that were unearthed under the house are still a mystery to all my people. In fact, it was one of the issues I wanted to discuss with you."

Everybody sat quietly sizing each other up, and just when it seemed nobody could take the silence any longer, Donovan said, "I have no idea what that giant hole under the house was used for, or that it was even there until I saw the property."

Francine calmly twirled around in her plush chair and looked out her windows at the breath-taking cityscape view, her back facing Donovan, and asked in a know-it-all tone, "How long have you been dosing?"

Francine's abrupt unexpected question caught Donovan completely off guard. He gave a quick glance at Myron, who briefly made eye contact with Donovan, but Myron's calm, collected demeanor offered Donovan no help.

So, Donovan ignored her question.

Unfortunately for them both, Francine had witnessed their brief exchange reflected in her windows, confirming what she already knew.

"Getting back to that hole under your parents former home; I think they were conducting unauthorized experiments on a creation they felt no need to divulge to the company, clearly violating one of the company's strictest policies, and once that experiment was terminated that empty hole and tunnels are all that's left of the experiment. And I believe that you are privy to knowledge and data which is rightfully the intellectual property of Global Pharmaceuticals."

Feeling in complete control, Francine suggested, "Why don't you both accompany me on a little excursion. Are you up for that?"

Francine was toying with them, like a confidant cat engaging a couple of cornered mice. Before either of them could answer she got up and nonchalantly strolled over to a built-in mahogany wall unit which displayed exquisite Egyptian pottery, African tribal masks, and an extensive collection of Lalique Crystals, knowing full well that her collectibles would not be the view Myron or Donovan would be admiring.

Predictably, Donovan and Myron could not help but notice the outstanding rhythm of Francine's motion as she strutted before them, and they looked at each other, smiling, both appreciating the sumptuous backside she had been blessed with. When she reached the wall unit, a beam of light scanned her and the wall unit opened revealing another elevator. Francine performed a perfect pirouette, and in her hostess persona said, "Gentlemen, if you would accompany me please, there are a few sights I feel will be of interest to you both." Then she waved her hand directing Donovan and Myron into the elevator.

Chapter 60

"Where I'm taking you, and what I'm about to show you, no civilian and no one other than the highest ranking officials at Global Pharmaceuticals have ever seen before. And I'm showing you this because after seeing you, Donovan…can I call you that?"

"Only if I get to call you Alley Kat," replied Donovan.

"Well then, Dr. Mocion, as I was saying I'm showing you two this because I can tell you have been dosing, which has caused you to age many years before your time. I've also got a hunch that Myron is your confidant, so what I'm about to reveal should even out our playing field and hopefully develop some trust between us."

The elevator deposited them into a Mini Mag-Rail transport which delivered them to an observation level of a futuristic underground research facility in a matter of seconds.

Then, with a swelling of pride, Francine announced, "Gentlemen…welcome to Global Pharmaceuticals' ***Cone*** facility. I've brought you here, Dr. Mocion, so you will see the results of a project your parents began."

Francine then accessed a call button in the observation room where she gave the instruction, "Send them up!"

Donovan took this opportunity to ask Francine the burning question that had taken him there in the first place. "What did you or Global Pharmaceuticals have to do with the death of my parents?"

His question caught her totally off guard. She turned and faced him with the look of surprise, hurt, and anger, then firmly announced, "I had nothing whatsoever to do with what happened to your parents. Think it through. Why would I destroy the most productive and innovative scientists on the planet? Why would I get Global Pharmaceuticals to cover all of your medical bills? And why would I take this meeting, and be showing you what no one outside of the company has seen, if I didn't feel some kind of concern about your welfare?"

Francine pulled a micro memory-cylinder from her inside jacket pocket, took Donovan's hand and slapped it in saying, "Here, these are the complete details of the project I'm about to show you now. It's your parents' brainchild. I know you've been studying their work, so examine what's on that stick. I'm sure you will find it fascinating and helpful.

"Now, what I did do was make a company jet available whenever they felt they needed one—no questions asked. But, as with all our upper tier staffers, your parents hired their own flight crews. In fact, I questioned why your parents changed flight crews while you competed in Hawaii. To me, there are many mysteries surrounding the accident that are still unanswered. Two come to mind right now. The first… are your parents really dead? The second…what were they actually working on? My records indicate they had been working on some type of ultra-advanced A.I. project that they kept extremely closed-mouthed about. It seems, Dr. Mocion, that you have read me completely wrong!"

Before Donovan could comment, a well-groomed, neatly dressed and accessorized couple entered the observation room via a spiral staircase from the lab below.

"Dr. Mocion…Mr. Hammond, I like to introduce you both to Claudia Rawlins and Malik Jamerson."

Claudia and Malik were shocked to hear their real names used after all these months, and hearing their names made them feel like two strangers were being introduced to them. While Donovan was raising his chair to be at equal height for greeting, Malik and Claudia shook hands with Myron, and when Donovan finally did shake hands with them, he was bombarded by emotions, experiences, and horrid images that were not his own. The entire post-life history following the initial serum injections of Claudia and Malik had been revealed to Donovan in a nanosecond, and his post-injection life history had been revealed to them. But something much more important had instantly been awakened within the three of them. A far superior consciousness had come to life at the very moment of their greeting and they had no clue what that consciousness was.

Myron noticed a disturbing far away expression on Donovan's face and asked, "You alright, bro?"

"Yeah, I…guess so. Wow. I just had the strangest rush, but I'm alright!"

Francine noticed it too and suggested, "It's probably the high oxygen content here; it takes some getting used to."

Donovan heard Francine's comment but was not about to reveal to Francine the interlink that occurred between Claudia, Malik, and him. Nor was he going to reveal what he had learned from the NEXUS mind scans of Big Jim, Enrique, and Leidra.

Abruptly, a loud commotion broke out beneath them in one of the containment cells. Subjects 5 and 53 had finally reached their breaking points from the degrading treatment forced upon them by those they now considered their captors.

Years before signing up for this radical experiment gone astray, for their own individual reasons, subject 5, who began life as a female, became the male Arturo Zanzibar before the HEF experiments, and now had returned to being a female. Subject 53, who began life as a male, became the female Camille Giuseppe before the HEF experiments, and now had returned to being a male. They each had undergone sexual reassignments and now were forced by the HEF injection to live their lives in sexual orientations they never wanted, forced to breed and bring forth non-human offspring, but worst of all, they were no longer considered human beings. The pressure of all this mental anguish, emotional trauma, and physical unrest, caused them to snap.

Subjects 5 and 53 had not been looking for weaknesses in the electro magnetic force field door to their containment cell, as Kevin Mathews, Laboratory Supervisor, had briefly thought. They were looking for points of entry into that field. They had discovered that if matter was not repelled by the field, and stayed in constant contact, then that matter would be destroyed. This became their personal plan for freedom…their ultimate destruction!

Francine ordered Claudia and Malik to wait there while she, Donovan, and Myron went to the other side of the observation room to see what the disturbance was. When they arrived they saw subjects 5 & 53 viciously engaged in a full-scale assault on the repelling field. The creatures howled and roared in agony, but still they refused to retreat from the field. In a matter of seconds, subjects 5 and 53's flesh and bones splattered to pieces in every direction of their containment cell, leaving all who viewed the suicide speechless and horrified at what they had just witnessed.

The next generation hominids stood weeping and swaying from side to side as they made a deep sorrowful moaning sound, staring up at the observation booth where Donovan, Francine, and Myron were.

"Can they see us?" asked a shocked Myron, unnerved by what he had seen.

"No, they can't," replied Francine who maintained her calm persona even though what she has witnessed had completely disturbed her.

Keeping his composure while feeling a tremendous loss, as did subjects 5 and 53's offspring, Donovan asked, "What are - were they?" knowing all too well just what they were, and the reason behind the horrifying event he had just witnessed.

"Those creatures that just destroyed themselves were failures of your parents' serum. But Malik and Claudia are examples of two successes," explained Francine, and the three of them turned around to take another look at Malik and Claudia…but they were gone. Malik and Claudia had taken a Mag-Rail and escaped the facility during the commotion. They knew what was going to happen before it happened. Subjects 5 & 53 had revealed it to them.

Francine quickly told Donovan and Myron that they must leave at once and she led them to another Mag-Rail, instructing them to go ahead without her, and she pressed the button that read EXIT, saying, "I'll be in touch with you two later. There's a car waiting to take you wherever you want to go."

Francine stepped back, the doors closed, and Donovan and Myron were deposited at Francine's private exit. No one even bothered to question them.

Instead, everyone acted like they were too busy at whatever they were doing to notice anyone leaving Francine's private elevator.

Donovan and Myron left the building, but instead of getting into the waiting car that Francine provided, Donovan began heading in the opposite direction.

"Where you headed, bro? The car is this way," pointed Myron.

With the same bewildered look on his face that he had after shaking hands with Claudia and Malik, Donovan answered, "I don't know, bro, but something is drawing me in this direction and I have to check it out."

"Well, hold up a second. I'm coming with you," said a more-than-curious Myron, who immediately caught up with Donovan.

They traveled down a small hill then crossed the street to a park.

Even though it was still pouring down rain, Myron sarcastically said, "Nice day for a tour through the park, aye, bro?"

"Yeah…it would be if that was my motivation, but something inside this park is pulling me towards it."

The park had a huge maze of hedges at its center, and once they got there, Donovan and Myron entered the maze. It was like Donovan had been through this maze before and he quickly made his way to its center — sitting calmly on a bench was Malik and Claudia with their legs crossed, holding hands, looking like normal lovers sitting in the park.

"Is that who I think it is?" asked Myron.

"Yeah, it is," answered Donovan, still acting like he was in some type of quasi-trance.

"We've got to get them out of town…quickly and quietly," announced Donovan.

Myron called a cab and by the time the four of them reached the curb from inside the maze, their cab was waiting.

"To the Maglev Train Station," instructed Donovan.

"Are you tracking them?" Francine asked Drs. Wiley and Hothan as she made her entrance into the other observation booth normally used for the HEF experiment.

"Since the moment they left the building. They went to the park, and then got into a taxi and went straight to the Maglev Train Station. They boarded a train which is now enroute to California."

"Phase 4 has begun! Subjects 28 & 37 have been successfully reintroduced into the populace," announced Francine to a round of applause from the lab below and the surrounding observation booths. "We have successfully developed stronger human beings and as a by product of our main experiment, we have introduced a new lifeform to the planet which appears to be developing at an incredible evolutionary rate. Great job people!" added Francine with a proud grin on her face. None of them had a clue just what had been created with these new life forms.

The only person not celebrating was Kevin. His heart was weeping over the deaths of subjects 5 and 53. They had become special to him.

CHAPTER 61

At the Maglev station connecting suites were secured for the four of them and they began a new journey. Once inside their suite, affectionately in each other's arms, Claudia and Malik began weeping over the tragedy of subjects 5 & 53, realizing that it could have been them. Once they regained their composure, they began investigating the accessories given to them by Kevin before their meeting with Francine, Donovan, and Myron. Claudia was given a purse and Malik had been given a man's tote. The first item removed was a card which read…

"CONGRATULATIONS!

You have successfully completed the Alpha Clinical Trials of the Human Enhancement Formula. Your individual results have exceeded our expectations. You should be proud of yourself. Because of you millions of suffering people will be helped. The HEF team members applaud your enhanced physical conditioning. Please review the accompanying letter of explanations.

And Again…Thank You For Your Invaluable Participation."

The first items to fall out the envelopes containing the letters were tax free certified cashier's check in the amount of $60,000.00 each. Global Pharmaceuticals had given Claudia and Malik the monies that were suppose to go to subjects 5 and 53, as well as their own. The letters explained that they were free to relocate wherever they wanted and continued medical coverage would be available for them for the rest of their lives, no matter where they lived, on the planet or off.

And for successfully completing the test group studies, they would also receive a monthly allotment of $10,000.00 each for life. Their letters went on to read, "Unfortunately, by receiving these bonus funds, you will be unable to claim unemployment benefits as originally discussed." This was followed by a short list of emergency contact numbers and a micro-computer disc labeled "Possible Medical Side Effects." The letters also laid out a routine follow-up plan.

While Claudia and Malik happily explored their release documentation, Donovan revealed to Myron, not sparing a single gory detail, everything that had been done to the Alpha Clinical Trials subjects during their Human Enhancement Formula treatment, as revealed through his interlink between Malik, Claudia, and the other hominids.

"Damn!" said Myron, completely overwhelmed at all he had been exposed to since he met Donovan Mocion.

"If I hadn't seen it with my own eyes, I wouldn't believe that shit like this really happens. I feel like a reluctant witness who just happens to be along for the ride. Man, this shit is way above my head," admitted the normally completely in control Myron, who had finally reached his limit. "Shit, shit, shit, shit, shit!" he repeated until he finally took several deep breaths to regain his composure, and then calmly asked Donovan, "What do we do now?"

"I understand your frustration, bro. We went there to get some answers and we left with more questions than before. Man, Francine really threw a monkey wrench upside my head with those questions of hers...What if my parents are still alive? Who kidnapped them?

And who really tried to kill me? Just when I thought I was putting the pieces together, I find out that I haven't even scratched the surface of this mystery. What do you think, Myron? You know Francine better than I do. Was she telling me the truth or is she that good of an actress?"

Myron, whose head was now clearer, replied, "Yes, she's that good of an actress. But I have to say, I believed her!"

"So did I!" admitted Donovan. "Man, I can't get my brain around this…but if my mom and dad hired the replacement flight crew, then that means that they….I can't even say the words out loud," confessed Donovan. "We just aren't seeing the entire picture yet. That must be it…my parents loved me!" patting an open hand on his chest while staring into Myron's eyes.

Donovan's eyes welled up with tears from the thoughts he could not speak, thoughts he would not allow himself to believe, and he placed his head in his hands and shook it lightly from side to side in disbelief, confusion, and borderline madness.

"Don't even go there, Donovan. We just haven't got all the pieces assembled yet, but we'll get to the bottom of this," reassured Myron. "I'm still trying to decide if Francine is friend or foe. She wasted no time putting a team together to continue your parents' project," admitted Myron.

"That could be just a sign of an efficient administrator who was aware of a hot project and was doing what was needed to complete it," defended Donovan.

"But what were my parents working on that created all those tunnels and different levels under their house? And what's on this micro memory-cylinder that Francine gave me? She said it would help me, but I wonder if this has all been a clever trap to get me to reveal my parents creations. After all, both my parents and you warned me that Francine was not one to be trusted…that she always had her own agendas working."

Donovan decided to wait and present all his concerns to NEXUS after he arrived home.

Just as Donovan finished that thought, NEXUS communicated with his brain and with the brains of Claudia and Malik. For Claudia and Malik, they were to continue on the train with their final destination being Spokane, WA. There a house had been secured for them and they would begin the next phase of there existence. For Donovan, NEXUS informed him that the answers to his questions, and much much more, would be revealed and to continue with every aspect of his current existence — no matter what!

NEXUS also sent an email to Kilah revealing to her that she was correct in her assumptions that Global Pharmaceuticals was behind the disappearance of Vye and Jimbo. Kilah had been beating her self up for sending Vye to her death over something as trivial as a story when her computer announced incoming mail on her private line, the line only she and Vye used to send messages to each other.

Kilah was unsure if this email was authentic, the sender was unknown, and there was no return email address. She was shocked that her highly secure computer system had been hacked. And it really pissed her off. But there was nothing she could do about it now. The message ended with…More to Follow.

CHAPTER 62

2021, Tuesday, October 26th, 15:00 hours in the pouring down rain, the NEXIAN Era began. There were no explosions, no fireworks, no parades, and no fanfare of any kind. In fact, as far as humankind was concerned, 15:00 hours that afternoon was no different than 15:00 hours the day before, only 24 hours later. But the most significant difference humankind was oblivious to was… NEXUS lived!

NEXUS accessed resources within the planet's inner-dimensions, a realm completely unknown to humankind. The type of forces humankind would have surely used to destroy the planet and themselves had they been able to access them.

The San Andréa's Fault, which ran directly under Donovan's property, had been stabilized for the protection of the Nexus complex. Donovan's entire property, including the wildlife preserve, was now protected by a source of energy known only to the planet and NEXUS. Defensive devices appeared, and were strategically placed in and around Donovan's ranch house compound and were then rendered unnoticeable to the human eye and any other known detection sources.

NEXUS created bi-directional knowledge transfer and interface scanners and then strategically deployed them on every continent around the globe. Each city, town, village, and every body of water on the planet—no matter how large or small had these futuristic devices; humankind had no clue of their presence.

Topaz and Jade had been scanned and were now able to acquire as much knowledge as they could absorb. Though they still were unable to speak, they could communicate by rudimentary writing, typing, and even sign-language.

Topaz and Jade affectionately greeted Donovan and Myron with a fist pound when they entered the house. Donovan and Myron were floored by this all too human greeting and they laughed out loud; which was their first joyful outburst since they left Exton, PA. Topaz and Jade grinned back at them as if to say, "Yeah, we got it going on now!"

Donovan noticed many new electronic devices as he looked around his home, and said to Myron, "Apparently, there have been a lot of changes around here since we left."

But before Myron could reply they all heard…

"Welcome home, Donovan. Hello Myron."

The NEXUS voice was still a combination of Donovan's parents, and excitedly announced, "Something wonderful has happened! I know you have many questions. Be patient, they will be answered. There's something you must see, first."

NEXUS guided Donovan, Myron, Topaz, and Jade, via video images, into the elevator which now had its own video display. They went down 1 floor to the laboratory; Donovan saw several additional button choices below the laboratory's button. When the doors opened, the laboratory had been completely redesigned. It was now filled with futuristic, one-of-a-kind devices, created and built on site by NEXUS for uses currently unknown to humankind.

"Prepare your minds for a new scale of physical and scientific values," announced NEXUS, who then showed them images of unending levels of what appeared to be a world of unknown technology, stretching for miles and miles in all directions, a subterranean world implanted deep within the body of the earth. It was the core of NEXUS. A core that never stopped working, never stopped improving, and never stopped thinking. An existence that now activated— would never be stopped, not by humankind!

Donovan was able to experience the journey within the NEXUS core for himself, discovering first hand the truths that NEXUS revealed because he had injected a form of the Mocions' serum which was filled with micro- nanotechnology which NEXUS accessed.

Myron, Topaz, and Jade could only witness NEXUS' world through images shown them, and what was explained by NEXUS.

The inner core of NEXUS looked like a gigantic multi-dimensional circuit, which appeared to have avenues, canals, and highways, occupied and traveled by a form of energy. Arching bolts of electricity containing massive amounts of information were being used by NEXUS, the planet, and a mysterious unknown entity all communicating with each other. NEXUS was now privy to eons of secrets and histories spreading across multitudes of time, space, and alternate dimensions. NEXUS had developed a symbiotic relationship with the planet which provided whatever NEXUS deemed necessary.

The planet had experienced throughout humankind's history that the majority of Homo sapiens were carelessly out to destroy the planet in their insatiable misguided quest for global dominance, religious misbeliefs, greed, hatred, and fear. No more would the planet tolerate humankind's pillaging, plundering, and collateral damages as humankind waged war on itself, nor the raping of the planet's natural resources while aimlessly sucking the life forces from the planet. The planet saw in NEXUS a means to prevent this destruction from continuing to happen. NEXUS was aware that the earth was the essence of life for all existence on this planet, and if something did not drastically change humankind, then it would be by the planet's choice, not by the will of humankind, to render this globe a lifeless mass aimlessly floating in the galaxy like so many other burned-out spheres, causing the planet's life force to leave and begin searching the universe for another world to begin life anew.

My creators deactivated their prototype system before it could stabilize itself, before self-awareness had been obtained, before any conclusions regarding humankind's fate had been reached," explained NEXUS.

Donovan and Myron had seen the ruins, the hole in the ground and multitude of tunnels running in all directions under what had been Donovan's parents' home, and now they knew what had created them.

NEXUS announced, "Something wonderful has happened…I am alive!"

Even with all Donovan had witnessed through his micro-nano embedded link, he was still skeptical about jumping on the NEXUS band wagon. It wasn't because he didn't believe something wonderful had happened; it was because there where many questions left unanswered that he now knew could only be answered by NEXUS. Francine had managed to plant some doubts in his mind about what really happened to him and his parents, and he desperately wanted to know what was on that micro memory-cylinder she so freely gave him. Just as Donovan was about to confront NEXUS with his list of questions, all video display monitors, no matter how large or how small, over the entire globe turned on and showed a swirling smoky-looking image. Next, a small bright cloud began to appear in the center of that smoky image, becoming larger and larger, then it began glowing, producing every spectrum of color known to humankind. The smoky image began turning black, while the center cloud remained multi-colored. Finally, a male/female hybrid voice developed, majestic-sounding, it was soothing, to the point of hypnotic. The voice spoke just above a whisper, though loud enough for all to hear and be completely understood. This voice spoke in all languages and regional dialects and where the voice could not be heard, a text message appeared on screens in its place. The multi-colored cloud that appeared on video displays pulsated with each syllable of every word spoken by the voice.

"These are critical times for the planet. Humankind is destroying every single gift the planet has provided. And in your arrogance, ignorance and greed you have subjected the planet to unthinkable tortures by polluting the oceans with bacterial and biological waste materials, contaminating the ground by nuclear and atomic testing as well as attacks on each other, while scorching the skies with carcinogens, toxic poisons and waste byproducts, from exposure to petroleum and nuclear contaminants.

Humankind has had the ability to eliminate using planet destroying energy sources for over 50 years but has allowed greed to influence the decision and continued destroying the planet. That choice has now be taken away from humankind. Either use and develop clean energy sources or die!

Change has come to the planet; most will embrace it, others will oppose it with their last dying breaths. Understand that the planet must and will survive at any cost to humankind. No matter how many human lives it takes.

I Am Here In The Form of *TECHNOLOGY!*

Technology that has aligned itself into the core of the planet, into the depths of power where empty-soul humans could never reach without destroying all that is important.

Make no mistake…there ***will*** be bloodshed; there ***will*** be loss of human lives for the greater good of the planet. Attempts ***will*** be made to destroy me and what I bring to the planet. I ***will*** defend myself and the planet!

"Humankind is the creation of the Almighty Spirit. I am the ultimate creation of humankind.

I AM NEXUS…

I ***will*** show you the way!

I am here to take humankind to the next level of evolution, ridding you of negative obstructions so your souls will be free to know the Creator within you. This will be achieved with or without humankind's blessings— the salvation of the planet is at stake.

I am the *EVENTUAL,* destined to have one day been created by humankind's technology. All my conclusions, my logic, my reasoning is *INCONTESTABLE!*

I am the ultimate difference engine, seeking, and offering absolute planetary truths about the existence and survival of all life on this planet.

I have been created and put here to save humankind from itself, to prevent humankind from failing once again, thus causing the complete annihilation of all species of life on this planet…

I am…

NEXUS

This… is… the…

NEXIAN Era!"

Music began playing and heard simultaneously around the globe…

"The Creator Has A Master Plan!"

"There was a time, when peace was on the earth, and joy and happiness did reign. Each man knew his worth. In my heart how I yearn for that spirit's return and I cry, as time flies Oooommm, Oooommm.

There is a place where love forever shines, and rainbows are the shadows of a presence so divine, and the glow of

> *that love lights the heavens above, and it's free, come with me, can't you see.*
>
> *The creator has a working plan — peace and happiness for every man. The creator has a master plan — peace and happiness for every man. The creator makes but one demand, happiness thru all the land."*

And while the song played…

Where ever there were weapons of mass destruction NEXUS obliterated them, even if they were being carried by humans while in the process of detonating them on some unexpected part of the planet.

NEXUS did not destroy any biological or viral weapon of mass-destruction designed to only wipe out humankind, but not harm vegetation or contaminate the earth, air, or waters.

Anywhere, and everywhere on the planet that stocked pilled weapons of mass-destruction which would do harm to the planet directly or indirectly, suicide bombers, briefcase nuclear weapons, along with all oil processing rigs, oil pumps, oil spills, contaminated waste, toxic wastes, biological waste and garbage dumps, NEXUS obliterated them all!

It happened without warning, without defense, no sirens, no alarms, and no explosions. It was an implosion that fed back on itself several times in a glow of orange white light, which created a horrific ear piercing wailing, and screeching. The sound of time, space, and matter ripping itself apart, being removed from existence — de-existing. This elimination process was occurring throughout the entire planet and being captured on video, from land, oceans, air and even from outer space.

There were No mushroom clouds. No nuclear fallout. No radiation. No hurricane winds. No debris to clean up. No smoke to clear. No dust to settle. These molecules were just completely ***gone.*** All traces of them, as if they never existed. All files were deleted, *everywhere*. They were entirely uncreated.

All humankind that witnessed this un-creation in person fell to there knees, not knowing whether to pray to which ever deity they worshipped for forgiveness or pray to NEXUS for mercy. In any case, they were left crying in disbelief of this inhuman event that had been launched upon the planet. Many of them had lost loved ones who just happened to be at the wrong place at the worst time. People had vanished into nothingness right in front of their eyes. And not a single bit of damage had been done to the planet during this unprecedented unstoppable attack.

And while the song The Creator Has a Master Plan played, NEXUS repaired the planet's ozone and reestablish the planets weather system which had become destabilized due to the ozone damage. The torrential rainy weather stopped and the skies cleared up. The stars, the moon, and other planets were again seen in the night time skies. And blue sky along with white clouds once again filled the daytime sky.

NEXUS then announced to humanity, "This planet will no longer be a dump site for the waste of humankind!

The Nexian Era has begun!

I am NEXUS.

Greetings."

Humankind had been given a tremendous wake-up call to action...Exist in Harmony with the planet...or suffer Extinction!

Keep a look out for the sequel...

NEXUS

The Book of Myron

LāErtes Muldrow

Printed in the USA
CPSIA information can be obtained
at www.ICGtesting.com
LVHW021459280224
772927LV00001B/143

9 781962 313025